Murder in Sun City

Sidney W. Frost

Published by Sidney W. Frost
153 Cattle Trail Way
Georgetown, TX 78633
sidfrost@suddenlink.net
http://sidneywfrost.com

Printed in the United States by CreateSpace.com

Editor: Lisa Lickel

Background Cover Photo and Design by Kera'sKreations
Couple Photo: © Wavebreakmedia Ltd | Dreamstime.com
Goblet Photo: © Vladakela | Dreamstime.com
ISBN: 0-9903181-2-5
ISBN-13: 978-0-9903181-2-5

DEDICATION

For the United States
military veterans who
served our country honorably
and for those who help them
through the rough times.

CHAPTER ONE

Margie waved as I parked the red double-decker bus, now a bookmobile, in front of Sharon's house. She lived in a pleasant neighborhood of Sun City called Mills Creek Estates. I had to look again to be sure, but I believe she had been crying.

This was my first stop of the day for a service I had initiated in coordination with the public library less than a month before, so I was still getting to know my new friends in Sun City, an active adult retirement community. I had high hopes for finding people my age who loved books.

I climbed out and gave her a hug. "Are you okay?"

She held on a little longer than usual. "I, I think so, Liz."

She'd been my first patron when I started the route

three weeks ago. I didn't know her well, but I could tell she was troubled. I pushed away and looked into her eyes. "You've been crying."

"No." She brushed at her eyes with a gloved hand. "Must be from the cold."

I knew she needed to talk. "Why don't you wait in the bus and get warm? I brought those books you asked for."

"Okay." Margie didn't look at me as she spoke. "I guess you should visit Sharon first."

I'd only seen Sharon twice before. Once in the bookmobile, and once in her home. She was the one who needed a friend. I would have thought Margie would know that, living next door the way she did. I stepped into the library and picked up the five books I'd brought for Sharon, along with a white paper bag.

Margie moved back to give me space. "What's in the bag?"

"Some orange scones for Sharon. Just a little thing to perk her up some."

"Scones? For Sharon?" Margie seemed hurt.

"Hey. Come with me. There's enough for all of us." I motioned for her to carry the scones.

Margie took the paper bag and followed as I walked toward Sharon's front door.

Before pressing the doorbell I noticed the door ajar. I turned toward Margie, who shrugged. I pushed the door open the rest of the way. "Sharon? It's Liz and Margie. Okay if we come in?"

Sharon's dog snarled from behind a stack of boxes, and caused me to freeze. "Nice doggy. Don't you remember me from the last time I was here?"

I held the books with one hand and extended the other for the little poodle to smell. She barked again, louder this time, then ran through the two rows of boxes and disappeared.

"Sharon! Where are you?" I followed.

There was a narrow path between waist-high stacks of boxes. Five grandfather clocks lined the wall. "Did Sharon just move here?"

"She's been here for about a year."

"Really? So you knew she was living with all this junk? No one in the neighborhood said anything or offered to help?"

Margie looked as if I'd slapped her. I'd been told I was too direct at times, but I had always said what I felt, and I was too old to change.

"I guess not. I didn't know about any of this clutter and mess. No one on the block mentioned anything to me about visiting Sharon. The neighbors I've talked to said she was a loner and they didn't know anything about her."

I shifted the books from one hand to the other and continued through the maze. "We need to see if she's okay."

"Maybe she's gone."

"With the front door open?"

"It's a little strange, but it happens."

"I don't think so. Not with a dog in the house."

"Hmm," said Margie. "Probably not."

We walked through the living room portion of the maze and followed the right turn into the family room toward the kitchen where Sharon and I had coffee a week earlier. Before we got there, I heard the dog whimper. The sound came from behind a stack of boxes near the fireplace. I peeked over them.

"Oh, no."

Sharon lay on the floor with her head near the hearth, the dog licking her face.

***

He watched the back of the house and waited for Princess to come out. She always did about this time of day. Something was wrong.

Peeking around the tree while standing in the damp icy grass reminded him of when he'd served two tours of duty during the Vietnam War, both times on river boats that had wandered across the border into Cambodia. He'd done his time and kept his mouth shut about the missions. He just wished the Navy had done the same for him when he returned to Cambodia after the war to settle some scores. That's when the nightmares began.

Today, everyone knew about PTSD. James shook his head in disgust. Post-Traumatic Stress Disorder. There wasn't anything named so fancy when he'd served. Veterans from his time were expected to get over it. Mother and Dad helped until they died. His inheritance went to buy the boat, but it hadn't been the money maker he'd hoped for. He was on his own now with little to show for all he'd done for his country.

He shook his head to quit thinking about the war and focus on the house. But the thoughts wouldn't go away.

Staring at the back windows of the Sun City house finally paid off and quickly brought him back to reality. But what he saw wasn't what he had hoped to see. Two women, and neither one was supposed to be there. Where was Wanda Jean? Where was Princess? What was going on?

CHAPTER TWO

I dropped Sharon's books and ran to her. The dog growled more savagely than before, but calmed when I gently stroked Sharon's head. Her skin was cold and stiff. I sensed she was gone. She had on a short-sleeved white T-shirt with "Panama" embroidered in red across the front. Odd shirt for this time of year. Odder, still, were matching bruises on her biceps.

"Is she…?" Margie went silent.

"I think so."

"Feel for a pulse."

I reached for Sharon's wrist, causing the dog to growl again, but softer now. I placed my fingers firmly inside Sharon's wrist and waited. Nothing. "We need to call 9-1-1."

I turned to Margie. Her eyes were huge. There was

no doubt this time, she had tears in her eyes.

Sharon looked peaceful, and I wanted to hug her one last time. But if her death wasn't due to natural causes, I didn't want to mess up any evidence. Instead, I said a short prayer. "Dear God, wrap your loving arms around this lovely lady."

Margie turned and walked quickly toward the door. "I'm sorry. I've got to get out of here."

I started to respond, but she was gone. I needed to call the authorities, but my phone was in the bookmobile where I'd left my purse. I turned to leave then remembered the dog. She was quiet now. With a little coaxing she let me pick her up. I guess she knew there wasn't anything we could do for Sharon. I petted the dog gently before taking her with me to the bookmobile.

When we got there I settled down in the swivel seat on the passenger side and pulled out my phone. I wished my husband was here. Samuel had a steady calm about him I adored. Although nothing like this had happened in the short time we'd been married, I knew his patience would be perfect for this situation.

"What's your emergency?"

"I think I found a dead person. I mean, I *did* find a dead person."

"Where are you?"

"I'm outside the woman's house in a mobile library."

"Where is the deceased?"

"In the house."

"What's the address?"

I looked out the window to check the house number.

"It's 312 Mills Creek Drive. In Sun City."

"Why do you think the person is dead?"

"She was lying flat on the floor with her head on the hearth. I felt for a pulse and didn't find one."

The 9-1-1 operator continued. "What is the deceased's name?"

"Sharon Coleman."

I could hear the sirens and wondered if they were for Sharon. Probably. The fire and EMS station were nearby.

"What is your relationship to the deceased?"

I wasn't sure how to answer. "I'm her librarian."

The operator paused. She'd probably not heard that relationship before. "Why were you there, in her house?"

"I was delivering books and found her front door open. When she didn't respond, I went in."

"What is your name?"

"Liz Helmsley."

The operator paused again. "I'm showing that you are calling from a phone registered to Liz Siedo. Is that you?"

"Yes. I've remarried and haven't changed my name on the phone yet."

"Okay, Ms. Helmsley. Please don't touch anything, and stay there until the police arrive."

A fire truck arrived while my ear was still warm from talking on the phone. It parked behind us. Two men and one woman jumped out and ran into the house. Sharon's dog had curled up near the heater and closed her eyes.

An EMS vehicle arrived shortly afterwards. Two more emergency workers entered the house. They certainly got here quickly and moved with great speed. Too bad there wasn't anything anyone could do for poor Sharon.

The firefighters exited the house just as a man wearing a suit and tie walked across the yard to the front door of Sharon's house.

I opened the front door and leaned out to listen.

"Hi, Joe," one of the firefighters said. "There's nothing we can do here. The woman is deceased. We'll be heading out, but EMS will stay for as long as needed."

"Thanks," the man said.

The man called Joe walked toward me as the fire truck departed.

"Ms. Helmsley?"

Sharon's dog alerted and let out a low growl. I picked her up and held her close. "Yes. Call me Liz."

"I'm Detective Joseph Bratton. You're the one who found the body, right?"

"Yes." I patted the dog's head and she relaxed in my arms.

"I'm going inside now, but I'd like to talk to you more. Would you mind hanging around here for a few more minutes?"

"No, sir. I don't mind. I'll wait right here."

Margie returned with a picnic basket and pulled out two mugs and a thermos. "I see the emergency crew has left. Did you learn anything from them? Is Sharon really…you know?"

She poured tea and passed me a cup. She still had the bag of scones and handed one out for me.

I put the dog on the floor and gave her one more pat

on the head before I took the scone. I felt concern for Margie and stared at her for a moment. After the way she'd run out of Sharon's house, I was surprised to see her so calm. Could she be in shock? I'd better keep an eye on her. "Yes. She's definitely dead."

We were silent for a time, sipping our tea. After a while Margie picked up the dog and fiddled with its tags. She looked at me. "Princess," she said.

The dog cocked its head and locked her eyes on Margie's face.

Margie gave her a pat on the head. "Yes. You know your name, don't you? Funny how little I know about my next-door neighbor. I knew she had a dog, but that's about it."

"I remember her name now that you read her tags. Poor dog."

Lieutenant Bratton knocked on the door.

"Come on in. No need to knock." I wanted to hug him, but knew it would be awkward due to the purpose of his being here. It's just my nature. I'm a big hugger, even though I know it makes some people nervous before they get to know me.

He pulled out a notepad and held his pencil near the paper. "You are Liz Helmsley, right?" He looked at me.

"Yes. I'm the librarian."

He jotted in his notepad and then looked at Margie.

"This is Margie. She lives next door. She was with me when we found poor Sharon on the floor."

He made more notes. "And your last name?"

"Cummings." Her voice cracked as she said it.

He made a note and turned to me. "How did you

happen to find her?"

"Delivering books." Oh, my. Where did I leave those books? "The front door was open, so we went in. Me and Margie. We found Sharon flat on her back near the fireplace. We couldn't find a pulse."

He looked at his notepad. "Did either of you know the deceased?"

We both nodded in unison.

"Do either of you know her next of kin? Someone to take care of the remains?"

I looked at Margie and we both shook our heads about the same time. Everyone should have a next of kin. I wondered if Sharon had anyone. Dear Lord, help me find her loved ones.

"I haven't known her long," I said.

"She kept to herself," Margie said. "I don't remember seeing anyone else here."

Bratton jotted something in his notepad then looked at me. "In that case we'll get the medical examiner to pick up the body until we can find her relatives."

He made a quick call, giving the address and particulars before our conversation continued.

"What about an autopsy?" I asked.

"The medical examiner will decide," he said, "but I don't think we need one. I suspect she fell and bumped her head. It happens more than you might think. Excuse me for saying so, but when people get older they sometimes lose their balance and fall. If they fall in the wrong place, it can be fatal. I know of three similar deaths, two on the same street not far from here."

"What about the bruises?"

He looked at me and pulled out his note pad and pencil again. "You mean the ones on her biceps?"

Margie looked at me with a look that said she hadn't noticed the bruises.

"Yes," I said. "A bruise on one biceps could be anything, but two matching ones is suspicious. The bruises were about the size of a thumb. It made me think someone had held her tightly while facing her. I didn't look, but there are probably finger marks behind her arms."

He stood and put away his note pad. "We'll ask the ME to check them."

Before he got to the door, he noticed the small bulletin board. He stopped and stared at it then looked at me as if for the first time. "Is that you with the president?"

I grinned. "Sure is.

"I remember that case. So you're Liz Siedo."

I hugged him. Not for being recognized, that happens all the time, but because I hug everyone. "It's Helmsley, now, but that's me."

"I read about you. Aren't you the library director in Austin?"

"Was. I sorta fell into the director's job after a series of unexpected events. Then last year I married a Georgetown farmer and gladly gave up my position in Austin to move here."

"You just got married?" Margie looked me over as if trying to form a question that didn't include my age.

"My second marriage." I didn't think it necessary to tell about my years as a widow nor tell them about the husband who drank himself to death. That all seemed so long ago and irrelevant.

Lieutenant Bratton looked at me as if in awe. "Well, welcome to Georgetown. We're fortunate to have such a celebrity in our city." He turned to Margie. "Did you know Liz here is famous for solving crimes?"

Margie's eyes nearly popped out of her head. "I didn't."

Bratton bent over to look through the driver's window. "There's the ME. Thank you ladies, both, and I'll call if I have more questions."

***

We watched from the bookmobile as several people came and went for close to an hour. When I saw two men with a fold-up stretcher walking toward the front door, I knew the investigation must be finished.

Margie and I went out to watch, and several neighbors joined us.

"What happened?" one asked.

"Is she okay?" another asked.

Margie shook her head solemnly and everyone knew what she meant. One woman I didn't know covered her mouth, another seemed to be uttering a prayer.

The two men with the stretcher came out and wheeled Sharon's body toward the waiting vehicle. Lieutenant Bratton walked behind them. When they got to the street, I stopped them with an upraised hand. "May I say goodbye?"

One guy looked at Lieutenant Bratton. He nodded.

They opened the body bag to where I could see her face. She looked peaceful, as if she were sleeping. I hoped I would look as good when my time came. I gave her the hug I'd wanted to give her earlier. Not my usual bear hug of course. I touched her cheek with mine. I gave each of the men a hug also. They didn't know what to do, as is often the case when I hugged someone. They were stiffer than poor Sharon. But they quickly recovered and completed their job of loading her body into the back of the vehicle.

Lieutenant Bratton stayed and talked to the neighbors who had gathered. I noticed one moving away before he got to her. I poked Margie, nodding my head toward the woman who hastily retreated. "Who's that?"

Margie looked around. "Joan Kelly. She lives three houses down. Looks like she doesn't want to talk to the police."

I made a mental note of the woman's name. Not sure why. We went back inside the mobile library while the detective continued to talk to the neighbors.

"You know," said Margie, "I didn't see those bruises you and that detective mentioned. Now I know why that detective recognized you." She pointed at the photo on the bulletin board. "Did you really save the president's life?"

I smiled. "Not by myself." If Margie knew about Chris and Percy and the Vengeance Squad, and what all we'd done, she'd really be impressed. But, no sense bringing that up. We'd all retired. Angela, who happened to be my dear husband's niece, married Chris and they moved to England. She worked for the government. Chris did contract white hacking while writing a book. Percy graduated from the University of Texas and worked as a guidance counselor for drug and alcohol addicts. His wife Jane helped us on the last case, but she was busy raising a family and working as a hospital chaplain.

Lieutenant Bratton came in the front door of the bookmobile with his notepad in his hand. He looked at his notes. "Ms. Helmsley, you said you hadn't known the deceased long. When did you two meet?"

"Two weeks ago."

"This is a fancy vehicle. An old double-decker bus from England, right?"

"Yes it is."

"You work for the public library?"

"Yes. The bookmobile is privately owned. The city library furnishes the books."

He jotted something in his note pad. "I see. So you own this bus?"

"Yes."

He nodded appreciatively and made another note. "What can you tell me about Ms. Coleman?"

"The neighborhood library service is new and this is only the third time I've been here. The first time, Sharon came aboard and checked out a couple of books. She also asked me to bring her some other books the next time I came."

"Did she talk about her family or tell you anything that might help us find her next of kin?"

"No. She didn't mention a family. Didn't say much at

all that first day. She talked a lot the next week, even invited me in for coffee and cake. She didn't mention any family members. I didn't ask. Figured I'd do that this week."

"She asked you into her house?"

"Yes."

"Was it...?"

"Dirty and stacked with boxes?"

"Yes."

"It was. Just like today."

CHAPTER THREE

He stayed hidden while the police and emergency workers were at Wanda Jean's house. He sneaked a peek from behind a tree every now and then to see if the strangers were gone. All the government activity around the house made him nervous. He didn't trust any of them. Not local, state or federal. He wondered if Wanda Jean was okay. He hoped he hadn't hurt her. He'd been relying on her for most of his food needs for the past month. Maybe longer. He'd been having trouble with time lately. And Princess. He hoped she was okay.

Something dreadful must have happened. Otherwise there wouldn't have been a need for all the sirens and flashing lights. Was he to blame? Surely not. That's something he would've remembered.

He knew it'd be safer to wait until dark to leave the

nature preserve, but hunger gnawed at him. Except for those government types, it should be safe to go for food. Most Sun City residents never ventured into the environmentally-sensitive areas where he'd been forced to live lately. The law-abiding citizens took the warning signs as gospel.

He made his way to the hiking trail, hoping no one would notice him. He dressed like everyone else in the area, but he suspected few would brave the cold weather today.

He followed the path until it ended on Sun City Boulevard. From there he took the sidewalk to Del Webb. He needed a few bucks for a sandwich at the City Market. He checked his pockets and found only coins. Wanda Jean had showed him where she kept some cash, but he hadn't needed any then. It was too risky to go back to the house. He walked on past the market, crossed Del Webb and went to the fitness center. He didn't enter through the front door since the woman at the desk would ask about an ID card he didn't have. He'd tried saying he'd lost it, but then she wanted to know some number. He didn't want to face her again. That's why he entered through the back door near the pool area like he'd done several times since. No one there to ask embarrassing questions.

In the men's dressing room, he found a wallet in an open locker and extracted a ten-dollar bill. He never took large amounts. Most of the people around there didn't know how much cash they had and wouldn't know if some were missing.

He left the way he came and made his way to the City

Market for a sandwich.

***

I felt a little guilty taking the dog with me when I headed home. Perhaps I should have said something to Lieutenant Bratton, but thought he might be required to call animal control and the little darling would be heading to the pound instead of the farm.

Besides, Princess seemed happy riding with me in the bookmobile. She had napped most of the way, but she sat up with ears at attention and looked out the front windshield when I turned into our driveway.

I parked near the barn and turned off the engine. Princess alerted at the change and followed me out of the bookmobile. It was a little icy, so I picked her up and carried her to the house.

The scent from Samuel's pipe greeted me as I opened the back door. Princess must have smelled it also. Her nose twitched as she looked at me for an explanation. "It's okay, baby. You'll be safe here." I couldn't believe how quickly she'd learned to trust me. She must know that her mistress would never again hold her or feed her.

It scared me some when I first learned Samuel smoked, mostly out of concern for his health. I soon got over my fear. He was seventy-two and had smoked pipes all his adult life. It wasn't worth talking about. I did pray for him every day, though.

As I shut the door, Samuel walked toward me with his arms open. "Welcome home, luv. I worried about you driving that monster vehicle on icy roads. So I'm especially glad to see you tonight all safe and sound."

I'd hugged many people over the years, but Samuel was the first one who'd hugged me back with the same intensity. But today I worried about squashing poor Princess. I pushed the darling dog out toward Samuel, stopping him in his tracks.

"What's that?"

"Don't worry. I'm not going to keep her."

"I should hope not."

Princess cocked her head. I put her on the floor and she went to Samuel, smelled his shoes, then went to the stove and lay down close to it.

"Look at that. I think she's found a home."

Samuel looked at me with raised eyebrows. "Not for long, I hope."

With the dog out of my arms, I moved to Samuel for the hug he'd intended. He was reluctant, but warmed to it quickly.

Afterwards, I took a cereal bowl out of the cabinet and filled it with water for Princess. I needed to tell him about poor Sharon, but not until I had taken care of her dog. I wasn't sure what I had to feed the dog and wished I'd stopped at the store for dog food.

Princess roused herself, sniffed the bowl, took a sip and then leaped into Samuel's lap.

"Well, Princess likes you."

He faked a scowl, but he looked more pleased than not. "Princess, huh? This is not a proper dog for a farmer. Too dainty, she is." He scratched her ears and got a lick in return. "Where did you find the runt?"

"That's what I need to tell you about. I had a little shock this morning...."

"What? What happened? You didn't slip and fall on the ice, did you?"

"No. Nothing like that. It was after we got inside."

"We?"

"Margie was with me."

"Another patron?"

"Yes. Guess what happened when we got inside the house."

"What?" Samuel sat on the edge of his chair in anticipation, causing Princess to shift to stay on his lap.

"We found Sharon Coleman, one of my regular patrons, d-e-a-d."

"D-e-a-d?"

I put my forefinger to my lips and nodded toward Princess. "Yes."

"I see. You're talking about the dog's owner. And why can't we say the word?"

I leaned my head at the dog again.

Samuel laughed. "If this dog is that smart, it can surely spell, too."

We both laughed and Princess cocked her head. "I guess, but I didn't want to upset the little dear."

"What happened to Sharon?"

"We don't know for sure. The detective thinks she may have fallen and hit her head on the fireplace. But, there were some strange bruises on her arms. Discolorations a person wouldn't get from falling."

"Now, now, luv. Angela told me about your Vengeance Squad and all your adventures. Don't get yourself all worked up over an accidental death. Let the police sort it out."

"The Vengeance Squad disbanded when Chris and Angela got married."

"Good. No need for you to worry about poor Sharon. I'm sure it was an accident."

"I guess. Still, it bothers me that the police will probably not check out the contusions on her arms."

He leaned back in his chair and grabbed the remote. "Time for the evening news, luv. Have you thought about dinner?"

I jumped up and moved toward the refrigerator. "Yes, of course. I made us a tasty King Ranch casserole this morning before I went to work. All I have to do is heat it up and make a salad. Won't take long." I bet Princess would like it, too. I should've stopped for dog food on the way home.

"Umm. Casserole sounds wonderful."

I kept it to myself, but I couldn't get Sharon's death out of my mind the rest of the evening. I decided to call a friend in Austin first thing the next morning. He'd know what I should do.

CHAPTER FOUR

He watched Wanda Jean's house the rest of the day. All was quiet after the emergency vehicles left. Princess must be gone. Otherwise, she would have come to the fence to see him.

A car drove by and slowed near the house, and he reached for his rifle. For just a moment he thought he was in Cambodia hidden in the brush, much like he was today. There was no gun at his side. No war. Still, something was wrong and he wasn't sure what. That's what made his situation unbearable, causing his head to pound so hard he thought he might pass out. He was alone and forgotten. Just like in Cambodia. Fighting the enemy without help from his unit, or his country.

That quack doctor had said the headaches were caused by trying to control the uncontrollable. Drugs were the solution, he'd said. The doctor also said the war was over and there was nothing he could do about it.

He waited until darkness to go to the library to warm up. He turned on the gas fireplace, grabbed the *Williamson County Sun* which he read in great detail. Afterwards he found a book to read and sat in the easy chair closest to the heat. He left five minutes before closing.

It was too cold to sleep at the campsite on the banks of Mills Creek so he went to the loft. He laughed at the name he'd given his hideout. Actually it was the outdoor restroom between the fitness center and the crafts buildings. He'd read the signs and knew the facilities were mostly used by people playing outdoor games, bocce ball, shuffleboard, horseshoes, and such. In this weather none were used, day or night, so he had the place to himself. Still, he looked around for anyone who might challenge his right to be there.

Moonlight broke through the trees and cast a grayish glow on the walkway to the loft. The light made it easier, but he could get to his hiding place in the dark of night. He moved a chair close to the four-foot high wooden railing. Next, he placed one foot on the chair and the other on the railing. He was sixty-seven, but as agile as he'd been in the war and he planned to stay that way.

At the end of the railing stood a six-foot high rock wall that surrounded equipment behind the women's restroom. He mounted the rock wall from the railing and climbed onto the roof of the small building. He crossed the roof and reached down for the two by three-foot slotted metal cover on the side of the attic used to ventilate the area. The vent came off easily even though it looked secure. When he first found this hiding place, he'd removed the screws and attached a wire in the center of the metal cover. The wire was attached to a brick inside the attic area. The weight of the brick held the vent in place. He pulled the cover out now, and turned it sideways so it would fit into the hole. He climbed into the attic and replaced the vent, letting gravity and the weight of the brick hold it in place.

He turned on his flashlight and looked around. Everything was in place. His sleeping bag was unrolled on one side of the area with a bottle of water and a few snacks next to the bed. There were also several empty gallon-sized water bottles for emergency use when he couldn't go down to the men's room. He extinguished the light as soon as he was sure his belongings were secure. It wasn't a good idea to draw attention to his hideout by leaving a light on for long. When he stayed at his creek side camp, he often read before going to sleep, but he didn't when he stayed in the loft.

He didn't need the light to finish getting ready for bed. Although he slept in his clothes, he emptied his pockets, took off his shoes, and removed the knife and its sheath from his right calf.

***

The next morning, after my second cup of coffee, and after Samuel left the house to do whatever farmers do during the winter months, I called the Austin Police Department. Or, I should say, I called the police chief's private cell phone. As head of libraries in Austin, I got to know the other department heads, including Tom. In fact, I knew him better than the others because of my involvement in criminal investigation. Even though his official stand was to discourage me and my friends from interfering with his cases, I think he secretly appreciated our help. True or not, he was always available to answer my questions.

Tom picked up on the first ring. "Liz, my dear. What can I do for you?"

"Good morning, Tom. I just missed hearing your cheerful voice. How are you doing?"

"About the same, I suppose. Except I miss your hugs. I'll tell you one thing, though, it's a lot quieter here since you married and moved away. Still, we stay busy."

"According to the news you're busier than ever. You seem to be interviewed more than I remember."

"You're right, and I need to warn you some reporter is due here any minute with what she's calling a hard deadline. I'd love to talk to you, but I'm afraid this isn't a good time. Can I call you back?"

I thought about that for a few seconds, and wondered why I was calling. I didn't have anything specific to ask. Not yet. "That'd be fine," I said. "I just wanted to kick something around with you. No hurry, I guess. Unless they don't do an autopsy for some reason."

"Autopsy? What happened?"

"No. You're busy. Call me back when you can."

"Liz. Tell me. Did something happen to Samuel?"

"Samuel? Oh, no. He's fine. Healthy as a horse."

"Who died?"

"You probably heard I'm driving the bookmobile here now. Yesterday I found one of my patrons deceased in her house."

"Foul play?"

"I don't know. She could have fallen and hit her head. The police think it was an accidental death."

"Sounds like it to me. Older person, I suppose."

I cringed. Sharon was about my age. "I guess you could say that. What bothers me is that she had bruises on both biceps. It looked to me like someone had grabbed her and perhaps pushed her back, causing her to hit her head on the fireplace."

"Come in," he said to someone other than me. "Liz, my meeting is starting now. I'll call you later. However, I suspect the police will investigate as needed and, although I know I'll never get you to believe this, they'll probably solve the case without your help."

"I know," I said.

"Then, relax, and let them do it."

"Okay."

It was just like the old days. He knew I wouldn't even though I said I would.

***

When Tom called back, I was on my way to the bookmobile to give it a cleaning.

"Sorry it took so long to get back to you."

Princess barked and chased the chickens running free in the yard, then followed me into the bus.

"That's okay. I could hug you for calling back so

soon."

He laughed. "You hug everybody. Listen, I talked to the detective handling the case, Lieutenant Joseph Bratton, and I don't think you have anything to worry about. I'm sure they'll do a thorough investigation."

"What about an autopsy?"

"If needed. Let them look around first. Right now they're still trying to locate the next of kin."

"Any luck?"

"Well," he said, "no one has shown up to claim the body."

That was so sad. "What happens if she has no one?"

"Don't worry about that. They'll find some family somewhere. A sister or brother, or perhaps a distant relative."

I began to think about how I would go about investigating the case. Even if Sharon died from an accidental fall, she deserved to have someone find out what happened. What about the memorial service? Where would she be buried? Poor Sharon. It was going to be up to me to do all that if she had no family. I decided not to tell Tom. It would be hard enough to let Samuel know I'd decided to investigate Sharon's death.

"Okay. Thanks, Tom. If you hear anything else, though, let me know."

"You're not going to let it go, are you? I can hear it in your voice. You and your buddies are going to keep after this until you find someone to charge."

"What? Don't worry. I'm all alone here now as far as the Vengeance Squad is concerned. Chris got married and moved to England. Percy graduated and is working. It's just me. Not much little ol' me can do."

"Hah. I don't believe that for minute. Just be careful."

"Of course."

As soon as I ended the call from Tom, I punched in Percy's number.

"Hello, ma'am," he said.

"Percy. So good to hear your voice. I've missed you."

"Same here, ma'am."

I knew Percy when he was drunk and homeless, living on the streets, so I know how far he's come. He'd been hit by a drunk driver after he'd sobered up and planned to go back in the marines.

He was in a wheelchair now, but in all the years he and I had worked together at the library, he'd never spoken of himself as a victim. If anything, he'd say how much better his life had become. He married the chaplain who counseled him while he was in the hospital and they had two wonderful children.

"Percy, I miss the old days when I could call on you to do a little detective work. I know you're too busy now, but thought I'd bend your ear about a case I'm working on."

"What's happened?" he asked.

"I found a patron dead yesterday."

"No kidding?" I heard it in his voice. He sounded as if he missed investigating crimes as much as I did. Percy had used his time on the streets to blend in and change his appearance when needed. He's been a student of Chris and was nearly as good as his teacher in the field of computer forensics.

"Yes. I had some books she asked for and, when I got

to the house, the door was open. You know me, I went on in, and there she was. Gone."

"Homicide?"

"I don't know. Police think it may have been an accident."

"But you don't think they're doing enough to determine if it was an accident or not."

"Well, we need to give them time. I'd hate to have her body buried without determining why she had bruises on her biceps."

"Surely the medical examiner will look into that."

"I guess. The only reason I'm worried is that the police said it looked accidental."

"Do you want me to come up there?" I could take a few days off. Rearrange my schedule."

I thought about it longer than I should have. It would be easier to have Percy to kick things around with. But that wouldn't be fair to him. And, mostly Jane. "I'd love to see you, and I could use your help with the computer stuff, but no. Jane told me how much you enjoy your work. Just be prepared for some phone calls and dumb questions from time to time."

"I don't mind answering questions, anytime. However, you could get Michael to help with the computer investigation part."

All I could think of was why my grandson, who had served time in prison for driving under the influence, was now talking to an addiction counselor. Then I stopped myself. They were probably talking computers. That's all. I was so proud of the way my wonderful grandson had made it through the dark times and finished college. "Good idea. Is he, you know, okay?" The question slipped out before I could stop it.

"He's doing great. With that computer science degree plus the training he got from Chris, he's as qualified to help you as me or Chris. He's got a knack for hacking. Chris has contracted him to do some special jobs."

That surprised me. I wondered if Michael was having trouble finding a real job because of his prison record. If so, he hadn't said anything to me about it.

We said our goodbyes and I started the engine. Princess looked at me and then jumped into the passenger seat. She seemed to like her new home.

CHAPTER FIVE

He spent the day collecting money for a night out. It was his birthday and he'd done without life's little pleasures for so long it was time to splurge. He found most of his money in golf carts parked at the social center. Typically loose bills and coins, but a billfold or purse from time to time. Since he'd been living in Sun City, no one had reported money missing as far as he knew. At least there hadn't been anything in the *Williamson County Sun* about it nor had he noticed any stepped up security. He wasn't greedy. He only wanted enough for a pizza and couple of beers.

He selected the Pub for his big night out. The smell of hot food hit him as he walked in. Two women and a man sat on stools at the bar watching TV and a couple in a corner table were eating and drinking. The waitress took his order and he couldn't help taking in a deep breath of her perfume.

He looked at the other diners while he nursed his first beer and waited for his food. The trio at the bar talked about the game, but otherwise didn't seem to be together. A couple walked in about the time the waitress delivered his pizza. She knew them and told them to sit anywhere. They picked a spot near the front window.

He inhaled the aroma of the pizza before singing "Happy Birthday" in his head, and grabbed a huge slice of pizza covered with slices of crispy pepperoni. The cheese was hot and the point of the crust drooped, making it difficult to get it to his mouth. But, he managed and declared it the best food he'd had in weeks. Worth the danger of being spotted out in public. That was a constant fear. He didn't know what would happen if someone reported him for some reason. But there was no reason for them to.

His fear of exposure grew stronger as a woman from the bar walked over to his table.

"Hello, soldier. Want some company?"

He looked her over. She was about his age. Graying hair. Slender. Nice smile. He nodded to the chair next to his.

"Thanks." She climbed into the seat. "You look like military. I've known a few in my life. But the long beard begs the question. Were you or not?"

"I was. Navy. Patrol boats. We didn't have time to shave then and I kept the beard when I retired."

"Yeah. A veteran. Thought so. You gonna order me a drink, or not?" She reached over and grabbed a slice of his pizza and had the end in her mouth before he knew what happened.

"I got a better idea," he said. "Why don't we go someplace where we can be alone?" He talked big, but he planned to finish his pizza before he went anywhere.

She looked *him* over this time, imitating his offensive scan of her. "I'd have to be a whole lot drunker than I am now."

"Waitress!" he called out with his arm in the air, without taking his eyes off the woman at his table. "Me, too."

"Thanks." Her tone snarled her response. "I'm Ruby Best. Nice to meet you, sailor."

He sat there without acknowledging her for a few beats too many, debating on what name to use, then offered her his hand, seeking human contact that had been too little and far between for a long time. "James Johnson." He hadn't used his real name in so long it sounded strange.

They talked through three drinks, beer for him, red wine for her. He wondered how much wine costs in a place like this. Didn't matter, he didn't have enough money to pay for it whatever the price. As they drank she told him her life story, including the fact that she was a widow. He told her his story, too. Only difference was his was all a lie, including the part about living in the Mills Creek neighborhood.

She stood and grabbed her purse. "Okay," she said. "I think I'm drunk enough." Her smile told him she wasn't drunk, but she was ready to go with him.

He stood also. "Good." He patted his track suit pants.

"Oops. I left my billfold at home." He pulled out the bills and coins he'd stolen during the day and slapped them on the table. "Can you cover the rest? And leave Sadie a good tip, will you? I'll pay you back."

She laughed and shook her head. "I should have known." She dug into her purse and pulled out enough to pay the rest of the tab and tip.

"Where's your car?" she asked when they got to the parking lot.

"It's in the shop." He paused. "That's why I walked and why I didn't think to bring my billfold. I didn't plan on a sexy woman making a move on me."

"In your dreams," she said. "You walked from Mills Creek?"

"Of course. It's only two miles. Walking is good for you."

"Uh-huh. I don't know. Here I am talking to a man with no billfold and no car. Something's fishy about you."

He laughed. "Oooh, are you scared? Don't forget, I'm a veteran. You should be thanking me for my service."

She paused, staring at him for seconds before nodding toward a red VW Eos. "Okay. I might be crazy, but get in. We can park out front of my house. You can walk home from there since you love it so much."

After they parked in her driveway, he kissed her a few times and enjoyed it. She seemed to like it, too.

He pulled away. "I feel like a high school kid making out in the car. Aren't you going to invite me in?"

"No way, sailor," she said. "My husband's home."

"I thought you said you're a widow."

"I meant I'd like to be a widow. Big difference. Besides, you need a shower."

"I took a shower," he said. "But since then I walked to the fitness center and worked out."

"That explains it." She tossed him a pert look. "Didn't you see the shower room while you were there? Come back tomorrow night when my husband's out of town and you've cleaned up and we'll talk. I've got a proposition for you."

"Okay." He started to get out of the car when he got an idea. "I know this sounds strange having just met and all, but could I borrow your car to go to the VA tomorrow? Like I said, mine's in the shop and two of the buddies I rely on for situations like this are gone. Hunting trip."

She appeared to contemplate for a moment. "I don't know you that well, but you fought for our country and I appreciate that. What's your name again, honey?"

"James Johnson."

"Are you in the directory?"

He smiled. "Of course." He didn't know what she was talking about. He probably should find one of those directories if he planned to hang around there longer.

"Will I find a wife listed there, too?"

"No. Just me."

"Are you married?"

"I don't know for sure. I was. She disappeared two houses ago and I haven't heard from her in years."

"Okay, Jimmy. You can borrow my car. My husband is leaving in the morning for a business trip and I'll tell him I left it at the pub because I drank too much and got a ride home."

"Don't call me Jimmy." Only Wanda Jean could call him that. "My name is James."

Ruby laughed and got out of the car. "Bye-bye, Jimmy."

Her laugh caused his headache to return, but he kept his mouth shut. He had her car. There were ways to get back at her. He made a mental list of some of the more exotic ways as he drove away fast enough to cause the tires to squeal.

***

Today was my grandson's university graduation ceremony and I was so proud of Michael I couldn't stop smiling and applauding even though there were many other wonderful people crossing the stage to accept their diplomas.

"What's got you giddy, luv? You're going beyond the proud parent reaction. Or, in your case, the proud grandparent reaction."

I leaned into Samuel and looped my arm in his. "I know. But you don't realize how important this is to me."

"You told me about his having to spend some time in the nick. Is that why you're busting your buttons?"

"Nick?"

"You know, what you call prison."

"Oh, yes. Another of your funny English words. I prayed for him during that time, more than usual. My prayers had to do with wanting him to learn something from being incarcerated. He could've gone either way when he got out. So, yes, I'm proud of how he's turned his life around. He did it on his own."

"Yep. Probably didn't want to get sent back to the nick."

"Oh, you." Samuel spoke the truth, but I knew he didn't say it to be hateful. He was making a joke. "Still, Michael changed and took control of his life. I know it wasn't easy for him."

"Now that he's finished school, he can get a job and start paying his own bills."

"I wanted to talk to you about that." I gazed into his eyes to make sure I had his attention. "I'm sure Michael will find the perfect job soon. Computer forensics is popular, but job opportunities are limited. Most of the places that would hire him are in other states."

"It'll be good for him to get out on his own, you know."

"You're one to talk. Your whole family worked the same farm for centuries."

"That's different. Besides, I'm in Texas now."

I pressed my cheek into his shoulder. "I know. I'm glad you are. Here's what I want you to consider. I need someone with Michael's talents to help me on the bookmobile. Not permanently, just until he finds a job in his field."

"Wait a minute. Are you thinking about hiring someone to help you, a volunteer, do your job? Are you talking about paying him or is that something the library would do?"

"We'd pay him. It could be a small amount to help

him out and make him feel he's earning an income. Just until a real job comes along."

"We, mostly you before I came into the picture, provided the funds for him to go to college. Isn't that enough?"

"That's plenty. I agree. He has a contract to do some work for Chris, but, as I understand it, that's part-time work. I doubt if it'll pay enough to live on. Can't we help a little longer? I could use his cyber skills. You know I don't get along with computers."

Samuel leaned back and locked his eyes on mine. "Now I see what's going on. You're getting involved in that woman's death. That's the only reason you'd need access to the Internet."

"It's not the *only* reason. When a patron requests a book, that interwebby thing lets me see if the library has it, and tells me if it's checked out or not."

"Still, you're a volunteer. How are we going to pay Michael if there's no money coming in?"

"I've thought of that. Now that he's out of school, I think we should invite him to move in with us while he's looking for work. If he does, then we can sell my house in Austin." After I married Samuel and moved to the farm, we let Michael stay at the Austin house to be close to school. It was Samuel's idea for Michael to find a couple of roommates to help pay the expenses. Thanks to the experience, Michael learned to take care of a home and manage his money.

"Hmm. That sounds like a good idea. What about the students living there now? Your renters?"

"They're all graduating and moving on."

"Well, then. Let's do it. But, for the boy's sake, set a deadline. He needs a proper job and place of his own."

"I agree."

"Good. How does three months sound?"

"How about six months?"

He shrugged. "It's your money."

I kissed him on the cheek. "Thank you for understanding." Now, if only Michael would agree.

CHAPTER SIX

He'd slept in Ruby's car at a rest stop on I-35. He enjoyed having a different place to sleep even though the tiny car wouldn't let him stretch out. It took all his reserve to stay with his plan to drive to the nearest VA office and not head south where he could be free again. There was too much at stake to leave now. Besides, how long would Ruby wait before reporting her car stolen?

When he got to the Olin E. Teague Veterans' Medical Center in Temple the next morning, without an appointment, he spent most of the morning in the waiting room hoping to see a psychiatrist. When his name was finally called, they handed him an appointment card for two months in the future.

"Or you can come back in a month," the receptionist said, "and see if there's been any cancellations."

"Deaths, you mean. Look, I won't be here that long."

"I'm sorry." She stared at him. "You're not suicidal, are you?"

He looked at her with disdain. "I mean I won't be in this part of the country. You've got my records on that computer. Check it and see why I need help today."

"I'm sorry, sir. There's nothing I can do."

He turned and walked toward the door. As soon as he was out of the clerk's sight, he went to the psych area and found a comfortable seat with lots of old magazines.

Several hours later, he heard what he'd been listening for.

"Mr. Loomis?" The nurse waited and called the name again. "Last call for Mr. Loomis."

No one moved. He held on until the nurse turned around and walked away. That's when he stood. "Did you say Loomis?"

She stopped and spun around. "Are you Loomis?"

"Yes. I'm sorry. I was reading a magazine and didn't hear you at first."

She looked at the file she carried. "Okay. What's your social?"

"Uh…fours, sevens. I don't know. That's why I'm here. I'm getting everything confused."

"Okay. Follow me."

They stopped at the scale and she weighed him on the way to the exam room. She checked his blood pressure and pulse then departed.

He waited alone until the doctor came in with the file in his hand. He stared at James. "You're not Steve Loomis. Who are you?"

"Loomis isn't here today and I can't seem to get an appointment. This time slot is available so why not use it."

The doc stared at the ceiling as if considering what to do. He opened the door as if to leave, but paused. "Brenda, get me…." He glanced at me. "What's your name?"

"James Johnson."

"Print out the file for James Johnson." The doctor closed the door and held out his hand. "James, I'm Dr. John Carlson."

James nodded and shook his hand. The doc's friendliness made James smile.

When the paperwork arrived, the doctor flipped through it and read the notes from his last VA visit, probably in Houston, or maybe Dallas. "You've lost a lot of weight since you last checked in. Are you eating okay?"

"I try to."

He looked him over. "Your blood pressure is high, too. Are you working?"

"No. I'm retired."

"Good, but you need to keep active."

"I walk a lot."

"Are you still taking Paxil?"

"I ran out."

"I'll write you a prescription."

"Do you have any samples? I've moved so much and changed bank accounts, I'm waiting on my pension to catch up to me."

The doctor pulled out a key, dug around in a cabinet

and came up with a handful of samples.

"Are you still at this Galveston address?"

"No. Uhh, yes, yes."

"Are you sure?"

"Yes. I hesitated because I'm traveling, seeing the world, more or less. I sleep mostly in an RV, but my mailing address is Galveston."

"So, any new problems or concerns. Or did you come to get more meds?"

"That's about it." James paused. "Except, I've had some pretty bad headaches lately."

"What kind of headache?"

James pointed to the top right side of his head. "I don't know. There are times when the pain is so severe I want to scream."

"How long does it last?"

He shrugged. "A few minutes at the most, I think. Sometimes I fall asleep." He wanted to tell the doctor he wasn't sure but thought he may have passed out a few times. He decided not to bring that up.

The doctor looked at his medical file and read more. "I see you've been in some campaigns that could cause anyone to have headaches."

"Yes, sir. You might say that."

"But to be safe, we need to get you an MRI. I can't work you in today, but we'll put you on the top of the list. If you don't hear from someone about an appointment within a week, call me." He handed James a card.

James looked at the card and saw the doc had given him a phone number other than the main VA line. Could he trust this guy? What would happen if he told the truth? What if he talked about his concern about Wanda Jean? The doc'd probably lock him up. But then, maybe he needed to be locked up. He sure didn't need an MRI.

"Thanks, Doc."

He ripped the card into pieces and dropped it in the first trash receptacle he saw on his way out of the building.

Leaving Temple, he checked the gas gauge and turned right toward Dallas instead of left to get back to Sun City. He needed to return Ruby's car, but he figured she wouldn't report it stolen for a couple of days, maybe longer. That would give him time to look up an old friend and spend the night in a real bed.

***

It turned out that Michael loved the idea of working in the bookmobile and he was ready to begin right away. A quick look at Google and we found all he need do was take a written test for his commercial driver's license. He downloaded the manual, studied it, and passed it all in the same day. The next week he was driving the bookmobile.

I sat in the passenger's seat as he drove us to the first stop. I don't know when it happened, but I realized he was no longer my little grandson. With his gradual maturity, the fact that he looked like his father hadn't hit me until today. He had a full head of brown hair just like his dad had when he was Michael's age. It was combed neatly on top, but curled around the sides, covering his ears. No facial hair, not even the day-old beard some young men wore today. He seemed a bit too slender to me, but my friends commented on his muscular appearance.

He dressed like his father, too. Khaki pants, blue shirt, and black leather shoes with rubber soles. The shirt brought out his blue eyes.

"Gigi? What's up?" he asked, grabbing a quick glance my way.

"Nothing. Just thinking how proud I am of you."

He smiled, returned his gaze to the road.

Michael had one characteristic his father never had, perhaps only because the craze came later. Michael seemed to always be fiddling with his smart phone. I was glad to see he could get by without it while driving.

It was the Monday after he graduated and we spent the day parked in Meadow Lake, the neighborhood across the way from the Mills Creek Estates where Sharon had lived.

It was nice having my own bookmobile, and my agreement with the city library was that they would provide the books and I'd do everything else, without an expense to the city. My reputation and my love for bookmobiles was well known. Librarians all over the state, and probably elsewhere, had heard about the red double-decker bus that'd been converted to a bookmobile. I'd purchased it for the Austin Library in England and had it shipped over. When I retired, the new director retired the bookmobile as well, claiming it was too costly to maintain. When it was put up for sale, my English husband Samuel bought it as a surprise for me. He'd thought we'd store it at the farm and bring it out occasionally for parades and such. Instead, I worked the deal with Georgetown and put it back in service.

It was for fun, and I tried to think of it as part time, so we only stopped in three Sun City locations. Perhaps we could increase the service with time, but I wasn't sure there was a need. The Sun City Library had an excellent selection of the latest books, fiction and nonfiction, as well as CD books and DVD movies.

Still, people climbed aboard our little bus library because of curiosity. Today we had at least a dozen visitors. Two checked out books and five turned in requests for books we had downtown but not on the bookmobile.

When it was time to close up for the day, I told Michael we needed to stop by Sharon's house to retrieve the books I'd left there.

Michael looked at me with a frown. "Do you think you'll be able to get in?"

"I don't know. Probably only if the police are there, but it's close by. Let's try."

When we arrived, there were no cars and the house seemed to be empty. Thinking about my last visit made me so sad I started to tell Michael to drive on by. But, I didn't. I wanted to find those books.

We parked in front and climbed out. It wouldn't hurt to look around a bit to see if we could get inside. The police hadn't posted those yellow tapes that said "do not cross" or whatever.

Michael joined me, Princess followed, her ears a little taller than usual as if on full alert. I tried the doorbell, but, as expected, no one answered. I checked the doorknob. Locked. I headed back toward the bookmobile, but when I looked around for Princess, I found her standing outside the garage looking as if she was waiting for me to open the door.

Michael laughed. "Looks like Princess is used to going in right there."

The dog sat below a keypad on the frame of the garage. "Okay, Princess. I see it. But, it doesn't help. Not unless you can tell me the code."

"Try 1-2-3-4," a voice said.

I turned to see Margie behind us. She sure had a way of sneaking up on people.

"Really?" Could it be that simple? I punched in the numbers and the door lifted up out of the way, leaving room to walk into the garage.

"Yeah. Most people tend to use something easy to remember."

"Thanks. Margie, this is Michael."

"Nice to meet you. Your grandmother has told me all about you. Congratulations on getting that college degree. That's an accomplishment to be proud of."

"Thank you, ma'am."

Seeing Margie gave me an idea. "I stopped by to get those library books I left the other day. Do you want to go in with us?"

"No. Can't. I'm late for a doctor's appointment as it is. Go on in." Margie waved as she walked quickly toward her house where her car waited in her driveway.

Princess went to the door that opened into the kitchen. Michael paused to admire the baby blue

Cadillac that looked older than me. But, unlike myself, it appeared to be in mint condition.

I saw a button on the wall near the door where the dog waited. I pressed it and the garage door closed. No sense drawing attention to what we were doing. I believed they called it breaking and entering.

We went into the kitchen and I made my way to the family room where I'd last seen the books. Princess worked her nose around the place where we'd found Sharon's body.

"I know, Princess. You miss her, don't you?" I turned toward Michael. "This is where we found her."

The dog whined and sat down.

I spotted the books I'd left. All but one. I couldn't remember which one it was, but they were all on South American art and collectibles. Had I miscounted or had the detectives moved it? I could check the library records to verify it, but I was sure there had been five books. I placed the other books near the door to the garage while we searched the house for the missing book. Princess followed, but she disappeared after a while.

When we got to the master bedroom I couldn't resist a quick look in the closet. I didn't know what I was looking for. I never do when I'm investigating a crime. But I found something interesting.

"Michael, look in here."

He joined me in the large wardrobe closet. "What'd you find?"

"See the men's clothing there?"

"Yes. Is that a problem?"

"I don't know. Could be. The police are looking for a next of kin."

We searched the rest of the house for signs of a male occupant, but didn't find anything. There was only one toothbrush in the master bath and none in the guest bathroom. Even though Michael turned up his nose, I looked through the dirty clothes hamper. Nothing masculine there either.

Michael turned to leave, then stopped. "I saw the books next to the garage door. Do you want me to take them? I'm going out to the bookmobile and check for e-mail."

"Sure." I knew he must be bored stiff looking around someone's home.

I found Princess lapping up water from the toilet, so wasn't surprised when she went to the patio door to go out.

I followed her to keep an eye on her. The metal fence looked like it was merely decorative. The chicken wire attached to the fence kept Princess from escaping. As I visually checked the fence, I locked on to something I didn't expect to see. There was a man peeking around a tree at me.

Princess must have seen him, too. She ran toward the location with her tail wagging. But before she got to the fence, the man was gone. I ran to where she stood and saw the back of a man in camo clothes running away. It was a strange sight for Sun City. Princess wagged her tail more robustly at first, then turned and walked slowly toward the house.

"Come, Princess. It's time to go home."

***

He'd worn his camo jacket and hat and was nearly invisible. Nothing showed except one eye and half his face. That silly woman still spotted him. He could tell by the way she stared at him.

He wondered who the woman with the piercing eyes was and why Princess was with her. He would've liked to hold a staring contest with that nosy woman, but he was afraid Princess might give him away. He never ran from the enemy without a good reason.

He raced without looking back until he was in the forested area, at his special place. He stopped and looked back to make sure she wasn't behind him. He didn't think she would walk past the sign saying to stay out of the environmentally sensitive area where he lived now, but he wasn't sure.

When he was far enough away to not be seen, he stopped and listened before he walked the rest of the way to his campsite.

CHAPTER SEVEN

Back in the bookmobile, I told Michael about the face I'd seen in the woods.

"Probably some inquisitive neighbor."

"I don't think so. A neighbor wouldn't peek around a tree like that, dressed in camouflage, from an environmentally sensitive area. He just stared at me, knowing I could see him. And, you know what is weird? I think Princess knew him. She didn't bark the way she does with strangers. She walked right up to the fence, wagging her tail."

Michael frowned. "That *is* peculiar. She's pretty picky about who she likes and doesn't like, especially strangers. Remember when she first met me? She growled and wouldn't let me get close to you. It took days for you to convince her I was okay."

"I know. Makes me wonder if that man has come up to the house before."

"Doesn't your friend Margie live next door? Ask her if she's seen anyone out in the field behind her house."

"Good idea." I looked out the window. "I wonder if she's back from her doctor's appointment. I suppose she'll stop by to say hello when she gets home. If we miss her, I'll ask her tomorrow. Right now, I've got a computer question for you."

"Shoot."

I nodded toward Sharon's place. "Is there a way to learn who owns this house?"

"Sure. What's up? Don't you think Sharon owned it?"

"I'm thinking about the men's clothing we found in her closet. That made me wonder if the property is in her name only."

Michael typed faster than I thought humanly possible and leaned back to wait for the results. He smiled and turned the screen around for me to see.

At the top of the display I saw the heading Property Detail Sheet and a string of letters and digits that didn't mean anything to me. Two lines down were boxes labeled for owner's name and owner's address. I stared at the contents of the name box before I read it aloud. "COLEMAN COMMA DENNIS AND SHARON."

I looked at Michael. "I was right."

"You sure were."

"Is this information available to anyone? You didn't hack in to obtain this, did you?"

"This is public information."

"Something the police could find?"

"And probably have."

"Hmm. Will this tell us if Sharon or Dennis Coleman own any other property?"

Michael moved the laptop around and typed more. "This is the only property in Williamson County. Let me check the surrounding counties. They all have separate databases."

He typed away.

"Nothing in Travis County. Nothing in Burnet County. Ah, here's one."

"What did you find?"

"Bell County shows a listing for Dennis and Sharon Coleman. It's for a house in Salado. Let me check the map."

"You don't need a map. I know where Salado is. It's not far from here. I went to the Stage Coach Inn there once with some friends from Austin."

"I'm checking for information about the house." He typed more. "The appraisal district website shows it to be six thousand square feet."

"That's huge." I looked Michael in the eye to let him know how serious I was. "I want to go to that house. How about tomorrow?"

"Fine with me. I'm working for you."

Before we could finalize our plans for a trip to Salado, Joan Kelly came in. I recognized her as the neighbor who had suspiciously departed so fast the day Sharon died. The one Margie said apparently didn't want to talk to the police.

I tried to give her a hug, but she twisted away. Must be shy. "You're Joan, right?" I asked.

She hadn't visited the bookmobile before and raised her eyebrows as if to ask how I knew who she was. "Yes."

I answered the unspoken question. "Margie mentioned your name."

A slow nod let me know she was satisfied with my explanation.

"Can I help you find anything?"

She quickly scanned the area. "Not really. I read about the bookmobile service in the local paper and wanted to see what you have to offer."

"Look around. See if anything catches your eye. If you don't find what you want, we can get it for you." I pointed to my grandson, hunched over his laptop at the back desk. "Michael, there, is connected to the main library and can tell you if they have a book you want and whether or not it's checked out."

"Interesting. But, like I said, I'm not here for anything in particular."

I decided to try an experiment. "Have you seen Dennis lately?"

Michael smiled and slowly shook his head.

Joan wrinkled her nose in a way I couldn't interpret.

"Pardon me? Dennis who?"

"Dennis Coleman. Sharon's husband."

"Husband? Really? I didn't know she was married. I only met her once and thought she might be a widow."

"You met her? When? Where?" From what Margie told me, no one in the neighborhood knew Sharon.

"She came to the house one morning, barefoot and frantic. She was incoherent at first, but I finally learned she had an important appointment, with a doctor I think, and couldn't find her shoes. She got control of herself soon after telling me her situation and appeared to be somewhat embarrassed. Anyway, that's when she asked if she could borrow shoes from me."

"How odd."

"I know. I hardly knew her and she wanted to wear my shoes."

"What did you do?"

"I gave her a pair. What else could I do? She never returned them and I never asked her about them. Quite frankly, I didn't want them back."

"Did she say why she had no shoes?"

"She claimed all her shoes disappeared after her daughter had visited. She was pretty mad."

"Did she mention the daughter's name?"

"I don't remember it if she did. She seemed especially angry about the theft since the young lady was supposed to be in some kind of religious order."

The neighbor who'd avoided the police as well as my hug didn't have a problem gossiping about her neighbors.

Before I had a chance to think more about gossiping, another patron came aboard and Joan left without so much as a wave.

I gave the new arrival a quick hug. "Hi, Ruby."

Ruby wasn't a regular and she didn't live in the neighborhood. The first time I met her she'd arrived in a golf cart. She'd said she saw the bookmobile from the golf course across the way. That prompted her to visit. She'd been there a few times since, but I don't think she'd ever checked out a book.

Today, she apparently didn't have time for greetings. "Have you seen James?"

"I don't believe I know a James."

"Bearded guy. Looks like an older SEAL. He said he'd been in the Navy."

I thought about the bearded guy back behind Sharon's house. "No. Why do you ask?"

"I let him borrow my car to go to the VA yesterday and I haven't seen him or my car since."

***

James sat on a bench near the pond behind the community activities center, and tossed his jacket on the bench beside him. The sun's rays warmed him. Giant golden koi swam in clear water that had nearly froze the last time he was there.

He opened the book he'd found at Wanda Jean's and began reading. The title of the book concerned him and he wanted to find out what she could have learned if something hadn't happened to her. As usual, he found it difficult to concentrate for long. It was probably the pills that VA doc had given him.

After scanning the same page several times, he closed the book and looked around. Off to his right he noticed a computer kiosk. He walked toward it, curious about its purpose.

It turned out to be a guide to where bricks were located in the Williamson County Veterans Memorial Plaza a few feet away. He looked for his name, knowing he wouldn't find it. After all he'd done for his country he should be listed.

He went back to the bench and tried reading again. It was calm there and he needed to stop thinking about the way he'd served during war and how no one cared.

"Where's my car?" Ruby leaned in so close to him he stood and moved back, almost tripping on the rocks surrounding the pond to get away.

"I left your car at the pub. Isn't that where you told your husband it'd be?"

She had her hands on her hips and he could tell she was angry. "Yeah. I found it. The keys were on the floorboard. Anyone could have stolen it."

"You told me to put the keys there and you found the car. Why are you angry?"

"You idiot. You were supposed to bring it to the house last night. I told you he'd be out of town." There was the start of a smile on her face, but it disappeared before he was sure.

Still, he knew what she meant. He stayed overnight in Dallas and left the car at the pub so he didn't have to see her. He couldn't handle getting involved with anyone right now. Especially a woman. "Oh, that. I'm sorry. The VA kept me in the hospital overnight and I didn't have a way to call you." Lying got easier all the time.

"Kept you over, huh. Where, in the looney bin? You're a liar and, by the way, there's no James Johnson in the Sun City directory. Who are you?"

***

Samuel agreed to keep Princess for the day while Michael and I went to Salado to see Sharon and Dennis Coleman's home. Michael started to climb into his car, but I pointed toward the bookmobile.

He looked at me and I knew he had a question. "I'm just wondering. Is it okay with the library for us to drive this vehicle to Salado?"

"Sure. The bookmobile is my private property and we're not getting paid."

He looked surprised. "Oh. I thought you said I'd get paid. That's okay."

"You *are* getting paid."

"Who's paying me?"

"Samuel and I are. I need the computer help and you need an income until you find a job."

He smiled. "Thanks. I hate to see you putting up the money, though. I promise to find a job as soon as I can. But, you know, it has been fun working together. With you raising me and all, you were more like my mother than my grandmother. Now that we're coworkers, I discovered you're a lot smarter than I thought you were." He smiled again.

"Oh, you. But I understand what you're saying. Since I raised you I blamed myself for all your trouble with alcohol and drugs."

He looked at me seriously. "I know you did, and I'm sorry for that. I don't know if either one of us could have done things differently. I'm okay now, you know."

"Yes, I know you are. I'm sorry I couldn't do much of anything for you during that terrible time. You had to do it yourself."

"You did fine. The important thing is you never stopped loving me. That was what I needed from you most."

Silence reigned the rest of the drive along with my thankfulness for my loving grandson.

When we got to the house, there was a black pickup piled high with boxes backed into the driveway. I looked for a driver or passenger, but the truck cabin appeared empty. "Are you sure this is the right place?"

Michael checked the note he had made when he'd looked up Sharon's property on the tax assessor's page. "This is it."

"Looks like someone is moving out."

"Or burglarizing the place." He pulled out his phone. "Want me to call the cops?"

"We don't know enough to call the police. What if it's Dennis or some friend of the family?"

"I guess it could be, but be careful."

"Look, the front door is open, let's go see who's here."

"Okay, but I think we should call the police first."

"In a minute. Write down the truck's plate number."

"I have a better idea." Michael used his phone to snap a photo of the pickup and then moved in closer to photograph the license plate.

"Good job." I felt like a proud mother seeing my grandson in action on our first investigation together.

It was a new house built to look like the homes I remembered from the 1950s. It had wooden sides and a wide, steep wooden stairway leading to a large front porch complete with a swing built for two. Before we got to the top step, a man carrying a packing box walked out of the house. When he saw us he dropped the crate and hustled down the steps two at a time. He reached the truck and had the motor running in a matter of seconds. All before I had a chance to see his face. The tires squealed as he drove away and the box stacked highest in the truck bed tumbled off and landed on the driveway. I was glad Michael got a photo of the truck's plates when he did.

"Now you can call the police. Tell them what happened and give them that plate number."

"I can do better than that. I'll send them the photos of the truck."

"You can do that?"

"Sure. As can most of the population."

"Good. Wait for them to get here and I'll take a quick look inside."

He waved an arm at me as if he wanted me to wait. I ignored him and entered the house while he called the police. I probably wouldn't get much chance to nose around after they arrived.

What I saw didn't surprise me. There was a bunch of grandfather clocks and other antique-looking pieces of furniture plus a maze of moving boxes filling the living room. There were a few gaps here and there, probably from the boxes the dark-haired man carried out to his pickup. Hmm. I must have gotten a better look at him than I thought. He'd had dark, actually black, shiny hair, combed back. His face was white, nose thin, eyes brown. He probably didn't get out in the sun much. Blue denims and light blue shirt, no coat, cowboy boots. Wow. It amazed me to think how much the human eyes could record in such a brief period of time. Who needed one of those fancy phones with cameras?

I made a quick survey of the rest of the house. It looked like no one lived there. Boxes filled every room except the bathrooms and they looked unused. No towels or toothbrushes and the closet was empty.

"Gigi?"

Michael found me in the master bathroom.

"The police are here. We better wait on the porch for them." He looked a little jittery.

"Did you see all the boxes?"

He nodded, gently took my arm and walked toward the front door. "Yes. It's just like the Sun City place. Now, we need to get out of here."

I followed his lead, but didn't understand the urgency to go. "And did you notice the fireplace hadn't been used?" It looked new. Not a smudge anywhere on the white stones inside the burn area.

He pulled me a little faster. "We better leave before the cops come in with guns blazing."

"They wouldn't do that. You told them we were here, right?"

"Yes, but..."

We walked through the front door onto the porch in time to greet two policemen. Their guns weren't blazing. Both were still holstered. I have to admit, though, they looked a little anxious.

"Are you Michael Siedo?" the one with sergeant's stripes asked.

"Yes. I'm the one who called. And this is my

grandmother, Liz Helmsley."

The sergeant looked around us into the front door. "What were you doing inside the house?"

Michael stepped forward. "As I said in my call, we found the front door wide open. We went in to make sure no one was hurt."

"Did you find anyone?" the other policeman asked.

Michael looked at me since he hadn't searched much of the house. "No. But, there are so many boxes in there, you may want to check out the place yourself."

"Is that your vehicle?" The sergeant nodded toward the red double-decker bus.

"Yes," I said.

"You two wait there while we check the house."

CHAPTER EIGHT

We left the bookmobile at the house and went with the officers to the Village of Salado Police Station. They were polite, but I had the feeling we didn't have a choice about going with them. What a nuisance. We needed to get back to Sun City and open the library service. At least we got to look in the Salado house and frighten away whoever hauled those boxes out.

When we got to the station, we were told to sit on one side of a table with the two police officers across from us. Before we had time to say anything, another officer came in. The policeman introduced him as Deputy Moore of the Bell County Sheriff's office. Moore looked like he needed a hug, but I resisted due to the circumstances.

Michael spoke first. He sounded irritated. "Look,

we're happy to help and answer any questions, but don't treat us like criminals. We're the ones who called you. We reported the man coming out of the house. We provided a description of him and his pickup. Why are you holding us?"

"Now, son, jus' relax." The deputy sat at the table with the two police officers. "Surely a smart man like you can un'erstand why we're curious about how ya'll happened to be there at the time that man came out of the house."

"We explained that." Michael got so frustrated, I wondered if he still held some ill feelings toward the law because of his time in prison. We'd have to work on that.

"I know," the deputy said, "but I haven't heard the story. Please indulge me and we can all get out of here."

I patted Michael's arm. "Michael, let me tell these gentlemen what led up to our being here."

The deputy looked more at ease, as did Michael.

"I'm the bookmobile librarian in Georgetown. A few days back, I found a deceased person at a home where I delivered books."

One of the policemen passed the deputy a sheet of paper. "This is the report Georgetown PD sent us on the death of Sharon Coleman."

The deputy studied the paper before turning back to me. "Okay. What caused you to drive to Salado and to the house in question?"

"We were looking for Sharon's next of kin. We did a computer search and found that she owned a house here and so we came to look for a Mr. Dennis Coleman who is shown as joint owner of both houses."

"I see. But why are you doing this and not the Georgetown Police?"

"I suspect they're doing it, too. They have access to the same information we do. Isn't that right, Michael?"

"Yes, ma'am."

The deputy turned to the police officers. "Have you heard an'thing from Georgetown about the deceased having a house in Salado?"

"No. But when we talked to them to get the info on the death there, they started asking why we wanted it. So, I told them. They acted surprised."

The deputy looked at me. "I strongly urge you two to leave this investigation to the police."

"Yes sir." I wondered if I could do that. Right now, though, all I wanted to do was get back to Sun City.

"Yes, sir," Michael echoed. "But, don't you think someone should try to find that guy in the black pickup?"

The deputy stood. "Don't worry about him. We had him in custody before you two got to the station."

"We are grateful for your help in identifying him," one of the police officers said.

I was relieved to hear about the arrest. "Was it Dennis?"

"No. We're still checkin' it out, but he claims to be an antique dealer who bought some items from Mrs. Coleman. Says he has receipts for ever'thing he took from the house. We'll be verifying that of course."

"Did he mention Mr. Coleman?" I asked.

"I've already told you more than I should. Only

because you helped us so much."

The sergeant stood. "Yes. Thank you both for your assistance. We'll give you a ride back to your bus and you can be on your way."

I couldn't help think the police wouldn't know what was going on if we hadn't gotten involved. Even so, we still didn't know where Dennis was and that was the main purpose of our trip to Salado.

***

We got back to Sun City in time for our scheduled afternoon stop in the Cowan Creek Activity Center parking lot. We'd missed the stop in Margie's neighborhood, and I wanted to tell her what Joan had said about Sharon's daughter. Although we didn't know much yet, we should also tell Margie what we'd learned about Dennis. Besides, I wanted to ask her if she'd seen anyone in the woods behind her house or, more specifically, behind Sharon's house. We'd have to wait until tomorrow for all that. Come to think of it, I guess we should've told the police what we know about the possibility of Dennis and Sharon's daughter. We'll have to do that when we learn more.

While we waited for patrons to come aboard, I called Lieutenant Bratton at the Georgetown Police Department to tell him about the house in Salado and how we found it. He wasn't interested.

"Ms. Helmsley, I must urge you to not get involved in this case. We know about the house in Salado and we're searching for Dennis Coleman. All we need to do is find the deceased's next of kin and notify them of her death. I know you're trying to help, but this case is closed. There's nothing else to do."

"Closed?" I couldn't believe my ears.

"Yes. The Medical Examiner didn't find anything suspicious and has ruled the death accidental."

"Are you sure?"

"Absolutely."

Michael frowned, but he could only hear one side of the conversation.

"And you know about the men's clothes in the closet? The antique dealer? The daughter in the convent." I wasn't sure about the convent part, but I took some liberties with the facts to pique the lieutenant's interest, mainly because he irritated me.

"The investigation is complete. It was an accident and we're looking for her relatives. If there are any, we'll find them. Good day." Lieutenant Bratton hung up.

He stuttered enough to make me think he didn't know as much as he thought he did. His concern seems to be wrapping things up quickly rather than solving a crime. I stared at the phone a second before disconnecting. I hadn't told him about the face in the woods.

Michael smiled and slowly shook his head. "Convent?"

I shrugged. "Could be. We don't know what Joan meant about Sharon's daughter being in some type of religious order. Sounds like a convent to me."

Michael laughed. "We don't know if Sharon had a daughter. Have you considered Sharon may have had mental problems? It's not normal to have a house full of unopened boxes and it's not normal to have to borrow shoes from a neighbor. Perhaps she made up the daughter to explain why she had no shoes, or couldn't find any. Perhaps they're all packed away in some of those boxes."

"I know. Even if you're right about all of that, we have to keep searching. Lieutenant Bratton said the case was closed. Her death has been ruled accidental. All they're doing now is looking for next of kin."

"I take it you don't agree with the ruling?"

"How can you ask that? Maybe it was an accident. But, I don't think they should rule out a possible homicide until they've talked to her husband and daughter. And, the man I saw out behind the house. Plus the antique dealer."

"They'll probably talk to them all, if they can find them."

"Yes, but they won't be looking for a killer. They'll be looking for someone to bury the body and take care of her estate. That's different."

"So what do we do now?"

"Nothing. All I want to do is go home and have a big dinner with you and Samuel. Do you realize we skipped lunch?"

"I do." His stomach growled as if on cue. We both laughed. "Ready to close up and head home?"

"Let's go."

***

James silently scolded himself for allowing Ruby to invade his privacy. He wished he'd never talked to her at the pub. Before that, no one had noticed him. He'd been able to go anywhere he wanted without fear of being recognized. No longer. Now he watched for her everywhere he went. He didn't want to leave Sun City before he finished what he had to do, but he didn't like having to constantly watch his back.

By the time he started thinking about turning in for the night, a fine mist covered the area. It wasn't as cold as it had been last week, but the heavy, damp air grew into a steady drizzle. Normally, he would sleep in the loft when it rained. But that was too close to where Ruby had discovered him. She could be stalking him right now. She could climb up to his hideout or call the police and tell them he was there. There was no telling what she might do. He hadn't let anyone get to him the way she had since he'd returned to the States.

He walked away from the fitness center where his loft hideout was located and strolled toward his campsite behind Sharon's house, stopping frequently along the way to see if Ruby was following.

Everything was wet, including the sleeping bag he'd left open. He looked toward Wanda Jean's house. Why not? No one was there. It would be warm and dry. He could leave before anyone discovered him in the morning.

He thought out a plan as he walked toward the house. He'd sleep in the closet that had the attic access, and hide upstairs if anyone came in the house. The closet would be comfortable. He could shut the door and turn on the light. That way he could read the book he'd found.

He jumped the back fence and walked directly to the patio door. He took out the key Wanda Jean had given him and unlocked the door, half expecting Princess to greet him. He went to the master bedroom closet and changed into the dry clothes he'd left there.

Before long he relaxed with his book on South American art and collectibles. The perfect distraction for the thoughts that had bugged him since seeing Ruby.

CHAPTER NINE

James woke refreshed. He hadn't slept so deeply in at least a week. He moseyed around the house as if he had a right to be there. Made a pot of coffee and took it the bathroom with him. He found a pair of scissors and clipped his beard until only stubble remained. Then he used soapy water and a razor to remove the rest. The sink was furry with the wet hair. He scooped most of it out with paper tissues and threw it in a trash container he found under the sink. The rest he managed to wash down the drain.

He stared at himself in the mirror. Not bad, he thought. Only nicked himself in a couple of places. He'd had a beard for a long time and looked different without it. Younger, perhaps, but at the same time, his neck showed signs of aging. He'd shaved to look different.

First Ruby, now that librarian. She'd seen him out back as he looked around the tree. He didn't want to make it easy for her to recognize him and he didn't want to stay in hiding.

James checked the sink again and wondered if he should've gotten out of the house sooner. There was no telling who might show up. Nothing was the same with Wanda Jean gone. He should have left before sunrise and taken the scissors and razor with him. He could have used them in the fitness center or any of the rest rooms in Sun City without caring if anyone saw him. Now it was daylight and he could be seen coming out of the house.

He washed his dishes and the coffee pot before he looked out windows on all sides to see if anyone was watching the house. When he checked the front window he saw that his fears had been justified. The big red bus was parked at the curb and Margie, the woman who lived next door, was waiting for its door to open.

***

Michael stopped in front of Sharon's house in Mills Creek Estates and opened the bookmobile door for Margie. I was glad to see her. I hadn't had a chance to talk to her about what we'd learned from the tax assessor's database.

"Good morning, Liz, Michael." Margie jumped in without spilling a drop from the coffee cup she carried.

"Good morning." Michael and I responded in unison.

"Didn't see you two yesterday. What happened?"

"We were in jail." I stretched the truth a bunch.

Michael laughed. "Well, almost."

Margie sat on the bench and leaned in, sipping her coffee. "Really? What happened?"

I hadn't known Margie long, but I knew the type. She loved gossip. Anything we said to her would be broadcast to the entire neighborhood. I also knew she'd share anything she heard from others with me.

"We were in Salado checking out a house owned by Sharon and saw a man getting away in a pickup piled with boxes from the house."

"Sharon had a house in Salado? How'd you know?"

"Michael used his computer magic to find out."

"Wow. So how did you end up nearly getting arrested?"

"We called the police to report the man who ran, and they took us in for questioning. Mainly to find out why we were there."

Michael turned toward Margie. "They didn't arrest us, but we felt obligated to go with them."

"How long did they hold you?"

"Not long, but it caused us to miss the stop here yesterday."

Margie shook her head. "She couldn't take care of one house, let alone two."

"There's more. The computer showed a co-owner for both houses. His name is Dennis Coleman. Have you ever heard of him?" I studied her for a reaction. It was hard for me to believe Sharon's next door neighbor didn't know about him.

"Dennis?" She scrunched up her nose as if trying hard

to remember. "I saw a man a couple of times, but he usually came through the backyard. That's a little odd now that I think about it because there's nothing behind our houses except the woods. In fact, it's a protected area. No one's supposed to be out there."

"That was another question I had for you. When I was here the other day picking up the books I'd left in Sharon's house, I saw a man back there myself."

"Do you think it was Dennis?"

"I don't think so. When he saw me he turned and ran away. Princess seemed to know him, though."

Margie was silent for a few seconds, holding a hand to her head. "That's strange. You'd think he'd use the front door. Especially with his name on record as a co-owner." Margie paused. "You know, one of my neighbors said they thought Sharon had a husband who didn't move here with her. She said he'd decided to move into an assisted-living facility in Temple. As far as I know, he never lived here or even visited."

"Interesting. Your neighbor didn't happen to say where, did she?"

"Yes. The Royal Gardens in Temple."

"Good memory." I was surprised she hadn't mentioned this to me before when we were wondering if Sharon had a next of kin.

Margie smiled. "I'm known as the main source of information for our neighborhood. A good memory is a must. I wouldn't want to tarnish my reputation."

***

James watched the library bus from Sharon's house. Margie was probably talking about him. She was the nosiest woman he'd seen around there, other than Ruby. He peeked through the edge of the drapes covering the living room windows on the street side of the house. He knew this would be an ideal time for him to scoot out the back door. His only fear of leaving earlier was that Margie might be looking in that direction. Now that he knew she was out front, he should go.

He had to be vigilant to keep from getting caught. But part of surviving had to do with knowing your enemy. He stood looking out, hidden, but still feeling exposed. Why did the librarian keep returning? It seemed every time he was there, so was she.

On the other hand, what could she do, anyway? Not much. He could easily get away from her. She was overweight so he knew he could outrun her. There was something about her that concerned him. She walked with an air of confidence he didn't see often. She always had a smile on her face. What about that young man who was always with her the last couple of days? He looked strong, but not strong enough. There he was now, outside talking on the phone like he often did. Who was he calling? The police?

James thought about the day the police came. Was it because he hurt Wanda Jean? Is that why she wasn't there anymore? He hoped she was okay. If he hurt her, he didn't mean to. Why couldn't he remember? Wait. It wasn't Wanda Jean. That was his big sister's name. She'd been the only person in his family to care for him. The woman who'd lived in this house was Sharon. It was all so confusing. He didn't want to think about what he must have done.

He grabbed his book and went out the back door and ran, slowing down only long enough to grab the top of the fence with his free hand to propel himself over. He ran all the way to the fork in the creek to his campsite.

CHAPTER TEN

Michael dropped me off at the front entrance of the Royal Gardens in Temple. He had some computer stuff to do for Chris so he waited in the bookmobile while I went in to talk to Dennis Coleman. I wanted to find out if he was Sharon's husband, and see if he knew she was dead. If I could somehow work it into the conversation, I also hoped to get permission to look inside both homes for possible clues in Sharon's death.

As I walked through the lobby, I couldn't help notice the place was what I called upscale. The furnishings appeared to be expensive and the carpet pile deep. The ceiling vaulted high with chandeliers filling the room with light. Unlike similar places I'd visited, this one smelled clean. A few people sat in plush leather chairs and sofas near a huge limestone fireplace so large it wrapped around a corner and half the side of the room. Even though it wasn't cold outside, a stack of logs burned on a centered metal rack.

The desk gleamed so brightly it reminded me of one I'd seen at a library conference held in a pricey Dallas hotel back when I was on an expense account. The woman behind the desk, wearing a black suit with a red scarf around her neck, looked more like a flight attendant than an assisted-living facility worker. According to the tag on her blouse, her name was Annette.

"May I help you?" She smiled, probably hoping I was considering moving there myself. No way. I'd rather die on the farm, or in the bookmobile for that matter, than at a fancy home like this.

"Yes. I'm looking for Dennis Coleman."

"Is he expecting you?"

"No. I wasn't sure how to reach him to let him know, but I have some important information about someone he knows. Perhaps his wife, but I'm not positive."

"Do you mean Sharon? I was so sad to hear of her passing. I'd never met her, but Dennis talked about her so much I felt I knew her. According to him she was a wonderful person."

"I see. I didn't know Sharon was married."

"You mean since they were living separately? That happens sometimes. One spouse desires assisted living and the other isn't ready."

Two of my questions had been answered. They were married and he knew of her death. Now all I had to do was meet him and ask if I could nose around in his houses. I was even more curious about him now. Was Sharon's death a homicide? Was Dennis a possible suspect? Why did they live separately? "May I talk to him?"

"Certainly. He loves visitors. He's in the dining room having his mid-morning coffee. He's always at the first table on the right as you go in." Annette pointed at two white double doors; one open, one closed.

"Thank you." I walked through the opening and was surprised again by the elegance of the room. I was reminded of the few first-class restaurants I'd visited, mostly in connection with my job as director of library services.

The man sitting alone at the first table on the right watched me as I walked toward him. I also looked him over. He didn't look as old as I thought he would, and there was a youthful glow about him that reminded me some of Samuel. What caught my eye, though, was the smile on his face and the sparkle in his eyes.

Before I reached the table, he was on his feet holding a chair out for me.

"Hello, young lady. I hope you're here to see me."

Before sitting, I held out my hand in greeting but, like me, he was a hugger. Ours was an exceptional hug.

"Hello," I said as we broke apart. "I'm Liz Helmsley. Are you Dennis Coleman?"

"At your service." He held the chair as I sat then gently pushed it toward the table. "What can I do for you?"

I jumped right in. Sometimes bluntness can accomplish more than tact. "According to Annette, you know about Sharon's death."

"Yes, of course. I'm greatly saddened by her death. She'd been losing her memory for months, maybe longer. Still, it was a shame for her to die alone like that. I can't help thinking if I'd been there I could've helped somehow. Or, perhaps if I'd insisted on her moving here with me, the medical staff may have been able to save her life."

He was clearly remorseful, or perhaps a talented actor. "I'm so sorry. I didn't know Sharon long and wasn't aware of her memory loss."

"It was so gradual you'd have to know her a while to get a sense of the deterioration. I'm just sorry it led to her death."

"You're assuming it was an accident, then." I watched his reaction.

"Of course. That's what the police said." He stared at me, erasing the smile he'd had since I walked into the room. "What's your involvement in this?"

His smile returned even before I responded. I could tell he was used to manipulating people. He was not a tall man, probably closer to five than six feet, but his bearing was such that he probably drew attention to himself in any situation. When we'd hugged, I felt muscle in his arms and back. When he stood to offer me a seat, his posture was that of a younger man, or one who had taken care of himself.

When it came to assertiveness, though, I was once told I had enough for any two politicians. Some of it came out in my response. "Involvement? I'm the one who found her body."

He leaned back in his chair and looked up, took a deep breath, and turned on all his charm as he once again gazed at me. "Ah, yes. The library lady."

"That's right."

"Then you saw how Sharon lived. All that hoarding, if that's what it was, happened before her memory left her. I tried my dead-level best to get her to get rid of most of her junk and move in here with me. She wouldn't. Of course what she collected wasn't really junk. I just called it that. At last count I think she had ten grandfather clocks worth upwards of three thousand dollars each, maybe more. She took better care of her precious art and collectibles than she did herself. In addition to grandfather clocks, I believe she specialized in artifacts from South America.

"I was a captain in the Navy for more than thirty years, and would have made admiral if I'd gone to the Academy. Because of my job I spent a good deal of time away from her so I understood her need for a hobby. Somewhere along the way, collecting became an obsession with her. Do you know there are two houses full of her stuff?"

"Yes. I've been to the one in Salado." I may have sounded boastful.

My words, or the way I said them, caused him to guffaw. "Dear Liz, you are a character. When that Bell County Sheriff's deputy called, I had no idea the person he was talking about was you."

I couldn't help but smile. "That was me." I also couldn't help wondering why he didn't ask me more about what I saw in Salado.

"You sure get around, young lady. Now, what can I do for you?" He asked the question in a friendlier way than before. "Not that I object to visiting with a lady as nice as you, but I'm curious why you came all this way to see me."

"First of all, I wanted to know if Sharon had a next of kin. And, secondly, I wanted to bring you your dog." I added the dog comment without thinking about it much. It was the right thing to do even though I'd come to think of Princess as my own.

"What? I don't want that stupid mutt. Did you see what that animal did to Sharon's white carpets? They're mostly yellow now."

"Princess is with me and I would be glad to keep her if you're sure you don't want her."

"She's yours."

"Thank you. So you've been to the Sun City house?"

"Of course. I helped her move in."

"I'm curious. Were you two divorcing?"

He looked at me as if I had lost my mind. "Divorce? Of course not. We loved each other. She wasn't ready to downsize and I didn't want to take care of a house. I spent the last part of my military career in London being chauffeured everywhere I went and hobnobbing with flag officers while attending extravagant parties. My every need was taken care of. In other words, I was treated like royalty. I rather grew to like it." He pointed around the room. "Even though life is more subdued here, I am well cared for. This is a first-class establishment and the food is five-star. Well, perhaps one star by world standards, but excellent for retirees if you know what I mean. I could easily live out the rest of my years here and die happy."

"From what I've seen so far, I certainly understand why you like it here. What about your wife's possessions? What are you going to do with them?"

The question seemed to take him by surprise. "I have everything I need. My military pension alone is enough for me to stay here, or somewhere like it, for the rest of my life." He paused as if mentally looking through Sharon's possessions. "There is only one thing Sharon had that I want."

"What's that?"

"My baby-blue Cadillac. She took it away because she thought I shouldn't drive any more. I could use it here to go to the mall occasionally. And that's not all. I used to sit in that car with the windows down, smoking a cigar. I miss that."

"Is it safe for you to drive to the mall?"

"Of course. But because I don't choose to drive, I've got a friend who'll chauffeur me. He's only seventy-seven and still has his driver's license. Sharon knew that. She just didn't trust me not to drive. I could buy another car, but I loved that one. Do you think you could find it?"

"Yes. I know exactly where it is. It's parked in the garage at the Sun City house."

"Wonderful. That's all I want. You can get rid of the rest."

"Won't your daughter want some of the things?"

His eyes pierced, but only for a fraction of a second. "You have done your homework. How'd you hear about

Kim?"

"From a neighbor."

"Kim's living in a convent in South America. I can't understand how a military brat with all the luxuries she had could end up in a religious order, but she did. She seemed to enjoy our life of opulence in London, Paris, and Brussels. She never went to church that I know of and never told me she wanted to be a nun."

"Hmm. If she's a nun, I bet she took a vow of poverty and can't accept anything."

"Probably. I hadn't thought of that. Perhaps the convent can use the money, though. Might make Kim's life better somehow."

"Then you plan to sell Sharon's possessions and donate the money to Kim's convent?"

"No. I plan to entice *you* to do it."

CHAPTER ELEVEN

Dennis grinned from ear to ear. He was a man who clearly enjoyed surprising people. Even so, he seemed a bit too jovial for a person who had just lost his wife.

"Entice me to do what?" I could usually read people enough to know what they were up to, but this guy didn't do or say what I expected he would.

"Look, Liz. I can hire people to clean up and sell the houses. But, can I trust them? Even if I don't want anything, other than my Caddy, I don't want Sharon's possessions trashed or given to the wrong people. That stuff in the houses was important to her and, out of respect for her, I want to find the right home for what she accumulated. You can sell things and give the money to Kim's convent. All I ask is that you get all of Sharon's collectibles to the people or organizations who will appreciate what they're getting."

"Why me?"

"Because you care. I haven't known you long, but I know you are a woman of great integrity. And, I'll pay you for your service."

He didn't know me at all. "I don't want to be paid."

Dennis looked surprised. "I see. Well, how about if I donate ten percent of the proceeds to the library, or a charity of your choice. Plus, I'll pay all expenses. All you have to do is sell Sharon's collections, clean the houses, or have them cleaned, and sell them, too. No hurry. You can do it anytime you want. Of course, I'd like to see a list of what you find before you sell it. You know, just in case it's a family heirloom or some such."

I was beginning to believe he was serious. Why was I feeling suspicious of this man? Was it because of the daughter? "What if Kim wants some of the possessions?"

"Then we'll give them to her. But, I think you were correct in saying she isn't allowed to own much."

That seemed reasonable. I hadn't considered he would ask me to handle the closing of Sharon's estate. I had to admit it appealed to me for a number of reasons. Mainly because I wanted to investigate both houses in hopes of finding a clue to determine if her death was accidental or not. This would give me an excuse to be in the houses and perhaps find a cause of death before the body was buried. I gave a decisive nod. "Okay, I'll do it on two conditions."

"What's that, lovely lady?"

"I want something in writing from you giving me the authority to do what you've asked. A limited power of attorney should do the trick. Do you have an attorney who can draw it up?"

"Yes. There's one living here. His legal license is up to date and I'm sure Annette will take care of the paper work and notary. What else do you require?"

"I'd like you to request an autopsy on your wife's body."

His constant smile evaporated. "I'm afraid I can't do that." He stood and turned toward the door.

I thought he might walk away without explanation, but then he turned back and looked into my eyes.

"You see I had her body cremated. We had a little ceremony and spread her ashes here. The staff and my friends at the Royal Gardens gave her a delightful sendoff from a place she never wanted to live. Now she'll be here in spirit eternally."

"Cremated?" I couldn't believe my ears. How had Margie missed that? She claimed to know so much about the neighborhood. And, what about Dennis? He sure rushed to get rid of the evidence, if there was any.

***

When I got to the bookmobile, I didn't say a word. Michael stared at me as if waiting for my usual blow-by-blow description of meetings. Still, I had nothing to say.

Finally, he gave up on waiting. "So. Was it Sharon's husband or not?"

"Yes. And he's either the most charming person I've ever met or the best actor in the world. Also, we will have to give up on trying to get an autopsy of Sharon's body."

"He won't allow it?"

"He had her cremated and spread her ashes here."

"Wow. That was quick. Do you think he may have had anything to do with her death?"

"Like I said, he's a smooth talker. But, I don't see a motive. He talked me into cleaning the houses, selling everything and getting the assets to his daughter Kim or donating the money to charity."

The smirk on Michael's face told me he knew no one could talk me into doing something I didn't want to do. Charmer or not.

***

When we got back to Sun City we opened the mobile library in front of Sharon's house. It wasn't long before several neighbors stopped by to look at books. Some asked about Sharon's death. I loved to talk to anyone, especially when I had some inside information, but for some reason I kept my mouth shut about what I'd learned from Dennis. The neighbors would know soon enough when I started cleaning out the house. For now I wanted to digest this turn of events. Something felt wrong, but I didn't know what.

Around four o'clock, after everyone left, a man I didn't recognize climbed aboard. But I *did* recognize his odor. He smelled like the homeless people who used to hang out at the library in Austin, and before I became director, like the people I sometimes fed on the bookmobile.

I moved toward the stranger for my usual hug. "Welcome to our little library."

He turned toward a bookshelf, evading my attempt to get close to him.

"Thmmp...."

His voice was weak and I wasn't sure what he said.

He cleared his throat as if preparing to try again. "Thank you. I wanted to see what you have here."

I stood behind him as he stared at a shelf of books. The track suit didn't look old, and it was similar to those worn by many residents out walking. Still, the smell of unwashed clothing was stout. There was also the odor of wood-burning smoke. Surely there were no homeless in Sun City.

"Look around all you want. My name's Liz. Michael, there, is the driver and assistant librarian. Just let us know if we can help in any way." I tried to sound as cheerful as possible.

The man nodded without turning toward me.

I liked to get to know all my patrons. "What's your name?"

"James." He stared at a shelf of books.

"Nice to meet you, James."

I watched as Princess sniffed the man's feet. She must have caught the unusual scent as well. Odd, though, she wagged her tail as if she liked his smell. He ignored her.

"Is there anything in particular you're looking for?" Many people are reluctant to say what they want to read even though they have a specific subject in mind. Sometimes the information they are looking for is something personal. Others don't like talking to strangers.

James was the type who only needed to be asked. "Yes. Do you have anything on South American art and collectibles?"

His voice was stronger now and, as he turned to face me, I noticed his clean-shaven face. The homeless people I'd met before didn't shave often. Some never. Perhaps James wasn't homeless. Maybe he'd just returned from a camping trip and wasn't aware of the way his clothes smelled.

"Sorry, we don't." Strange. The books I had taken to Sharon's house and couldn't find were about South American art and collectibles. "I can bring some books on the subject day after tomorrow when we're here next. Would you like that?"

He stared at me just long enough for me to see the pain in his face. His look reminded me of some of the mental patients I'd seen while doing volunteer work. The blank stare. The inability to look directly into my eyes.

"Okay." He went out the door without another word and walked briskly down the street.

"Well, he's different." Michael hadn't said a word while our visitor was with us, but I knew he had listened and observed, as he always did.

"Calling him different is being polite."

"I don't have to mention the smell," he said. "It's still here and will probably linger for a while longer. In fact, I'm going to open both doors to get a breeze going. Clear the air, so to speak."

"Thanks." I waited for Michael to climb back in to ask

him about the book.

"Did you recognize the book he asked about?"

"I did. The same as the book that's missing from Sharon's house?"

"Yes. And here's another bit of information I just now remembered. Dennis said Sharon collected antiques."

Michael's eyes narrowed. "Are you thinking James was somehow involved with Sharon?"

I tried to make a connection, but the only thing they had in common was the type of book they requested. That wasn't enough. "I guess I am, but so far it's all intuition."

"I'm glad you're not trying to tie them together because of the book. Everyone on this block probably knows about art and collectibles, and most have the means to be collectors as well."

He was right, but of course that wouldn't stop me from investigating further.

***

James walked away fast. How stupid of him to go to that library. He didn't need books. He could get all the books he wanted at the regular library where no one would know him. Why had he gone there?

He said her name over and over again. Liz, Liz, Liz, Liz, Liz. She was the one who'd stared at him from Sharon's backyard when he had tried to hide behind the tree. She was the one who acted unafraid.

But she didn't know him. Even when Liz stared at his face, she didn't act as if she'd ever seen him before.

Getting rid of the beard did the trick. Maybe Ruby wouldn't recognize him, either. Was that why he had gone to the bookmobile bus? To see if Liz would identify him as the man in the woods? Yes. That had to be it.

He smiled. He could go back to the library vehicle. Next time he'd take his book and check it in. Wouldn't she be surprised? She didn't have a clue.

***

Ruby's voice was loud. Too brash for the small loft area where James stayed on cold or rainy nights. The whole neighborhood could hear her. "You know exactly what I want you to do. Don't make me spell it out for you."

James sat up. It was dark. Not even moonlight made its way into his hideout. How had she found him again? There was no way she could have climbed up here without his help. Had he brought her to the loft? Maybe. The pills made him forget things. If he'd invited her up, he'd have to burn the place down to cover the evidence.

"Pay attention," she said. "You know what I'm talking about. And you're going to do it. Right?"

"Ruby?" He didn't know where she was in the dark room, but her presence was strong. "How did you get in here?"

No response.

He reached around the side of the sleeping bag and found the flashlight he kept if he needed to get up in the dark.

She spoke again. "Don't worry, you'll get paid. I'll give you ten thousand up front and another ten thousand when it's done. If that's not enough, say so. Pardon me for not knowing the going rates."

He turned on the flashlight and searched the space around him. Every hair on his body was at attention as he turned the light a full 360 degrees and found no one there.

CHAPTER TWELVE

The next day Michael and I took the bookmobile to Cowan Creek Clubhouse, a place I loved because we always had many patrons waiting for books. I couldn't stop thinking about James and wondering if he knew Sharon. I would have asked him if he hadn't taken off so abruptly. He was a strange one. I hoped he would come back next time we were in Mills Creek Estates.

It wasn't long before all my attention was involved with planning the sale of Sharon's assets. Samuel shook his head and laughed when I told him what I'd gotten myself into, but I knew he'd support me. He knew I loved to work on projects, especially complicated ones. With two houses and tons of collectibles there would be lots to do. One chore would be to go through the boxes to see what was in each house. After we inventoried the findings, we'd need to find buyers. Perhaps that antique dealer we'd scared off in Salado would want to buy more of Sharon's collection. The police there seemed to think he was legitimate, but we could check him out to make sure. It was a good feeling knowing that the money from the sale of Sharon's estate would do others some good.

But what about Kim? No matter what Dennis said, I still wanted to talk to his daughter.

"Michael, can you use the interwebby to find people?"

"Sure. Who are you looking for?"

"A Miss Kim Coleman. Dennis said she's a nun and lives in a convent in South America."

Michael nodded. "Okay. I'll see what I can find. Let me warn you, there's probably not much information online about nuns."

While I watched, he typed rapidly, paused, and leaned into the screen. "Well, I stand corrected. Turns out there's a mountain of information about convents in South America. So much so, it'll be difficult to find Sharon's daughter. We'll have to e-mail each convent and ask if Kim is in their order. And I don't think they'll tell us."

"You mean you found some convents in South America already?"

"Yes, but you do realize how big South America is? And I don't know much about Catholic Church hierarchy, but there seems to be a variety of groups of convents."

Michael turned the screen to where I could see what

he had been looking at.

"Look at this. Servants of the Lord and the Virgin of Matará, the Religious Family of the Incarnate Word." He waited while I looked over the screen. "There are hundreds of convents around the world in this one order. I can limit the view to show only those in South America, but the list is still long. I'd say at least fifty. If we know the city she's in, I'm pretty sure we could get a message to her."

"I bet Dennis would know. I'll call him."

"Good idea. Did he give you a phone number?"

"Hmm. No. Can you look that up?"

"I can find a number for the Royal Gardens."

"Perfect. I'll ask Annette how to reach him."

Michael found the phone number and I talked to Annette who found Dennis and put him on the line.

"Hello, dear Liz." He sounded as happy as he had before. I still wished he'd show a little more remorse about his wife's death.

"Sorry to bother you again so soon, but I'd like to contact Kim regarding the estate and I realized I didn't know how to reach her. Can you help?"

"Normally I could tell you exactly how to contact her. Not now. After you and I talked yesterday, I realized I hadn't told her about her mother's death. The two of them never got along, and I don't think they'd talked to one another in years. Still, I was obligated to let Kim know."

"How did she take it?"

Michael looked at me and seemed to be trying to follow my side of the conversation. I should have punched some button so he could hear Dennis, but I could never remember which button was which.

"I didn't talk to her."

"What? Why?" Dennis never seemed to say what I expected.

"She'd flown the coop. MIA, Deserted. No one at the convent knows where she went."

"What are you going to do? Could she have been kidnapped?"

Michael raised his eyebrows.

"I doubt it. The convent said it looked like she packed up her belongings and moved out. Even told one of the sisters goodbye."

"When did this happen?"

"They said she left the night of December 28."

I quickly computed Kim could have been in Sun City by the time her mother died. "And no one has seen her since?"

"I don't know yet. I just learned she was missing. I'm going to try to find a phone number for Arthur today and see if he knows anything about Kim."

"Arthur? Who's that?"

"Arthur Duncan. Kim's old boyfriend. I think she joined the convent to get rid of him, but the last time I talked to her, she let slip that the two of them were in contact."

I wrote the boyfriend's last name on a piece of paper while holding the phone to my ear. After handing the note to Michael, I continued the conversation with Dennis. "Do you know how I can reach him?"

"No. The last I knew he worked in Austin. He said he

was an antique dealer, but I think he only handled flea market stuff."

"Hmm, antique dealer in Austin, you say?" I repeated this for Michael who typed away on his computer. "Well, thank you, Dennis. I'll see if we can find Mr. Duncan and ask him about Kim. If I learn anything, I'll give you a call. What's the name of the convent where your daughter is?"

He stuttered. "Uh..., uh, I can't remember. Not sure I ever knew. Somewhere in South America."

His voice changed. He was full of energy again. "Do you have the houses ready to sell?"

I laughed. "You're kidding, right? I haven't thought about that yet." Sorry, Lord. That was a little white lie. "But, don't worry, I'll take care of everything."

"I know you will. And I realize you haven't had time to get started. Don't forget, I want an inventory list before you sell anything."

"I haven't forgotten. Goodbye, Dennis."

"Goodbye, Liz."

Michael looked up from his computer. "Jackpot. There's only one Arthur Duncan in Austin listed as an antique dealer. Probably the same guy we saw running out of Sharon's Salado house. Here's his address and phone number."

I gave him a sitting hug. This wouldn't be nearly as much fun without Michael's help. What I loved most was how close we had gotten. Instead of the parent figure always helping him become the man I knew he could be, our relationship was now more like that of close friends.

***

James slipped out of the loft before sunrise to lessen the likelihood of being seen. Not because he had someplace to be. His mind was on what happened during the night. He gulped down one of the pills he got from the VA psychiatrist. Then wondered if he'd already taken today's dose. After walking around the block near the ballroom, he settled down on a bench in back of the building facing the Veteran's Memorial.

Ruby's voice had sounded so real he was surprised she wasn't in the attic with him. He'd heard voices before, but only when he was awake. Maybe this time it had been a dream. When he'd been with Ruby at the pub and out in front of her house hadn't she said something about wanting him to kill her husband? That wasn't a dream. Did she actually say she wanted her husband dead? Not really. She did hint about it, though. That doesn't mean she was serious.

"I said I'd like to be a widow, sailor, and that's what I meant."

Fear spread through his body the second time in twenty-four hours. He turned and scanned the area. Where was she?

He saw no one.

That voice wasn't a dream. She was somewhere nearby taunting him. Even though his heart was about to burst out of his chest, he casually walked to the concrete wall twenty yards away and looked over it, hoping she was hiding there. If she wasn't, the only explanation was that the hallucinations were stronger than ever. The meds weren't working this time. They probably gave him placebos.

He searched every place a crazy lady might hide, but without success. Perhaps she said something and then quickly disappeared. But, wait, she couldn't have said what she did without reading his mind. He laughed and relaxed before remembering he may have said it out loud. His life had gotten so confusing.

"Forget her. Think about something else," he said out loud.

If she wanted someone to make her a widow, it'd be easy. She said she left the car keys on the floorboard. Or did he say that? Didn't matter. All a hitman would have to do would be to break into the garage, find the keys and start the engine. After they'd gone to sleep, of course. He'd read a story in the *Williamson County Sun* about a couple dying that way.

"Wouldn't that kill her, too?"

"Yes. She deserved to die. She's the real killer. She's the one who offered twenty thousand dollars to have her husband killed."

"Well, then. Sounds like a good plan to me."

James smiled. His blood pressure seemed to be down to normal, but he decided to go to the fitness center and check it anyway.

"Are you sure the carbon monoxide will reach the bedroom?"

"Hmm. I think so. I better do more research." He changed directions and went to the library. He could check his blood pressure later.

***

I punched in the phone number Michael had found for the antique dealer Dennis mentioned and waited.

"This is Arthur Duncan. How may I help you?"

"Mr. Duncan, my name is Liz Helmsley. We've met, but you may not remember me. You were running fast when you passed me on Sharon Coleman's front porch in Salado." I regretted my words, but it was too late to take them back. Not because it wasn't fun to say, but because he might get scared and disconnect.

But he didn't. "I can explain that. When I heard about Mrs. Coleman dying, I thought I better pick up the items I'd purchased. I have receipts for every item I took. The police cleared me of that little incident."

"I know. I'm not accusing you of anything." Not yet, anyway. I'd called to find a way to reach Kim. Now it occurred to me that he could be involved in Sharon's death. Or, perhaps he could benefit from her death. I'd need to see those receipts he mentioned, but for now I wanted to concentrate on finding Kim.

"What do you want, then?" He sounded more defensive.

"I've been hired by Mr. Coleman to find his daughter Kim and close out the family assets related to Sharon. He said you might know how to find Kim."

"Dennis hired you? Strange. I offered to do that for him."

Dennis hadn't mentioned Arthur's offer. "Yes. He wants me to sell everything and give the money to Kim or a charity she names."

"Sell everything? I…I was negotiating with Mrs. Coleman about buying her antiques."

"Well, now, you'll need to negotiate with me. But the reason I'm calling is to find out if you know how to reach Kim. Mr. Coleman said you two have remained in contact since she became a nun."

"Nun?" He laughed loudly. "She's not a nun."

I wished Michael could hear what Arthur had said. I held my hand over the phone's mouthpiece and looked at Michael. "Can you make this phone talk out loud so you can hear this?"

He took the phone, punched a button, and nodded.

I leaned in close to the phone as he held it. "What do you mean? I thought she lived in a convent."

Arthur laughed. "She's lived in several convents in South America. Kim is an IT specialist and she has a multi-year contract to install computer systems for them. Some of the convents are remote so she sleeps there instead of driving miles to the nearest hotel."

"Seems strange that convents would want computers. I thought they didn't like technology?"

He laughed again. "Yes, you'd think that. Kim told me they're having trouble getting novices to join them. Especially if they have to give up their electronic friendships. Now the convents provide Wi-Fi, e-mail, texting, Facebook, Skyping, all sorts of technology, just to keep up their ranks. I understand they do require quiet times as well."

"So, have you heard from Kim lately?"

"She called in December saying she was on her way

to the States. But, I thought she'd changed her mind or something. She never came to see me or called again. She hasn't answered my calls."

"Does it seem odd to you for her not to contact you for so long?"

"Not really. She's a pretty independent character. She has no reason to let me know where she is. She was out of the country for a long time and may have stopped to visit friends on her way home."

"Well, if you hear from her, please give me a call."

"I sure will. And I hope you'll let me buy the estate's assets when you're ready to sell."

"Of course. We'll let you bid. I'm obligated to get the best price. However, I'm also looking for the right buyer. Mr. Coleman stipulated that buyers must have an appreciation for the items in the estate."

"I've sure got that. Appreciation, that is." Arthur sounded anxious to convince me he would be the best buyer. "When can we meet?"

"How about next Tuesday at the house in Sun City. Are you familiar with it?"

"Yes. I've been there several times."

"Okay, then. Is ten in the morning okay?"

"I'll be there."

"Good. Oh, by the way, how did you hear about Sharon's death?"

"Uh…I think I read the obituary in the paper."

"Okay. Goodbye."

I pressed the off button on the phone and looked at Michael. "There was no obituary."

CHAPTER THIRTEEN

The next day Michael parked the bookmobile in front of Sharon's Sun City house two hours earlier than usual to start emptying the place and getting it ready to sell. Princess went with us and reminded me we should go in through the garage.

Dennis had given me keys to both houses along with the limited power of attorney, but I wanted to check on the car first since I'd promised to get it to him. I punched in the not-so-secret code 1-2-3-4 and the garage door lifted. Princess walked to the door to the house and waited for someone to open it.

"Okay, Princess, I see you. We're going to check the car first." She didn't seem to care.

Michael walked around the vehicle. "I'm not sure why anyone would want to keep this old car. It might be a classic, and it's in good shape. Still, it's old. No telling what will go out next. Plus, the paint job is faded and there's probably rust everywhere. The tires aren't bad, but could use some air." He opened the front door and climbed in. "The leather seats are worn, and the whole car reeks of cigar smoke. Didn't he say he could afford to buy a new car?"

"Yes, but I can understand why he'd want this one. People get attached to their things. Especially men and their autos. Besides, they don't make big cars like this anymore."

"It's big all right, and probably weighs three tons," Michael said. "I bet it gets less than ten miles per gallon. If I had the money, I'd just as soon get attached to a new car. One that's not only nicer, but cheaper to take care of."

I leaned in on the driver's side to see the dashboard. "Can I drive this car to Temple and deliver it to Dennis? You could drive the bookmobile and pick me up there."

Michael climbed out and looked at the vehicle closely. "I don't think so. The registration is two years old and the tires are partially flat. I bet the battery needs charging or, more likely, to be replaced. There's no telling what else is wrong. The gasoline may have turned to water by now and the oil could be more like tar."

Such a pessimist. "Just a minute. I know where the key is."

Princess waited patiently at the door. When I opened it she jumped in ahead of me. The Cadillac keys were on the kitchen counter next to the refrigerator where

Dennis said they'd be. I grabbed them and took them to Michael.

"Here you go, my Doubting Thomas. See if it starts."

He laughed. "If it does, you owe me a latte next time we go to the coffee shop."

"Deal."

He climbed in and turned the key. It not only started, it purred.

Michael scratched his head and let it run for several minutes before he turned off the motor. "All the gauges looked normal."

I nodded and smiled.

He scrambled out. "All I can say is someone must have been driving and maintaining this vehicle without updating the registration."

"So it's in good enough shape for me to drive it to Temple, right?"

"Without registration? You'd be taking a chance on getting stopped. Why don't we hire a tow truck to haul it? Let Coleman pay for it and then he can take care of the inspection and license. He's the one in a hurry to get the car."

I had an itch to drive it, but Michael was right. Seems I'd said that a lot lately. I gave him a quick hug. "Okay, spoilsport. We'll do it your way. It'll give Dennis something to do. Even though he seems to enjoy where he lives, I suppose it could be boring at times."

We were in the house when I thought of something. "Let me have those car keys for a minute. Before we call a tow truck, we better check the trunk. It'd be like Sharon to use every nook and cranny around here to hide her collections."

Michael laughed. "I doubt she would have put anything in the trunk. She would have used the garage first, I would think. There are no boxes in the garage. In fact, there's nothing but the car."

I hadn't noticed, but realized he was right. "Let's check it anyway. With the power of attorney, I have certain fiduciary duties, you know."

When I got to the garage, James, the man who'd asked about books on South American art and collectibles, stood admiring the car.

When he saw me, he smiled. "What a fine-looking vehicle. That's a 1975 Cadillac Sedan DeVille."

"James?" For a moment I thought he might not be the man I thought he was. What was different? Then I realized that when I last saw him he was cleanly shaven. I ticked off the days on my fingers. Now, he had a three or four-day beard, a combination of black and gray growth covered his face.

He paused briefly while holding his gaze on me. "I'm sorry. I didn't mean to surprise you. I brought something for the library, but you weren't there. When I saw the garage door open, I decided to look for you here. I love this car."

There was something about this man that made me uncomfortable. "Just a minute." I opened the door to the house. "Michael. Come see who's here."

Michael came out and so did Princess, wagging her tail. I wished she wasn't so friendly to strangers.

I turned to James. "We don't open for another two hours. But as long as you're here, let me show you the books I found for you."

"I appreciate you doing that," James said. "Maybe next time. Today, I only have time to give you this."

He held out the book I recognized as the one missing from Sharon's house.

I took the book. "Where did you find this?"

"It was in the Sun City Library. I go there often and I noticed it wasn't marked the way the others were. It says Georgetown Public Library, not Sun City Library."

I held the book on the edges. "You're right. This one came from the bookmobile. Thank you for noticing and returning it."

He smiled. "I'll come back another day to look at the books you found for me. Can't stay today. I have an important meeting to go to."

With that he turned and walked away.

When he was beyond hearing range, I turned to Michael. "Get me an evidence bag."

He stared at me with the look he gets all too often. "What are you talking about?

"This book has that strange man's fingerprints all over it and I don't want to obliterate them with my own. Grab one of those plastic bags I carry for when we buy stuff at the farmer's market."

"Oh, *those* evidence bags." Michael may have been laughing, but I couldn't see his face. He jumped in the bookmobile, and came back with a large plastic bag.

"Thanks." I dropped the book in while he held the bag open. "Now, we need to call the police and tell them what we have."

"What do we have?"

Michael could be so naïve at times. He looked so grown up since he graduated from the university I sometimes forgot he was my grandson and hadn't had too much experience. "The fingerprints, of course. James is involved in this case in some way. I just don't know how. Remember when Ruby came looking for him? The man she described was the same man I'd seen over the fence behind Sharon's house on the day of the murder, and—"

"But, there was no murder. The death was ruled accidental. The police aren't going to care about his fingerprints. Not now."

"They should. Just because they've decided to call Sharon's death accidental doesn't mean it was. It just means the investigators didn't find anything to prove a murder took place."

Michael shook his head causing me to try again. "If we can find some evidence that foul play occurred, then the ruling can be changed."

"But the body was cremated."

"That's okay. I don't think an autopsy would tell us anything new."

"How does this book with James' fingerprints on it prove anything? At best, it will show he was in the house after the body was removed."

Hmm. That was a good question. Maybe I could make a detective out of this kid after all.

"Now you're thinking, son. You're correct. The book wasn't in the house until after the murder."

"You mean death."

Stubborn, but he could learn.

"If you say so. But, if you recall, the book was not there the next day, meaning James was probably inside the house the night after Sharon's death. Either he had a key or he knew the garage door entry code."

"Everyone on the block knows the garage door code."

"Probably. I'm betting James wouldn't risk being seen going in on the street side of the house, though. I think he has a key and came in through the back where there was less of a chance of being seen. So, he had the opportunity to be in the house prior to her death."

Michael paused and I could almost see his brain working.

He finally spoke. "I see where you're going with this, but I still don't think the police will care whether his fingerprints are on that book or not. He said he found it in the Sun City Library. Perhaps he did. That means another person could have taken it from the house and turned it in. The other unknown person had the same opportunity."

Boy, he was good.

"Yeah, well, we'll see what the fingerprints tell us. Who knows, James may be wanted in three states for breaking into little old ladies' homes, befriending them, and pushing them down onto their fireplaces."

He laughed. "I guess that could happen. But first you have to persuade the police to check the prints."

I picked up my phone and clicked on Lieutenant Bratton's number.

***

Bratton wasn't as excited about the fingerprints as I was, but I convinced him to come get the book. Probably since I offered to deliver it to the station if he didn't. For some reason I didn't think he wanted me there. If he only knew how close I'd become with the police in Austin, he probably wouldn't feel that way.

While we waited, Michael and I finally got to inspect the trunk.

Michael popped open the lid and stepped back in awe. "Well, I'll be. Look at this."

I stood next to him peering into the storage space but all I saw were some wooden crates. "I told you there could be something stored in the trunk. What do you think is in those boxes?"

"Wooden crates like these are used to transport items packed carefully to prevent breakage. Or something heavy that might tear the usual cardboard container." He grabbed the end of the top container and lifted. "This one's heavy. I'm guessing it contains something precious."

"Wait. Before you open it, take photos of everything. I have a feeling we may need to remember this."

Michael took photos of the crates from several angles as well as several shots of the trunk. "We'll need tools to get this baby open. A hammer might do it. Do you think there's one inside?"

"Maybe. There are no tools here. Let's go look."

"What you doing?" Margie asked.

I almost jumped out of my skin. "Margie! Don't sneak up on people like that."

I turned to face Margie and block her view of the

opened trunk. Michael must have had the same thought because I heard the click of a trunk lid shutting gently.

Margie looked at me. "You are as white as a ghost. Is that because of what you found in that trunk? What is it?" She pushed around me to look, but Michael had made sure there was nothing to see.

I wasn't the best liar in the world, but I gave it a try. "It's nothing. You should holler before you get so close to a person. I'm still shaking from you slipping up on us."

"I'm sorry," Margie said. "I saw you two in the garage and wanted to see how the investigation was going. I didn't mean to startle you." She looked around me even though the trunk was closed. "What did you find? Is there a body in there?"

She had some imagination. "No. Nothing like that. Dennis asked me to inventory everything and sell it for the estate. So, we were checking the trunk to see if there were any assets in there."

"And? Were there?" She just wouldn't let it alone.

I looked at Michael, but he wasn't any help. He was suddenly interested in the garage door above us. "Don't know yet, but even if we did, I couldn't share private information like that."

Margie's eyes narrowed. "Dennis asked you to do it? That's rich. He never cared about Sharon's collections."

That surprised me. Margie had said she didn't know Sharon well and had only heard about Dennis through a third party. "When did he say that?"

"Uh…well, I don't remember. Maybe it was something I heard."

Why was she lying? I made a mental note to find out what Margie knew and when she knew it.

Michael, who apparently had finished examining the garage door, checked his phone. "Lieutenant Bratton will be here shortly. We better close the house so we can meet him at the bookmobile."

"Lieutenant Bratton?" Margie's eyes opened wide. "Why is he coming? I was right. You did find something in that car trunk."

"No. We called him on another matter. It has nothing to do with Sharon." I stretched the truth some, if I was right about James' connection to Sharon. "Come by day after tomorrow when we're here next and we'll talk." I led her out of the garage, with Princess on my heels, and left Michael to lock up.

When Lieutenant Bratton arrived, his smile made me think he was impressed we had placed the book in a plastic bag and labeled it with the information we knew about James. He reiterated the case was closed. That didn't faze me. So-called facts hardly ever prevented me from doing my own investigation.

As soon as Lieutenant Bratton left, Michael and I loaded the wooden crates onto the bookmobile to take them to the farm. It would be easier to examine them without snooping neighbors popping in. The drive home seemed longer than usual because I was dying to see what was in those boxes.

CHAPTER FOURTEEN

Samuel joined us in the barn and helped Michael place one of the crates on the workbench. He grabbed a large crowbar used for repairing fences and handed it to Michael.

"Do you know how to use one of these? If so, we'll let you do the honors."

Michael smiled and took the tool. "Thank you."

I loved Samuel even more for the way he treated Michael. What a wonderful friend and father figure he was for my grandson.

Michael slipped the straight end of the bar under one corner of the lid near a nail head. Once he worked the flat end of the bar between the pieces of wood, he pushed down on the curved end of the tool. The nails securing the lid creaked as metal tore away from wood.

He repeated this at several points until the lid was free. Samuel took it and laid it aside.

A piece of thick plastic sheeting covered the contents. As Michael pulled the sheeting away, I smelled the familiar odor of straw. I couldn't wait longer. I reached in and pulled out handfuls of straw, flinging it onto the floor.

"Go easy, luv. There might be something fragile in there." Samuel moved in closer. I could tell he was as curious as I was. However, he was more patient.

Something gleaming became more visible as each piece of packing was removed. Slower now, Michael and I worked the straw away from the objects until we could see the contents clearly.

Michael looked up. "What is it?"

Samuel stepped closer. "I'd say it's a matching set of communion cups."

I could see it now. "Yes, four communion chalices. They're dark, but I bet they could be made of silver if I gave them a good cleaning. I've got some silver polish in the kitchen. I'll go get it."

Michael held up a hand of caution. "Uh…let's wait on that. These are antiques. Until we know what we are dealing with, I think we should hold off on any type of cleaning."

The boy was getting smarter every day. "You're right," I said. "If these are antiques we should leave the cleaning to specialists."

"I agree," Samuel said. "Now, let's see what's in the rest of the boxes."

We left the chalices nestled in the remaining straw

and opened the next box, and then another, until all were open. We removed only enough of the packing to see and photograph the contents of each crate. When we finished, we had everything a church needed for communion plus three matching crosses, all apparently quite old.

We stared at our findings for several minutes before I realized I hadn't fixed dinner. "Oh my, Samuel. I'm so sorry. You haven't had a bite to eat, have you?"

"Don't worry about that." He nodded toward the opened crates. "This is an important find. I never gave dinner a thought. Of course now you brought it up, my stomach has begun to growl."

"Poor dear. I'd planned on frying up a batch of chicken tonight, along with mashed potatoes and that creamed gravy you like so much. But, to speed up the process, why don't we have breakfast for dinner."

"I love breakfast," Samuel said with a smile.

"Me, too," Michael said.

"All right, then. Breakfast it is. Michael, will you make a list of everything we found?"

Before he could answer, my phone rang.

"Hello."

"Liz? Dennis here."

"Well, hello Mr. Coleman. What can I do for you?"

Michael and Samuel moved in closer to me. I pointed to the phone and Michael knew what I wanted. He fixed the phone so he and Samuel could listen in.

"Have you thought about getting that Caddy to me any time soon? I sure miss it."

"I have. In fact, there's a tow truck coming

tomorrow."

"Tow truck? Do you think that will be safe? I hoped you might drive it up here yourself."

"Can't. The registration is out of date. You can take care of that when the car gets there. Right?"

"I see. Yes, well then, towing is fine. Tomorrow, you say?"

"Yes. I'll call you as soon as I know it's on the way."

"Thank you, dear lady."

"You're welcome. Anything else?"

"No. Just missing my Caddy."

"Okay. Goodbye."

I pressed the disconnect button. "Yeah, I bet he's missing that car. More likely he's missing what was in the trunk."

"Wait a minute." Michael sounded confused. "Are you suggesting Mr. Coleman knew there were artifacts hidden in the trunk?"

"I am."

"What makes you think that?"

I tapped my nose. "Intuition. Something smells about all this."

Samuel smiled.

Michael persisted. "How would he know there was anything in the trunk?"

"I don't know for sure. Maybe he put it there. Maybe Margie called him and told him."

"Margie didn't know he existed until we told her."

"So she said. She sure sounded like she knew him today."

Samuel wrapped an arm around Michael. "Listen,

son. I've only known this lady for two years, but I've learned to believe her when she gets this way."

"I know," Michael said. "I usually believe her, too. But this time I've been involved in the investigation and I haven't seen anything that would lead to these conclusions. What if Mr. Coleman is merely calling to check on the car for no nefarious reasons? He'd asked about the car before Margie saw us looking in the trunk. Remember?"

"I do. And I can't explain my feeling that she knows more than she's letting on. That's why it's called intuition. Part of it is because of Margie's constant checking up on how the investigation is going. Why would she do that?"

Samuel began shepherding us toward the door. "Come on, now, what was all that talk a while ago about breakfast for dinner?"

Princess yipped at the mention of dinner and ran circles around me as we headed to the house.

***

When we got to Sharon's Sun City house early the next morning, the wrecker was parked in front with the driver leaning against the truck, smoking a cigarette. Michael parked behind the wrecker and we got out and walked up to the man.

He dropped his cigarette to the pavement and stepped on it. But smoke lingered around his head.

"Howdy, folks," he said. "You must be Ms. Helmsley."

"Yes. And this is Michael."

"Frank Young. Nice to meet you."

"You ready to tow the car to Temple?"

"Yes, ma'am. I'll just need you to verify my paperwork to make sure I get it to the right place and sign some releases in case I don't." He laughed.

"Okay. This car is special to the owner. It might even be called a classic."

Michael nodded.

"I understand, ma'am. You want me to take care and get it to the owner in one piece."

"Well, yes." Seemed that would be true for any car he towed.

"What kind of car is this?" he asked.

Michael answered. "It's a 1975 Cadillac Sedan DeVille."

"Must be a beauty. Does it run?"

"Yes," Michael said.

"That's good. I'd like to move it to the street before hooking it up. Tires okay?"

I took the question. "Plenty of tread, but you may want to stop at the City Market and check the pressure. It's probably been sitting here for months"

"Okay. Let's do it," Frank said. "I'm anxious to see this beaut. I may have to stop by the shop and get a cover for it. Wouldn't want no rock dings on a classy vehicle like that."

We walked to the garage keypad where Princess waited. I keyed in the code. The door lifted, but the garage was empty. Princess chased dust bunnies where the Cadillac used to be parked.

CHAPTER FIFTEEN

The blue Caddy purred as James drove slowly around the VA Hospital in Temple looking for a parking place. The crates were gone, but that wasn't his problem. He was glad the timing was right to "borrow" the vehicle. All he had to do was get it back before the library bus showed up again, and that wouldn't happen until tomorrow.

He loved the car. The Khmer Rouge took over Cambodia in 1975 when the car was new. He'd never forget that time of his life. He'd worked clandestinely in the country for three years after the revolution. He'd taken his job seriously and his handlers had said he'd done some outstanding work. His reports were to help bring an end to the Communist takeover, the genocide, and the social engineering the Communists tried to carry out. It wasn't easy for an American to move about in Cambodia unseen by the revolutionists and the Vietnamese invaders, but he'd survived. He had tried going from one work camp to the other, especially those with few guards, but he soon learned the prisoners who were forced into labor couldn't be trusted. Many were starving and would turn him in for a bowl of rice. Others had been so brainwashed they thought he was the enemy.

Even so he did his job and sent tons of information back until he was captured. He'd spent the last year of the Khmer Rouge reign in a prison in Phnom Penh. The memories jumped into his head so fast, and were so painful, he screamed to clear his thoughts. That was the most horrible year of his life. A time he wanted to forget, but couldn't. Still, he'd done much for his country and for the world. There were good memories as well as bad and the car reminded him of both.

He pulled into a parking place in front of the psych building and walked toward the door, thinking he should tell Doc Carlson about that prison someday. All he had was the official military record, the one without his secret assignment in Cambodia. Then he remembered he couldn't tell the doctor. He couldn't tell anyone. That was okay. He didn't like thinking about it anyway, much less talking about it.

He got to see the doctor this time without a hassle. It was nice to have a real appointment. James sat on a chair facing the one Carlson sat in. The doctor had a thick file folder in his hands and flipped through several pages.

"How did the medicine work this time? I gave you

Paxil, right?"

"Yes, sir. I think it worked." He remembered the voices, but didn't say anything for fear of not getting more meds.

"Remind me. What pharmacy are you using?"

"You're my pharmacy. I can't afford to get a prescription filled."

"What do you mean? I've got your file right here. You should be able to get these meds cheap."

"Should. If I had an address. If I had a bank account where my measly VA check could be sent."

Carlson looked at James' file. "Where are you living?"

"I'm staying with my brother in Georgetown. But, it's temporary. I don't know how much longer I can stay there." James thought about how hard it was to distinguish truth from lies. He probably should tell the doctor that, too. He couldn't, though. If he did, he might not get the meds. Right now, that was all that mattered. Without them, he didn't know what he might do. Besides, he had lived with his brother once. Not in Sun City. It was in Florida somewhere.

Carlson stared at James for what seemed like an eternity before he shut the file and let it fall to the floor with a thud. "Look, I don't know what's going on with you. But, I'm only going to give you enough meds for one more month. After that, you've got to come in for a full exam. Do you understand?"

"Yes, sir." Maybe by then he'd find another doctor. Right now he'd say and do whatever this one wanted.

The doc unlocked the cabinet where James had seen him take out the drugs the last time he was there. In an instant, James had one arm wrapped around the doctor's throat. He squeezed until Carlson went limp and then held on a little longer. It wasn't good if he called the MPs.

When he let go, the doc's body slumped to the floor. James took all the drugs he could stuff into his pockets and left.

***

As the tow truck driver drove away, I called Lieutenant Bratton to report the missing car. "It's a 1975 Cadillac Sedan DeVille. Baby blue with a white top."

"License number?" Bratton sounded irritated, but at least he took the information. He might help find the car. Dennis was the one who was going to be upset. Maybe the car would be located before we had to tell him anything.

"Hold on." I put my hand over the phone. "Michael, do you know the license number?"

He shook his head.

Back on the phone, I gave the news to Bratton. "We don't know. Can't you look it up? The car belonged to Sharon and Dennis Coleman, but the registration is a couple of years old."

"Okay, we'll put out a stolen car report. But, it'll take a while to get the info distributed."

"Can't you do it on the radio now? I promised to get that car to Mr. Coleman in Temple."

"Well, he'll have to wait."

Bratton was upset. I guess I should've called another

department besides homicide, but I thought it best to talk to someone familiar with the case.

I tried to soften my voice. "I understand. I just appreciate anything you can do to get that car back."

"I'll let you know as soon as I hear something."

"Thank you."

After I hung up, Michael didn't ask what Bratton had said even though I still didn't know how to put the phone on speaker. I think Michael got the gist of the conversation listening to my side of it. All we could do was wait.

We didn't waste time. As long as we were there, we started lugging boxes out of Sharon's house and storing them in the bookmobile for delivery to the barn.

The carpet installers were coming tomorrow so we needed to clear everything off the floors that were being carpeted. Michael estimated we'd need to make at least three trips to get all the boxes moved. There wasn't much furniture, but the carpet installers promised to move what there was to tiled areas or the garage. They also agreed to move the larger collectibles such as the grandfather clocks.

As we loaded the last of the cardboard boxes into the bookmobile, my phone rang and I saw who it was.

"It's Bratton. That didn't take him long."

I punched the talk button. "That was quick. Where'd you find the car?"

"Car? We haven't located the car. I told you it'd take a while."

"No car?" I repeated for Michael.

"No. I'm calling about the fingerprints. Can we meet?

I need to talk to you more about this James character."

"Fingerprints? The ones on the book? Sure, we can meet with you. Where? When?"

"How about the Coleman house? I may need to check it again while I'm there."

"That's fine. Actually, we're at the house now. I don't know if you've heard, but Mr. Coleman hired me to empty the place and sell it."

"Yes, I know about that. Can I meet you there now?"

"Sure. We were just getting ready to leave, but we can stay longer if you want."

"I'm on my way. I should be there in fifteen minutes."

"See you when you get here."

***

James decided to wait until dark to drive back to Sun City. He didn't expect anyone to be looking for the car, but if they did, the vehicle's main feature, its baby blue color, wouldn't be as noticeable at night. He'd seen an IMAX theatre on I-35 each time he drove into town. Ideal place to kill time. He parked in the back of the building in case someone came by looking for the Cadillac.

Sharon had showed him where she kept some cash in a kitchen drawer. She'd told him to use it if he ever needed a little money. When he'd picked up the car keys in the kitchen, he checked the drawer. There was only about thirty dollars left, so he took it all.

It was enough for the movie ticket as well as popcorn and soda. It was early so there weren't many people there. He watched the show twice to make sure it was dark outside before he left.

When he got to Sun City, he didn't go straight to Sharon's house to put the car in the garage as he'd planned. On impulse he drove to Ruby's house and parked across the street. The lights were on inside. He waited.

***

When Lieutenant Bratton arrived, Michael and I directed him toward the house since the bookmobile was so full of boxes I didn't want to explain. Not yet, anyway. Besides, he'd said he wanted to look around again. There was less chance of a neighbor stopping by the house than the bookmobile. Except for Margie. Lately she'd been showing up every day to ask how the investigation was going.

We stood at the counter separating the kitchen from the dining room. Even before Bratton said a word, I had this strange feeling he was going to tell us James was somehow involved in Sharon's death.

He cleared his throat. "The most prominent fingerprints on the book belong to James Johnson, as you suspected."

"I'm surprised he gave his real name," I said. "I'd been thinking he might have used an alias."

"There's not much information on him, other than he was in the military. Has he been back since he brought you the book?" Bratton turned his full attention to me.

"No. But he is supposed to return to pick up some

books."

"Gigi, tell the lieutenant about seeing him out in the woods the day Sharon died."

"What?" Bratton sounded surprised. "You never told me about that."

"Well, I wasn't sure it was the same man. Still not. The person I saw had a full beard, an untrimmed and wild beard. Besides, I only got a quick glimpse of him before he ran down the hill into the woods."

"Ma'am, we have reason to believe James is dangerous." He paused as if to let that soak in. "I'm not considering him Sharon's killer. In fact, I'm still pretty sure that was accidental."

"Then why do you think he's dangerous? He didn't look or act that way when he stopped to drop off the book. Mysterious or shy, maybe. I didn't fear him."

Lieutenant Bratton hesitated a moment as if trying to decide what he could say to a civilian. "He's wanted in Dallas for questioning. James' wife was murdered not long ago and his fingerprints were found at the scene."

I thought about what Bratton said, trying to change my mental image of James from a mild-mannered skittish person to a monster who could kill his wife and then go on as if nothing had happened.

"Did he not live there? Why is it suspicious to find a husband's fingerprints in a house where his wife lived?"

"We don't know for sure what the situation was between them. At this time, he's only wanted for questioning. No one has charged him with murder based on his fingerprints being at the scene. I understand there were no signs he had lived there and the neighbors never saw him around."

"Any children?"

"Two. They're grown. A daughter who is married and living in Orem, Utah, and a son on active duty in the Marines. They've been notified about their mother and neither have heard from their father for years. But, still, they both scoffed at the idea he might harm their mother."

I turned to Bratton. "So, I guess you're telling us all this so we'll keep an eye out for James and call you immediately if we see him."

"Yes. And more importantly, I'm telling you this so you won't take any unnecessary risks. Let's assume he's dangerous until we know otherwise. If he shows up, lock the doors and drive away."

Michael laughed. "It's not that easy. Usually we have a cart of books out on the street and we have steps to make it easier for the patrons to go in. I have a checklist of things to do before we can depart."

"Forget the list. If James appears, leave the cart and steps and whatever. Drive away and call me." Bratton sounded irritated. Not so much at Michael. More like he hadn't had enough sleep.

Michael nodded, looking to me for reassurance. "We can do that."

"Good. Now, let me tell you a little more about Mr. Johnson. This is all public information, by the way. He's a military man. Vietnam veteran. Retired in 1982. Since then, he's never seemed to find his niche. He's held a variety of jobs, the most recent one driving trucks across country, but that was years ago. When his parents died, he bought a boat and the government lost contact with him other than periodic sightings at VA offices around the country."

I couldn't resist asking Bratton about James' medical information. "We hear a lot about PTSD today and we're learning more about it than we knew in time for Vietnam veterans. Did they mention anything about it in his military record?"

"His VA appointments have all been for depression. But, we don't have any details. Part of his military record is sealed. All I know is he was in Vietnam up until the 1975 evacuation. There is nothing more until his discharge except that he was in the hospital for several months just prior to leaving the service. If there is anything recent, it wouldn't be public information."

"What does that mean, part of his military record is sealed? That's unusual, isn't it?"

"We see it sometimes. Normally it turns out the person had worked on some ultra-secret project that can't be discussed for the next fifty years or so."

I looked at Michael, wondering if his hacking skills would shine more light on the situation. Michael nodded as if reading my mind.

"Anything else we should know?" I asked.

"No. Mainly I want you to be careful. But, call if you see him."

"Will do."

CHAPTER SIXTEEN

James woke up and looked around. Though groggy from the pills he'd taken, he recognized where he was. He was in the back seat of the Caddy parked across from Ruby's house. He checked his watch. It was two in the morning, still time to get the car back where it belonged before sunrise. Before anyone reported it missing.

Something kept him from leaving, but he wasn't sure what. Then he knew. He jumped out of the car and ran toward Ruby's house. With one ear held against the garage door he could hear a car engine running.

Did he cause that? He couldn't remember. His mind had more questions than answers. Why would he do something so reprehensible? Was that what Ruby had hinted about? Was it too late to fix?

Ruby's red VW was parked in the driveway. He

climbed in and found her remote control button. Pressing it caused the garage door to open. He had the strangest feeling. Déjà vu? He went in the garage, opened the door to her husband's car and turned off the engine. What about fingerprints? Didn't matter. Ruby would give him an alibi, if she was alive.

He worked his way to the bedroom and shook the man, hoping he'd wake and help. He was alive, but drowsy. James got him to his feet and walked him to the front yard. The man had trouble standing so James helped him sit on the grass.

"Take some deep breaths," James said to the man who did as he was told until he fell to his knees vomiting.

Finally, he looked at James. "What happened? Who are you? Where's Ruby? Where's my wife? Please help her."

"Don't worry," James said, "I'll get her."

He ran back in for Ruby. He probably should've gotten her out first. Why hadn't he? Was it because it was her idea to kill her husband? Or had he dreamed that? He couldn't let her die.

When he got to the bedroom he spotted a mobile phone on the dresser next to the bed and slipped it into his pocket. He cradled her in his arms and carried her outside. Her husband, who sat in the grass, was coughing and spitting. When he saw her he helped James lay her down.

"Is she breathing?"

"Yes, but wake her and get her to take deep breaths while I call for help."

James pulled the phone from his pocket and punched

in 9-1-1. He gave the address and reported the carbon monoxide poisoning.

"Who are you?" the man asked again after James disconnected the call and handed the phone to the husband.

"I'm nobody. I heard the sound of a car running in the garage," he said, "and thought I better check on it."

"You happened by at two o'clock in the morning?"

"I couldn't sleep. EMS is on the way. Wake her and get her breathing."

As soon as James heard the sirens, he ran to the Caddy and drove away.

***

Michael and I got to Sharon's house the next morning and opened the garage door to prepare for the carpet layers. What we saw gave us a start.

"What's this?" Michael looked at me wide-eyed.

"It's back." For a moment I doubted my memory that the car had really been gone. It sat right where it had before.

"Well," Michael said, "I guess we should call Bratton and tell him he can stop looking for the missing Cadillac."

"I guess we should. We'll have to call the towing company, too."

"Better hold off on that until the police have a chance to check for fingerprints."

"Good point." I loved the way Michael thought more like a detective every day. We were going to make a great team.

He shut the garage door as if that would make the car stay where it should and I went to the kitchen to call the police. Princess disappeared as soon as we got there, but I knew she liked to run around the house. She was probably looking for Sharon.

Bratton answered on the first ring. "I was just going to call you," he said.

"Oh, what for?"

"Someone reported seeing an older baby blue Cadillac last night. Don't know if it's the one you're looking for, but there can't be many like that around Sun City."

"Well, that's why I'm calling. Ours is back in the garage."

"What?"

"Whoever took it decided to bring it back, I guess. I don't know how they drove it off and returned it without being seen by a neighbor. You may want to talk to some of the people in this area. Perhaps someone noticed the car on the street."

"That's interesting. I thought you'd probably never see it again."

"Why?"

"A car fitting its description was spotted during an attempted murder."

I motioned for Michael to fix the phone so he could hear. He did.

"Attempted murder? What happened? Hit and run?"

"No. Carbon monoxide poisoning. At this point in

time, it could be accidental. Don't know if you read about it in the paper or not, but a couple of years ago a Sun City couple died from carbon monoxide. The car in the garage was out of gas and the key was on. The theory was that they accidently left the motor running before going to bed and the HVAC system distributed the carbon monoxide throughout the house."

"Is that what happened last night?" My stomach turned, thinking about the victims. I sent up a quick prayer for their recovery.

"No one died this time. But they would have if a Good Samaritan hadn't come by at the right time."

"Really. Who was it?" I hoped Bratton meant James. I don't know why, but I so wanted him to be the one who saved those people.

"Don't know. According to the husband, someone helped him out of the house and went back and carried his wife out. After calling 9-1-1, the man left."

"...and drove away in a baby blue Cadillac," I guessed.

"Yes."

Michael smiled.

"So, whoever borrowed the car saved some lives last night. That's the Good Samaritan you're talking about."

"Yes, but he probably left because the car was stolen." There was a long pause before Bratton continued. "I'm not ruling out he tried to kill that couple, then changed his mind."

"I guess you're going to want us to wait on delivering the car to Dennis, right?"

"Yes. I'll come over and look at it today. Ruby didn't see it, but her husband Steve did. He wants to find the guy to thank him for saving their lives. I didn't tell him the car, or one like it, was stolen."

"Did you say Ruby?" I asked.

"Yes. Ruby and Steve Best. They're the ones our mystery person helped out of the house. Do you know her?"

I could tell by the look on his face Michael recognized the name, too.

"There's a woman named Ruby who visits from time to time. She's never checked out a book, so I don't know much about her, not even her last name. A while back she came in looking for James."

"James?" Bratton's voice was close to a whisper. "I didn't expect that. So there could be a connection between Ruby and James."

"Yes. At the time I didn't know who she was talking about. I hadn't met James."

"Did she say anything to you about him?"

"When I asked her to describe him, she said he had a long bushy beard and looked like an old military type. He'd told her he'd been in the Navy. At the time I remember thinking about the bearded guy I'd seen behind Sharon's house."

"But the man you know as James doesn't have a beard, does he?"

"I think I mentioned to you I thought at the time he'd recently shaved. When he came by yesterday, he looked like he hadn't shaved in several days."

"Did Ruby say why she was searching for James?"

I thought for a minute. Michael remembered first.

"Yes," Michael said. "She had let him borrow her car to go to the VA and he hadn't returned it."

"That's right," I said. "She was looking for him so she could get her car back."

"Hmm...that means he may have borrowed the Cadillac, also. You two have been a big help," Bratton said. "If you don't mind, I'll send some folks over to check the car."

"That's fine. We're planning to be here all day. The carpet layers are coming soon and I don't know how long that will take."

"Okay. Thanks again." The call ended.

***

James awoke to a wet tongue licking his cheek. After returning the car, he'd fallen asleep in Sharon's bedroom closet again. He jumped into action, knowing Princess wouldn't be alone. Pieces of the plan he'd worked on weeks earlier fell into place. The closet's built-in shelves served as a ladder to get to the attic access. He climbed them quickly, shoes in hand, without making a sound, and pushed the covering out of the way.

Having Princess there watching him wasn't part of the plan and he was afraid she'd start barking and alert the library people.

And, bark she did. However, he was in the attic with the opening back in place before anyone appeared.

He removed the hunting knife from his calf sheath and waited, knowing that interfering librarian would be there soon.

"What are you barking at, girl?" It was the woman's voice. "Michael, come here."

James hoped she didn't call for Michael because she'd seen something out of place. Something suspicious. What could be wrong?

"What's she barking about?" It sounded like the young man James had seen on the mobile library.

"I don't know."

"Probably saw a rat."

"There's no signs of rats. Besides, she's looking up."

"I don't see anything. Maybe there's a squirrel in the attic. That happens all the time."

"I guess," the lady said. "We better go."

"Go? I thought we were going to wait for the carpet layers."

The librarian didn't respond.

"Oh," the young man she called Michael said. "Yes, we better go."

James didn't like that. The woman must have communicated with Michael without words. That meant she knew or suspected something. Or, perhaps he was just being paranoid again. James didn't move for several minutes, trying to determine if they had left. When he was satisfied no one was close enough to hear him, he made his way to the front of the house and looked out the attic vents in time to see the library bus pull away from the house. He thought it odd that they left a cart of books in the street.

James took the opportunity to crawl back to the bedroom attic access and climb down, making sure to re-cover the hole. He went to the patio door and made his way to the woods.

***

"Remember what Bratton said to do if we saw James?" I asked as Michael sped away from the house.

"Sure do. He said drive away and call him. But, we didn't see James."

"I saw enough."

"All you saw was a tiny piece of pink insulation on the closet floor."

"Insulation that wasn't there before. Someone was in the attic. That was verified by Princess."

"Could've been a squirrel."

"The sound that got Princess' attention could have, but a squirrel wouldn't have dropped insulation on the floor. The only way that could have happened was if someone opened the access cover to the attic."

Michael slowed to turn right onto Sun City Boulevard. "Why do you think it was James?"

He was no doubt getting tired of me telling him it was intuition, but it probably was. I tried another reason. "Because we know James has been in the house before. He has a way of getting in. I wouldn't be surprised if he's the one who borrowed the Cadillac."

When we got to the City Market I motioned to Michael to turn in. "Stop here. I'll call Bratton as well as the carpet layers."

CHAPTER SEVENTEEN

Michael and I were standing beside the bookmobile talking to the carpet layers when Lieutenant Bratton came out of Sharon's house.

"It's clear," he said.

"Was I right? Was someone there?"

"Definitely. There's a part of the attic just above the closet that has a wooden floor for storage. We found some blankets and men's clothes. It appears someone has been living there. Also, the patio door was unlocked. I assume you hadn't left it that way."

"No. We open the door sometimes to let Princess go out to do her business, but we hadn't today. Do you think it was James?"

Bratton scratched his head. "Can't say. We'll look at that possibility. Two of my officers are searching the area beyond the fence, just in case."

I nodded toward the carpet layers' truck. "Is it okay for us to get started on the carpeting?"

Bratton paused as if considering his answer. "I don't see why not. I believe you spooked him and he won't be back. This isn't your regular day to be here, is it?"

"No. We're here for the carpeting job. Our regular library stop isn't until tomorrow."

"I think he knew that," Bratton said.

Michael nodded. "Sounds logical. If he lived here he'd probably know when it was safe and when it wasn't."

"Right," Bratton said. "Now that you've proved you can show up at any time, he'll be more cautious."

I didn't like the idea of being in the house with someone crawling around in the attic. "I think Mr. Coleman will spring for the cost of changing the locks on all the doors."

"Good idea," Bratton said. "Better change the passcode for the garage door as well."

Thinking about Dennis reminded me I needed to get the tow truck there again. "Are you finished looking at the car? I need to get it delivered to Mr. Coleman."

"All done," Bratton said. "My guys dusted it for fingerprints."

"Bet you find James drove it," I said.

Bratton nodded. "And that means he was at Ruby's house last night."

"And," Michael added, "he may have saved her life."

We all shook our heads over that. I didn't know what to think of James and would be glad when Michael found more information about him. But first, I wanted Michael to see if the artifacts we found in the car's trunk were reported stolen.

Bratton's officers came around the house and said they didn't see anyone out in the field. They didn't go far into the woods because it didn't appear to be habitable.

After the police left, Michael let the carpet layers in the house and I sat in the mobile library to make my phone calls. I called a locksmith first, then the towing company and Dennis. When I finished, I thought of one more person I should call.

The antique dealer in Austin answered on the first ring, and in the same way he did the last time I called him.

"This is Arthur Duncan. How may I help you?"

"Arthur, this is Liz Helmsley. How are you today?"

"Ah, Mrs. Helmsley. Are you ready to sell me Mrs. Coleman's collections?"

"I have a few items ready to sell, but I wanted to ask if you've heard from Kim." I made a mental note to ask Dennis that question, too.

"Not a word," Arthur said. "Now, what do you have ready to sell?"

"How about ten grandfather clocks? That's five at each location. Are you interested?"

"Sure," he said. "I'll take them. How much?"

"Dennis said they were worth about three thousand each. How does that sound?"

"Yikes. That's retail value. I have to make a little something off the deal. How about two thousand each for all ten?"

"Okay. But only if you can pick up all ten by Friday."

"I can do that."

"Good. We'll talk later about when you pick up the Salado ones. See you Friday."

"Wait…what about the rest of the collectibles?"

"We don't have anything else ready. We need to sort through the boxes and see what's what."

"I could do that for you," he said. "I could price each item for you."

I laughed. "I'm sure you could, but I'd prefer to do it myself."

"Do you have experience with antiques?" He sounded a bit testy.

"No. But I love old things."

"Hardly the proper credentials." When I didn't respond, he added, "Just give me a chance to bid on everything first."

"We'll keep you in mind." I didn't like his attitude, but needed to keep him talking to learn about Kim.

"You didn't find any…uh…wooden crates, did you?" Arthur asked.

"Wooden crates?"

Michael walked in time to hear me mention the crates. He smiled knowingly.

"As a matter of fact, we did." I didn't want to tell Arthur about what we'd found in the trunk of the car, but I wasn't a good liar. I learned early on, it was best for me to be truthful and work out the complications it caused as needed.

"You did? What was in the crates?"

"Oh, they contained a bunch of old church stuff. Didn't seem to be valuable. You wouldn't want any of that stuff. We'll give it to some religious museum or something."

"On the contrary. I would be interested in what you found."

"Really? Well, okay. We'll let you bid on it. I'm obligated to get the best price for the family."

Michael grinned and shook his head.

"Thank you. Oh, I'd also like to buy Sharon's baby blue Cadillac. Is it still available?"

"I'm sorry. Dennis asked for the car. Apparently, that's all he wants."

"I see." He sounded disappointed to hear the car wasn't available. "Well, see you Friday."

I disconnected the call.

"That must have been the antique dealer," Michael said.

"Yes, that was Arthur. I sold him the grandfather clocks and you heard the rest."

"All I heard from this end was that he sounded interested in the church artifacts.

"I know. Still, I have a feeling he knew about them before I said anything."

Michael turned toward the door. "You know what? I'm going to check those clocks to see if there's anything hidden in them."

"Good idea. When you finish that, how about doing some research on the Internet to see if any of those items we found in the wooden crates were stolen."

"Okay. I've been meaning to do that, but I've used all

my spare time doing my work for Chris."

"I know you're busy and still trying to find a 'real' job, but if you get a chance, would you ask Chris if he can find out more about James Johnson's military service?" I couldn't help think how nice it would be if Michael could stay and work with me. He was becoming a first rate investigator and, for some reason, there always seemed to be a lot that needed to be investigated.

"Sure. In fact, I'll do some digging on my own first, then ask Chris for help if I need to. That'll let me test my hacking abilities. But right now, I want to look at the clocks."

"I'll go with you." Once again, I liked the way Michael thought. I was proud of him for pointing out we should check the clocks, even if it was before I thought of it.

***

Sharon had not unpacked the grandfather clocks. There were no pendulums or weights. The chains were wrapped for shipping. The packing tape coming up from the base of the clock indicated there could be something stored there.

With help from one of the carpet layers, we laid one down so we could see under the pedestal. The area was covered with bubble wrap covered with tape.

"I wonder what's in here," Michael said.

"It's okay," the carpet layer who helped us said. "I used to work for a moving company. The space under the clocks are used to store the weights during shipping."

I wanted to tell him we would take it from there, but I could see he was excited about helping. A few more minutes of his time wouldn't hurt.

Michael removed the tape until the package could be removed. He opened the bubble wrap and exposed a beautiful, antique crucifix.

The carpet man crossed himself as he moved away from the cross. "Mary, Mother of God. What is that doing there?"

I patted him on the back. "Don't worry. I think someone sent it to us by mistake. We'll make sure it is returned to the church."

He kept retreating, eyes wide open, then he turned and ran out of the room.

Michael laughed. "What's his problem?"

"He's probably superstitious. I'll talk to him later, make sure he's got nothing to fear."

Michael held the artifact, still in the bubble wrap, where we could get a closer look. "This one matches the ones we found in the car trunk. Smaller, but from the same time period, I would guess."

I couldn't take my eyes off the cross. "It's beautiful."

"This means we should check the other four clocks." Michael rewrapped the cross and pulled the tape around the edge of the bubble wrap to secure it.

"Right. And we need to check the ones in Salado, too, before Arthur arrives Friday to purchase them."

Michael frowned. "Do you think he knows the artifacts are hidden in the clocks?"

"We can't say that with certainty." I suspected Arthur knew a lot more than he'd let on. "From his question about the wooden crates and the car, I think we can assume he knew about the artifacts in the car. But I'm the one who brought up the clocks. If he knew there was something hidden in the clocks he would have mentioned them before I did, and...he wouldn't have haggled about the price. Now, what do you need to check the rest of the clocks? I'm hesitant to call on our carpet layer friends. The discovery of the cross seemed to spook the guy who helped. Besides, I don't want too many people to know what we find."

Michael looked up the way he did sometimes when he was thinking. "The clocks are taller than I am and heavy. I can do it with the help of one more person."

"How about me?"

"With your bad back? Too dangerous. I can get one of my old roommates to assist. Max should be available. He doesn't start his new job for two weeks."

Michael paused. "I'm sure he'll do it for one of your dinners if it includes peach cobbler. And, he'll keep his mouth shut about what we find."

"Call him." I went over the peach cobbler recipe in my head, all my recipes were in my head, to remember what ingredients to buy. "See if he can come tomorrow and I'll fix that fried chicken Samuel's been asking about."

"With peach cobbler for dessert?"

"Of course."

"Okay. I'll give Max a call. Then I'm going to take what we found today to the bookmobile and check the Internet to see if any of the artifacts have been reported stolen."

"Good. What about the ones at the farm?"

"I've got the photos with me."

The doorbell rang.

"That's probably the locksmith. I'll talk to him and check on the carpet layers while you load those artifacts. Then call Max and do your research."

While the locksmith changed the door locks and the garage door password, the tow truck driver backed the Caddy out of the garage and hooked it on to his truck. He covered the car with a tarp he'd brought along this time and left without complications. I called Dennis to tell him his car was on the way. Everything was back to normal.

Then Margie showed up.

CHAPTER EIGHTEEN

Margie pushed past me to get to the grandfather clock, still on the floor. The crevice on the bottom was empty. "What happened? Did the carpet people drop it and leave it like this?"

I placed a hand in the small of her back and directed her toward the front door. "Margie, Margie, Margie, I'm trying to get this house ready to put it on the market. Let's go outside to talk so we won't get in the way."

When we got to the front door, she balked. "What's he doing?" Margie nodded toward the locksmith.

"It's standard practice to change locks when selling a house."

"Why? Did someone break in?"

"No. It's just safer. The real estate people showing the place want to make sure no one except the seller has a key."

I hated to be rude, but I think God knew how difficult Margie could be at times. "Well, nice visiting with you. We're heading out soon and there's so much to do, I can't talk to you any more today."

Margie didn't budge. "Sharon gave me a key. I guess I'll throw it away now." She paused, then looked at me. "Unless you want me to check on the house from time to time."

"Thank you, Margie. That's not necessary since we're in the neighborhood frequently. But, I'll keep you in mind." What a strange lady. She'd said she didn't know Sharon and now she confessed to having a key to the house.

Margie walked away, looking back every so often. I could see the pout on her face. She hadn't asked about the tow truck, but I was sure she'd noticed the blue Caddy being hooked up to the wrecker before the car was covered with the tarp.

Once she was in her house, I joined Michael in the bookmobile. "Did you find anything?"

"Sure did." He smiled.

"And?"

"Look at this." He turned the laptop's screen toward me.

"What am I looking for?"

"Don't you see? This is a photo of the altar area of a church before it was burglarized about a year ago. Do you recognize the chalice? The communion tray?"

I moved in closer to examine the image. "I see. They look familiar. Are you saying we're storing stolen items in the barn?"

"Yes." He switched to another image. "Here is a photo I took of the chalice we found in one of the crates stored in the trunk of the Cadillac."

The photo on the screen now showed a tarnished silver cup, one I remembered seeing when we unpacked the first crate of artifacts at the barn. "Okay, I recognize that one."

Michael switched back to photo of the lost chalice. This time, he zoomed in on the object in question. "Do you see the similarities?"

"Yes. They look the same. Both have etchings of the apostles on them. There are probably thousands like that around the world. How do you know the ones we found are stolen from that church?"

"I don't. What I do know is the ones we found *could be* the stolen ones."

***

After eating and washing dishes, Samuel and I read our books while Michael played with his computer. I knew he was searching for that sealed information from James' military records, and I wondered if I had pushed him too hard about that. The boy needed some down time. He should be reading a good book, relaxing, forgetting about work. Besides, did we really need to know what the Navy didn't want us to find out about what James did so long ago? Would having that information make any difference in the case? Was there a case?

"Samuel, let me know when you get to a stopping place, I want to ask you a question."

Samuel nodded and kept reading. "Uh-huh."

My brain worked so hard I couldn't read another word. Michael might not care about reading a novel the way I did, but he deserved some time off. He helped me all day and worked for Chris at night. I can't remember when he did something just for fun. I hadn't seen him watch one of his favorite TV shows since he'd moved in with us. On the bright side, though, he seemed to enjoy the work he did for Chris.

"Okay, luv. What's the question?" Samuel closed his book, marking his place with an index finger. That meant a brief conversation. What I wanted him to use was his paper bookmark which meant I'd have his attention for a longer time.

"Well, dear, it's not so much a question. I think I need you to listen and comment about what's been happening with the case."

He grabbed a paper bookmark and put it in place of his finger. I loved the way he could read my mind and it made me smile.

"I'm anxious to hear about it," he said as he placed his book on the side table on top of a half dozen magazines he hoped to read someday. "Should we see if Michael can join us?"

"No. He's doing some research."

Samuel got to his feet. "Mind if I freshen my tea while you talk?"

"No. Go right ahead." I rose and joined him and filled my teacup as well, then we sat again.

"You know about Sharon's death and the collectibles she had in Sun City and Salado. I think we also discussed Sharon's husband Dennis who lives in Temple."

"Right," Samuel said as he stirred his tea. "I also know about the artifacts you found in the trunk of the car Dennis wanted. You told me last night the car had been stolen."

"Okay. Since then the car was returned and towed to Temple."

"Good. Dennis should be happy."

"He is. At least he says he is. However, I have this sneaking feeling he had hoped the trunk would have been full of artifacts."

"I know you do, but why?"

"I don't know. At this point it's just a feeling." I took a sip of tea and continued to mull the case over in my head as I pieced it out to Samuel.

"By the way, Michael found reports on the Internet of stolen chalices and other communion pieces that look similar to the ones we found in the trunk of Sharon's car."

"Really? Did you tell the coppers?"

"No. Not yet. If we get the police involved now, everything gets complicated."

Samuel chuckled.

"What?" I asked.

"I think that means you're afraid to turn control over to the authorities." He laughed again. "You're afraid they'll exclude you from the investigation."

"No, it's not that. We're still collecting information.

Like today for instance, we found more religious artifacts in the base of a grandfather clock."

"You did?"

"Yes, and there are nine more clocks to check tomorrow. They're heavy so Michael's ex-roommate, Max, is going with us. Oh, and Max will join us for dinner tomorrow night."

"Ah, ha, working for food, is he?" Samuel smiled and raised his eyebrows. "What are we having?"

"I picked something you've been asking for. I'm sure the boys will enjoy it as well."

"What?" His eyes opened wider.

"Pan fried chicken with cream gravy, mashed potatoes and steamed broccoli."

"Mmm. And for dessert?"

"Peach cobbler."

He took a deep breath the way he did when he sat at the table for dinner. "Mmm. A meal fit for a king."

"Okay, now that your mouth is watering, let me tell you what else happened today."

"Wait. Before you go on. What have you done to secure the clocks? With people taking the car and bringing it back, the same someone could just as easily take the clocks. And bring them back empty."

"That's right. And, as you'll hear soon, we know someone stayed overnight at the house."

"What?"

"But, to answer to your question, we changed the door locks and the garage door code."

"Well, that's a start," he said as he leaned back in his chair. "But as I'm sure you know, locks don't keep criminals out. Now tell me about the break in."

My tea was cool now, but I sipped it anyway. "Okay. But first, I assume you'll want to hear where the car was seen during the night."

"Ah ha. That is a proper assumption. The plot thickens, as they say."

"Yes, it does. So much so, Lieutenant Bratton may reconsider Sharon's cause of death."

"Really? Why's that?"

"An EMS call came in a little after two this morning reporting carbon monoxide poisoning. When the responders got on the scene, they found a couple in their front yard gasping for air and vomiting. They're going to be okay, but, according to Bratton, they came close to dying in bed."

Samuel leaned in. "I suppose the Cadillac was involved somehow. Right?"

"Correct. According to the man EMS aided, some guy he didn't know carried him out of the house and then went back for the wife. The stranger called 9-1-1 with the wife's phone, and then he left in a..."

Samuel chimed in. "Baby blue Cadillac. And Bratton knew whose car it was because you'd reported it stolen."

"Right." The rest of the story had to do with James. This was the part that wasn't clear in my mind, the part I wanted to tell Samuel about and get his reaction.

Samuel sat back. "So, the question is, who stole the car? Is this person good or bad?" He held his hands out with palms up as if comparing weights. "He stole the car, but he saved two people. Then he returned the car. Do you know who the person is?"

Samuel asked the right questions. I just wish I had some answers.

I took a sip of tea. "We *think* it's a man named James Johnson. We know little about him. Actually, that's the research Michael is working on right now. He's trying to learn more about this mystery man.

"We got his fingerprints off a book he turned in when he visited the bookmobile. Bratton learned he had spent time in the Navy, but parts of his military record are sealed. To make things worse, Bratton said James was wanted for questioning in the death of his wife in Dallas."

"Sounds like a dangerous man. Are you safe getting into this man's history? What if he comes after you? Who knows, he may have tried to kill that couple with carbon monoxide and then changed his mind for some reason."

"We discussed that possibility and we're being extra careful. In fact, Bratton told us to take off if we see him. We did just that this morning."

"You saw him?" Samuel's voice cracked.

"Not exactly. In Sharon's house we found insulation on the closet floor that looked like the ceiling opening to the attic had been opened since we were last there. So we followed Bratton's admonition and hurried to the bookmobile and drove away, even left some of our stuff in the street. We called Bratton when we were a safe distance away."

"Good. Don't take chances." Samuel looked solemn. "What did Bratton do then?"

"He searched the house and said someone had been

in the attic recently. His detectives found men's clothing as well as blankets. They dusted the car for fingerprints before we sent it to Temple. Bratton liked my idea of changing the locks and garage code."

Samuel leaned back in his chair and went quiet.

I waited for a minute or so. There wasn't much more to tell. I hoped he understood what we had to do and would offer encouragement.

"I came into your life late, luv, but I think you know how much I love you. I would be perfectly happy if you'd stay home all day and read or start other hobbies that could be done here in a safe place." He smiled as he looked at me. "But, we both know that's not going to happen. I'd be crazy to attempt to change the person I love."

He stood and walked to me. Taking my hands, he pulled me close. "All this detective work you're doing scares me at times. James scares me. A lot. He sounds like a loose cannon. I would love it if he wasn't in the picture."

I kissed Samuel. "Please don't worry about me. We're being cautious about everything we do, and we'll be extra careful with James. We don't know for sure, but he may be suffering from PTSD, another reason his actions could be unpredictable."

He kissed me back. "I can't stop worrying. But, I trust your judgment."

"If you two are finished making out I have news to report about James' military records." Michael had entered the room before we realized it.

Samuel laughed and kissed me again. "Okay, that

should hold me for a little while. How about you, luv?"

I pushed away and turned to Michael, wondering if my face was red. "What did you find?"

"Absolutely nothing," Michael said.

CHAPTER NINETEEN

James had left Sharon's attic so quickly, he hadn't taken the clean clothes he'd planned to change into today. The ones he had on were beginning to smell rank. It didn't bother him so much, but he knew there was a better chance of being found out if he had that homeless person odor. When people he passed on the sidewalks did a double take, he knew it was time for a new set of clothes.

His need for a change of attire led him to the fitness center where he could take a shower and find something fresher to wear. Before going in, he found a spot out of the light near the outdoor pool and made sure no one was around to see him. He unbuckled the sheath he kept on his right calf and hid it with the knife near the gate at the fence that prevented children from entering the swimming area alone.

Disarmed, he entered the fitness center through the back door, making sure the woman at the front door didn't see him. Near the dressing rooms, he rifled through the box labeled "lost and found." He took a non-descript towel, but there were no pants and only one shirt. It didn't smell as good as the one he had on so he left it in the box. He didn't like to, but he'd have to look elsewhere.

But first, he took a shower. After a thorough cleaning and leisurely time enjoying the warm spray, he toweled off, dressed, and waited for the right person to come in. If he was going to take someone's clothes, the person would have to be about his size. He also needed to do it at the right time, when his mark was taking a shower for example, for maximum escape time.

While waiting for the right person to show up, James stood in front of the mirror and brushed his hair back with his hands. If he'd had a comb, he would have used it while watching in the mirror's reflection for someone to enter the area.

It wasn't long before he saw what he wanted. A man his size in a beige colored track suit came in and undressed. This outfit would be ideal for walking the paths where James traveled most frequently, and it looked like what other men wore around Sun City.

The man removed his outfit and hung it on a wooden peg next to the shower. When the man pulled back the shower curtain and went in, James walked casually over and grabbed the track suit off the peg.

That's when he realized something was wrong. He

hadn't heard the cascade sound in the man's shower as he expected. James froze, listened, and was soon rewarded by the sound of water pattering against the floor behind the plastic curtain. He grabbed the track suit and walked toward the door.

"Hey!" The man's voice echoed in the small tiled room. "You got my clothes."

James kept walking and didn't look back.

"Did you hear what I said?" The man hollered louder than before.

James left the men's dressing area, walked quickly past the door to the women's locker room, and on to the indoor pool. It was a long walk alongside the pool before he could get away, but he didn't think the naked man would venture out far. Not for a used get up such as what he'd stolen.

There was one swimmer. She splashed along, doing an Australian crawl, with her head underwater most of the time.

When James was halfway to the outside door the angry man ran into the pool area with a white towel around his waist.

"Drop those clothes," he screamed.

The angry man slipped and fell on the wet walkway beside the pool.

James laughed. Not because the man fell, but because he heard his mother saying, "See, that's why you shouldn't run around the pool."

The fall gave James time to get to the door. Before going out, he glanced back to see if anyone watched. So far no one had seen him except the man who was struggling to stand up. He was naked now because of the fall, but he scooped up the towel and wrapped it around his waist before continuing toward James.

James pushed the metal door open and turned to the right, speeding up the pace to put some distance between him and the angry man. Surely that guy wouldn't follow him outside for a cheap track suit.

The fitness center would close soon and most people had left. James made his way to the pool supply area. He decided to hide in the shadows of the bushes near the parking lot where it was lighter. He was not far from where he'd hidden his hunting knife, but he didn't want to move to find it in case the man in the towel was crazy enough to come looking for him.

"There you are!" It was the angry man. "Thought you'd just take my stuff and run, huh?"

He walked up to James and, instead of reaching for his property, he grabbed James by the arm and tried to force him back to the fitness center.

"What are doing?" James asked. "Just take these cheap, dirty clothes and get away from me."

"Oh, no. It's too late for that. I'm turning you in to the police."

"What?"

"You heard me. I'm making a citizen's arrest."

James couldn't believe the man. "Look, I thought these were mine." He held the track suit out to the man. "Take them."

"Nope. I'm going to teach you a lesson." He pushed James toward the indoor pool area.

James looked at his opponent a little closer to

determine his best response. He was probably in his seventies, but appeared to have the strength of a younger man. Good muscle tone in his shoulders and arms. James wouldn't be able to get away without using his military training. He wished he had his knife. That would scare the man away. All he had were his hands and years of survival experience. He flung the man's clothing to the ground to free his hands for combat and twisted out of the man's grip. Next, he moved to put some space between them. But, his advantage didn't last long. Before he got away, the man grabbed him again.

At some point in the struggle, James used an upward motion to slam the edge of his palm just below the man's nose. The man crumpled to the ground.

James grabbed the beige running suit and ran to his loft space over the restroom, about twenty yards from where the confrontation took place.

***

I couldn't believe Michael hadn't found anything about James' military record. My grandson was so good at that computer stuff. And when he got stumped, Chris always helped him.

"What do you mean? Were you unable to access the records or was there nothing there?"

Michael fell onto the sofa the way he did when he was a kid. "I couldn't get into the defense department computers. They had code I'd never seen before. I gave up and called Chris."

I sat in my easy chair and twisted to the side where I

could see Michael. "So, what did he say? Did he help you?"

"No."

"Chris didn't know how, either?" I asked.

Michael laughed. "It wasn't that. Turns out he wrote the security software for the defense department. It was his code blocking me."

"Oh, then," I said, "he can find the information we need."

"Of course he could," Michael said, "but he won't."

I wasn't sure I understood. "Did you say he won't?"

Michael nodded. "That's what he told me. Doing so would violate his ethics, not to mention his government contract. If he got caught, he might not find another white hacker job for the rest of his life."

"I hadn't thought of that," I said.

"Makes sense, I guess," Samuel said. "Although I don't really understand what Chris does." He looked at me. "Do you?"

"No, but it must be difficult." I turned back to Michael. "So, I guess we'll have to do without that bit of information. I'm not sure how we were going to benefit from it anyway, but my intuition told me it was important."

"Yes. I'm sorry," Michael said, "but, I do have some good news."

"What's that?" I wasn't sure anything he said would make up for not being able to find the information we needed.

"Chris offered me a job."

Samuel pulled off his glasses and began to clean

them. "I thought you already worked for him."

"I do. He gives me projects from time to time. This is something new. A special contract to test the new security software he's installed at the defense department. He wants me to try to break in. If I can, Chris will know where to strengthen the system."

I wondered how that could help us. "So, we can only get the information about James if you can break into the computer? What are the odds of that happening?"

Michael opened his arms. "I don't know. He's allowing me to try, but there's a strong possibility I'll not be able to make it through the security. He's the best at this I've seen."

"Well, why are you sitting here?" I asked. "Get in there and break in the defense department's computer. Wow, I never thought I'd be saying that to my grandson."

Michael didn't get up. "Actually, I've already tried. I recognized a lock-down sequence that makes the job of entering the system more and more difficult during a twenty-four hour period. I'll have to wait until tomorrow night to try again."

"That's okay, dear. I know you'll be able to do it. Knowing what I know about James, though, I just hope it doesn't take too long."

Michael looked at me sheepishly. "I'm sorry, but even if I break into the computer files and find the information on James, I won't be able to tell you any of it."

"What? Why?" I didn't understand what he meant.

Samuel peeked over his book with eyebrows raised

and then laughed out loud.

***

When James slept in the loft he would be up and out before sunrise to reduce the chance of being spotted. Today, something woke him. Was it because the sun was up? Maybe. But it could have been the voices. People were talking just outside the loft. He reached for his knife, but couldn't find it.

He dressed quickly and peeked out the movable vent. He heard the voices clearly, but he didn't have a view of what happened below.

He searched for the weapon again before a faint memory of hiding it near the fence came to him. He'd have to find it. But first, he wanted to figure out what all the ruckus was about. He took a chance and stuck his head out the vent opening to see if he could tell what was going on. He saw yellow plastic tape, the kind police used to keep people out of areas being investigated. Could it be because of the knife? He remembered hiding it, but couldn't remember why he'd forgotten to get the knife afterwards.

He shut the vent and listened.

"Who found the body?" It was a woman's voice.

"I don't know," another woman said. "By the time I got here the police had everything blocked off. All I saw was something covered by a sheet."

"I didn't see it myself," a man said. "But I heard the cleaning crew found a naked man in the grass near the gate. They checked to see if he needed help, and called

9-1-1 when they didn't get a response."

"Goodness," the first woman said.

James wondered why he hadn't heard the sirens. But what worried him most was the nagging feeling he'd recently had a confrontation with a man wrapped in a towel.

CHAPTER TWENTY

Max joined us at the farm for breakfast and would be back tonight for dinner after helping Michael with the grandfather clocks.

I met Max a couple of years ago, about the time I moved to Georgetown. He'd answered the "roommate wanted" ad Michael had posted on a bulletin board in the computer science department at the University of Texas.

Max was the type of young man every mother hoped for. He showed my grandson how to enjoy life and still be a decent young man. Max did something else I hadn't been able to do. He got Michael to go to church again. I need to thank Max's folks someday for raising such a nice young man.

We got to Salado about nine to look inside the

pedestals of each of the five clocks there. If any of them contained artifacts like the clock in Sun City did, we would remove the hidden items and put them in the bookmobile for transportation to the farm. Arthur was expected to pick up the ten clocks tomorrow, five there and five in Sun City, and we wanted to take out any concealed items before he showed up. And, we wanted to do it while Max was there to help with the heavy lifting.

Michael backed the bookmobile into the driveway and got as close to the front door of the house as he could. Max helped by signaling when to stop. The lots in the neighborhood were about two acres each, so we didn't expect any neighbors to wonder why we were there. As we walked up to the front door, I thought how nice it was to not have Margie showing up at every turn.

I unlocked the front door and pushed it open. "Come on in, boys."

What I saw made me gasp.

Michael saw it, too. "What happened to this place?"

Max looked around. "What? The boxes?"

Every box in the living room had been overturned, its contents spread about on the floor.

Michael called out from the dining room. "Uh-oh. All the clocks are on the floor and their bases are empty."

I entered the room where he was and saw the five grandfather clocks on the floor. Nothing in the pedestals. "To be honest, we don't know if these clocks contained hidden treasures or not."

Michael nodded. "Right. But based on Sharon's other house, I bet there were artifacts stored here, too."

"Didn't you tell me you'd been here once before?" Max asked.

"Yes," Michael said, "but only briefly."

Max pointed at the wall. "Was the wall ripped up like that?"

"No." I looked at where he pointed. "What's going on here?" The plasterboard had been pulled off the wall exposing bare studs on the bottom. I looked around and found the same destruction had been done elsewhere.

Michael walked to the wall. "It looks like whoever was here didn't find what they were looking for in the boxes so they started tearing into the walls."

I thought about that for a while. "That's possible, but we don't know if they found anything or not."

"True," Michael said. "So, what do you want to do now?"

I scanned the room. "We need to call the police."

Michael stared. "Call the police? What good will that do?"

"They can't do anything, probably. Dennis' insurance won't cover the damage without an official report being filed with the police."

Michael took photos of the overturned boxes and clocks. Max helped.

"Okay. Want me to call the police now?" Michael asked.

Before I could answer, something caught my eye. The floor seemed too high for the fireplace. No matter how I looked at it, something was wrong.

"Michael, come look at this. You, too, Max."

"What's up?" Michael asked.

"This floor."

"What about it?"

"It doesn't belong here. Everything indicates there should be a sunken family room at this location. The fireplace should be higher off the floor than it is."

Max walked to the wall near the fireplace. "She's right. It's clearly an afterthought. But, it could have been added to accommodate someone in a wheelchair."

Michael joined Max. "I don't think so. This wasn't done by a professional. See here? There's no baseboard." He looked at me. "Okay to pull up this floor?"

"I don't see why not. The walls have to be repaired. Why not the floor, too."

Michael took the poker from the fireplace tool rack and used it like a lever to pry a board loose. Max grabbed the floorboard and pulled it away. They both kept pulling until I could see I'd been right about the fake floor. Crates similar to the ones we found in the trunk of the Cadillac in Sun City covered the real floor.

The boys opened one of the boxes and displayed the contents gently on the carpet.

Max oohed and ahhed as he saw each new piece.

Michael was impressed also. "Look at this cross. I think this is the one I saw on the Internet that was missing from a church in South America."

Michael took photos of each box, one to record where the box was found and one showing the contents.

"Is it time to call the police?" Max asked.

Michael looked at me for a response. "No. This changes things. We should call the police, but I feel it is best to take these items to the farm where we stored the other artifacts."

We repacked the boxes and carried them to the bookmobile.

"Okay," Michael said. "We've got all the important stuff loaded. Do you want to leave the rest of this until we come back tomorrow with Arthur?"

I nodded. "Good idea. I think we should take what we have and get back to Sun City to check the clocks there while we have Max's help."

The boys climbed aboard the bookmobile while I locked the front door of house. As I turned toward the driveway I heard what sounded like a gunshot. Grass nearby popped out of the ground with each sound of the weapon.

Michael and Max ran out of the vehicle and took my hands. Michael led the way to the side of the bookmobile. "We'll be safe here," he said.

"Is someone shooting at us?" Max asked.

"Probably," Michael said. "Gigi tends to get into situations like this from time to time."

A number of shots increased and then Arthur came running across the front yard. He zigzagged across the open area as grass and dirt popped up around his feet. He rounded our vehicle and hunkered down next to us.

"I don't think they're shooting at us this time." I said, staring at Arthur. "Michael, call the police. What are you doing here, Arthur?"

To prove me wrong about where the shooter aimed, the next shot hit the upper deck of the bus and glass fragments landed close to us. It wasn't long before we heard sirens. The gunfire stopped. An engine cranked up and an unseen vehicle sped away.

Arthur smiled. "I came to pick up the clocks."

I looked at Michael the way I'm told I do when I think I've forgotten something and hope his youthful memory might help. But, I knew good and well Arthur was lying. "We agreed you'd come tomorrow. Why are you here today? Where is the truck you need to haul the clocks? Who was that shooting at you?"

His smile didn't fit the situation. "I know we said tomorrow, but I was nearby and thought I'd see if you were here."

"Nearby?" I asked.

"Yes," he said. "I was driving back from Dallas and when I got to Salado, I turned off to look at the house. Maybe I stretched the truth a little about hoping to find you, I really just wanted to drive through here for sentimental reasons."

I didn't buy any of it. "You're getting closer to the truth, but you've got a ways to go. If what you said was true, you wouldn't have parked so far away. Where is your vehicle, anyway? And you never did say who shot at you."

"I left my truck up the hill there because I love to walk along the road here. I'm not sure who was shooting at me, but I suspect it was Kim, Sharon and Dennis' daughter."

"And your girlfriend." Michael said. "Why would she try to kill you?"

"Kill me? I don't think so. You don't know much about weapons, do you, son. That was the sound of a deer rifle you heard. Kim can hit a deer a hundred yards away. If she'd wanted to kill me, I wouldn't be standing here talking to you."

"Then what was she doing?" I asked.

"Who knows? Letting me know she's here. Warning me to stay away. Any number of possible reasons. She's unpredictable."

A police car with tires squealing, lights flashing and with the siren decrescendoing pulled up behind us.

"Oh, dear." That was all I could think to say. If we were in Austin where the police chief knew me, I wouldn't be so concerned, but the only experience I'd had with law enforcement in Salado was not too good.

"What's wrong?" Michael asked. "This time you have that power of attorney from Dennis. We have a right to be here."

"Well…yes…but, I don't carry it around with me." I didn't want to mention the artifacts we found in front of Arthur but I was also concerned about what the police might do if they spotted them.

***

I shouldn't have worried about the Salado Police. They remembered me and were much nicer this time. From what they said at the station, I think they had talked to Lieutenant Bratton and Tom, the chief of police in Austin. They didn't search the bookmobile, and they let Michael drive us to the station.

They knew Arthur as well and let him meet us there. I was suspicious about why he'd left his vehicle so far from the house.

We made statements about what had happened. The police asked a lot of questions about Kim, but I had few answers for them. Arthur gave them some information about her, but I had no way of knowing the accuracy of his statements.

When the police finished with us, I told Arthur we'd meet him at the Salado house tomorrow to sell him the clocks. Afterwards, we'd all go to Sun City where he could pick up the ones there. I didn't tell him Michael and Max were going to check them for artifacts first.

"Arthur, I'm assuming you're bringing a truck and someone to help you load the clocks."

"Sure." He looked at Michael and Max. "I bet these two could help me."

"Max won't be here tomorrow," I said. "I guess you and Michael could lift a clock. Is that okay with you, son?"

"That's fine," Michael said. "The clocks aren't too heavy. Just bulky."

Arthur smiled. "All righty, then. I'll be here tomorrow at nine with a truck."

"Good." I was ready to get on the road and look at the other clocks. I didn't trust Arthur one bit.

After he left, the three of us piled into the bookmobile and headed for Sun City.

By the time we got to I-35 I felt immediate relief. Mainly because we hadn't been thrown in jail for stealing the artifacts. But I also thought about the possibility that Kim might be shooting at us back there at the house.

Michael must have noticed my attitude adjustment.

"You've got a smile on your face bigger than Dallas. What's up?"

"I was thinking. When I worked with Chris on a few investigations he always said when we got attacked it meant we were getting close to solving the case."

Michael smiled and shook his head.

***

The remaining four grandfather clocks in Sun City had religious artifacts hidden in their bases. With Max's help, we removed the treasures and transported them to the barn.

It was time to inform the authorities. They wouldn't be too happy about what we did. At the time I thought it was necessary, but looking back, I could see we'd transported stolen items from one jurisdiction to another. Hopefully, Bratton would help keep us out of trouble. I wasn't so worried about myself, but Michael couldn't afford more legal problems.

While I cooked dinner, I thought how best to report what we'd found. Michael and Max were in Michael's room searching the Internet for missing religious items that matched our discoveries.

My fingers were covered with flour stuck onto a layer of raw egg and milk when I felt Samuel's arms circle me from the back.

"That browned chicken looks and smells delightful."

I held up a battered hand. "You better be careful or I'll get this on you."

"I wouldn't mind." Still, he backed away and

examined the stove top more closely. "You *are* going to make cream gravy, aren't you?"

His love for my cooking made me smile all over. "Of course. You can't have fried chicken without gravy. Now, scooch over. I want to batter the chicken, not you."

I placed the rest of the battered chicken into the frying pan and washed the sticky goo off my hands.

His tone turned somber. "Can I talk to you, luv?"

"Yes, of course. Okay if I keep cooking while you do?"

"Certainly. I just want to ask what you plan to do with all the religious artifacts stored in the barn. I feel like we're doing something illegal and I've hardly broken in my green card. I don't want to get kicked out of the country now that I've found you."

He was right. Even though I knew it was time to report what we'd found, I'd been putting it off, hoping there was more to find. "I thought the same thing. Not getting you expelled, but about turning everything over to the police. They'll know who to notify. My only excuse is that we had to move fast to make sure the items were secured. I haven't told you yet about the fake floor where we found some of them. And, to top it off, we don't know who put them there. We don't know who we can trust."

I turned the chicken with tongs and adjusted the flame. The browned batter made me hungry. I don't know why we don't have fried chicken more often. It's messy, but so good. I found a loose piece of batter that was browned on both sides. I scooped it out and placed in on a paper towel to cool.

Samuel reached for the fried morsel.

I smacked him lightly on the arm. "Wait. That's too hot."

He made a sour face, but didn't pick up the fried scrap. "You can trust that Lieutenant Bratton."

A thought hit me. "Let's call him right now. He could join us for dinner while we tell him all about what we've found. You know I always cook too much food."

"Good idea," Samuel said.

I handed the tongs to him. "Watch this chicken a minute."

He grabbed the piece of fried batter I'd set aside to cool and popped it into his mouth and then took the tongs with a big smile. "Yes, ma'am."

I realized I hadn't told Samuel about being shot at, and hoped the boys didn't mention it before I did. I could do that later.

I called Bratton and, after hearing my proposal, he said he was on the way.

CHAPTER TWENTY-ONE

The boys and I told Bratton about the fake floor in Salado and the possible Kim sighting, along with the gunshots attributed to her by Arthur. Samuel's eyes popped open when Max told about the hole in one of the bookmobile windows. I knew Samuel would have more to say about this incident later.

Perhaps it was the food, or the way it tasted, but the conversation about artifacts and shootings dwindled.

Joseph, the name Lieutenant Bratton insisted we call him, raved about my cooking. Max chimed in as well. Samuel nodded knowingly at their comments and Michael couldn't understand what all the fuss was about since he hadn't known anything else.

Everyone loves compliments, me included. However, I know my strengths as well as my weaknesses and I've never depended on others for self-fulfillment. God provided me an abundance of happiness.

After dinner, Max picked up a stack of dirty dishes. "I know you want to talk to Joseph, so let me do the dishes."

I turned to see Michael's reaction.

He seemed to read my mind. "Good idea," Michael said. "You and Samuel take Lieutenant Bratton to the barn and show him what we've found. Max and I can take care of things here." He picked up two bowls in each hand and started toward the kitchen.

Samuel raised his eyebrows at me as he smiled. "Thanks, boys. That's kind of you."

Lieutenant Bratton grabbed his nearly empty bowl of peach cobbler before Max could take it and quickly spooned out the last bite. I think he would have licked the bowl if he'd been alone.

"Liz, do you think you might share this recipe? My wife has been trying to make a peach cobbler for years. Without success, I might add. She's not a Texan."

I laughed so hard I thought Samuel would slap me on the back to help me stop. "Not a Texan, huh? Well, I'm not, either. This is cobbler my grandmother taught me to make in Holly Springs, North Carolina. And, yes, I would be glad to share the recipe with your wife."

We finally got Bratton away from the table and walked him out to the barn. When Samuel pulled back the tarp covering the artifacts, I could see the lieutenant's eyes open wider.

"I had no idea," Bratton said. "When you told me

you'd found some religious artifacts that may have been stolen, I didn't realize how many you were talking about."

He walked around the table, taking in the various crosses, cups, plates, candelabras and other objects, all old and probably valuable.

I gave him time to circle the table. "I'm sorry I didn't tell you about this sooner. I knew once we reported the findings, we would have to turn them over to the authorities. However, we didn't know what else we might find. I wanted to discover it all and get it out of the houses before alerting the thieves. I think we achieved that today."

Bratton nodded as he took his eyes off the treasures long enough to look at me. "I understand. Ordinarily I would be upset that these items were moved. I'm sure it would aid the investigators to know exactly where you found each one."

"I know. We took photos before we relocated anything, but I understand the importance of leaving the items in place for the professionals. We were faced with the fact that there seemed to be people searching for the items as we discovered them."

"I was going to add that since you are considered a professional investigator by some important people, we can trust your reports."

"Thank you."

I looked at Samuel and he winked.

Bratton continued. "However. I'm going to have to get someone out here early tomorrow to pick up everything. You can send me your report and photos via e-mail."

I felt relieved. Not only had I been worrying about what the police might say, I had also been anxious about being responsible for the treasures. Knowing the authorities would take charge of them tomorrow was comforting. Only one more night and the artifacts would be out of our hands.

Bratton pulled out his phone and took some photos. "I think the FBI will be interested in this. They have a unit called the Art Crime Team. They work with investigators and international legal authorities around the world to recover stolen works of art. I'll e-mail these photos and see if I'm right."

Bratton helped Samuel replace the tarp to cover the artifacts. "Since this is not a homicide, I won't be doing the investigation myself. Some members of the special theft team will be here first thing in the morning. They'll know who else to include."

We waited outside the barn while Samuel locked the door.

Before I leave," Bratton said looking at me, "I need your help with a homicide matter."

I stopped and turned back to the lieutenant. "What's that?"

"I found another connection between Ruby Best and James Johnson."

"Oh, my," Samuel said.

"What is it?" I asked.

"On the night James' wife was murdered in Dallas, a car registered to Ruby was spotted nearby. The vehicle was videotaped in a grocery store parking lot near the wife's home. The police only recently saw the license plate on the store's surveillance video."

"You don't think Ruby had anything to do with that murder, do you?"

"Oh, no. Ruby told you James borrowed her car to go to the VA. All we want to do is find out what happened that night. She seems reluctant to talk to me. I think it is because of a fear of James. I wonder if you could meet with her in a non-stressful place and see what you can learn."

I needed to pray for Ruby, but I couldn't imagine her being a bad person. "I'm going to meet with a buyer for Sharon's clocks tomorrow morning, but I'll call Ruby and see when we could get together."

"Thank you. Maybe she'll talk to you."

That reminded me Michael and I wouldn't be home when the special robbery investigation team arrived in the morning. "Samuel, can you be here when the authorities come to pick up the artifacts?"

"Yes, of course."

It passed through my mind that Samuel would be happy to get the stolen goods off the farm.

Bratton lingered. "There's another bit of information I need to tell you about."

"What's that?"

"It's a long shot, but I'm telling you because I want you to be careful. A few days ago, the name James Johnson showed up as wanted in Temple. Seems a VA psychiatrist was choked and left for dead. His sample meds were taken."

My heart pounded for the doctor. "Oh, my goodness.

That poor man."

"James Johnson is a common name, but I have to look into the possibility that this was done by the same person we're looking for here. Especially because he told Ruby he was going to the VA when he borrowed her car and this happened near the time the Cadillac was missing."

I didn't want to believe our James would be capable of such a heinous crime. "Please let us know as soon as you learn anything that ties our James Johnson to the murder."

"Will do. In the meantime, be extra careful if you see him."

"Yes," Samuel said, "be careful."

Before we walked Bratton to his car, I went inside and dished up some peach cobbler. "Here, take this for your wife."

He looked disappointed.

"Don't worry. There's enough for you, too."

Max left shortly afterwards, still thanking me for a wonderful day. Not only the food, but the excitement as well. He'd never been shot at or visited a police station before and couldn't wait to tell his mother. I hoped she understood.

***

The red-glowing digits on the dresser clock said it was three fifteen when I woke up, not knowing why. I quickly determined it was because of Princess' low, this-is-serious growl. It was as if she made the sound just loud enough to awaken me without alerting anyone else.

I shook Samuel gently. When he was awake, I whispered, "Princess seems to think we have uninvited guests. I suggest we go check."

Samuel got up. There was enough moonlight coming in the windows for me to watch him. He paused at one window before he went to the closet and came out in his robe and house slippers. He also had his shotgun.

Princess was quiet now. Since we were awake and taking action I guess she was satisfied she had done her job. However, we didn't know what she'd heard or smelled.

Samuel came close to me and whispered, "From the window I saw some shadows moving around the barn door. Would you wake Michael while I go down? Tell him to bring his shotgun, loaded."

I dreaded that. Michael had only recently become eligible to own a gun in the home because of his prison time and had taken up shooting at Samuel's suggestion. Samuel had taught him gun safety first, but I knew even the most careful people had accidents from time to time.

"Are you sure?"

"Yes. Don't worry, luv. I'll watch out for him."

I woke Michael and explained the situation. We went to the kitchen door where Samuel waited.

The three of us huddled there. "I think someone is trying to break into the barn. Here's what I suggest. We open this door without making a sound. Liz, that means you have to hold Princess so she won't run out. Michael, you and I will go out and get into position, me on the right and you on the left. We sneak up on them at the barn door. Liz, you count to thirty, slowly, and then flip this light switch." He took my hand and showed the switch that turned on the lights above the barn door. "Okay?"

"Wait," Michael said. "What do we do then? Shouldn't we call the police?"

"We can call the police later. Right now we need to stop the bad guys from getting the treasures."

"What if they don't stop?" Michael asked.

"Then we shoot."

"Shoot?"

"Aim high," Samuel said. "Really high. Don't want to hit the barn."

"Oh," Michael said. "You want to scare them off."

"Yes. Don't shoot anyone."

I picked up Princess and held her a little tighter than usual and hoped she wouldn't bark. Samuel turned the doorknob and slowly opened the door. However, Princess didn't understand the plan for she wiggled and kicked until she was out of my hands and she went flying through the door, barking as loudly as she could as she ran toward the barn. So much for planning.

"Alternate plan." Samuel shook his head. "Follow the dog and shoot toward the sky. Liz, turn the lights on now."

Samuel and Michael went toward the barn. I couldn't remember which switch he'd showed me would light up the barn so I flipped them all. Light washed over areas I didn't know were part of the farm. Two people ran under one light with Princess at their heels. A shotgun went off and then another sounded. The runners revved up their speed. Princess stopped and headed back with what looked like triumph on her face.

It was late and we decided to wait until morning to call the police. Bratton knew about the artifacts, but I didn't want to try to explain them to anyone else this close to turning the items over to the authorities.

***

I woke at six and made a huge stack of pancakes, each one large enough to cover a dinner plate. I also fried up enough sausage patties for an army. Then I took two cups of coffee out to the barn where my men had stayed the rest of the night to protect the treasures. They had talked about taking turns staying awake, but when I got there, both were sound asleep, Michael on an old sleeping bag he hadn't used since high school, and Samuel in a chair at the desk. But, there was nothing to worry about. Princess was wide awake and standing guard.

"Who's ready for breakfast?"

They both sat up quickly.

"I am," Michael said.

"Me, too." Samuel rubbed his eyes.

Princess stood on her hind legs to get my attention.

I handed the guys a cup of java, still warm enough to steam in the cooler air. "Thanks to you two, and Princess, we made it through the night without another attempted break-in. Now we can turn everything over to the police and be done with it."

Samuel sipped his coffee then raised his cup. "I'll drink to that."

Michael stood. "Me, too. What's for breakfast?"

"Pancakes and sausage."

That got Samuel up and moving toward the door. "Sounds good to me. I think this place will be safe while we go eat."

Michael followed him. "Should be. Samuel, now that we know what can happen, are you okay staying here alone until the police arrive?"

Samuel stopped and turned toward us. "Thank you, son, for asking. Yes. I'll be okay. I doubt if anyone would approach here in daylight. All I have to do is stay awake. Perhaps you could leave that alarm dog with me just in case."

He laughed, but I could tell he was glad Princess had alerted us when she did.

CHAPTER TWENTY-TWO

After breakfast, Michael put the phone on speaker and I called Bratton to tell him about the uninvited guests who came to see us in the wee hours of the morning.

"They're not still there, are they?" The Lieutenant sounded more concerned than I expected he would. I liked that.

"No. After Princess woke us, we scared them off."

"That's good. How many were there?"

"It all happened pretty fast, so I'm not positive. I saw two people running away."

"Did they get in the house?"

"No. We're pretty sure they were trying to break into the barn. It was as if they knew where the treasures were kept."

"Had you told anyone what you have stored there?"

I looked at Michael and Samuel. Both shook their heads

"We didn't tell anyone." I thought for a few seconds. "Margie Cummings saw one of the grandfather clocks that had contained some of the artifacts and asked about it. And, before that, she may have seen some boxes in the trunk of the Cadillac."

"Margie, hmm." It sounded as if Bratton was taking notes.

I could tell him how she always sneaked up on me, but I didn't.

He continued. "Did you recognize the intruders?"

"No. They took off in a hurry when we turned on the lights. I don't know how anyone would know to look in the barn."

"One explanation would be that someone followed you home and watched while you unloaded the artifacts."

"Seems unlikely," I said. "You've been here. It's at least a quarter of a mile from the highway to the house. We'd know if someone followed us and got close enough to watch us carry the artifacts into the barn."

Michael nodded his agreement.

Bratton continued. "Not necessarily. You've got a lot of trees around the house and barn. Someone could have parked out on the highway and walked in with binoculars to spy on you."

I doubted that. "That's possible. But why were they here last night? Or, I should say earlier this morning. Two people couldn't take all the treasures we've got and walk that far to get to their car."

"Hmm. You're right. I think I'll come out there right now and look around. I'll send a team out to check for tracks and see where they lead."

"Michael and I need to leave before you get here. Samuel can show you around."

"I understand. After I've viewed the area, I'll wait with Samuel until the FBI arrives."

Samuel smiled.

"Thank you," I said. "Michael and Samuel stayed up to guard the barn after we scared off the intruders. They're both tired, I'm sure." I looked at them and Michael nodded. Samuel, the one who had fallen asleep while on watch, a matter I felt shouldn't be mentioned, gave a so-so sign indicating he wasn't too tired to continue the watch.

"I'm heading that way now." Bratton sounded as if he wanted to be sure the treasures were safe.

"Okay. Michael and I are going to Salado to meet Arthur and help him load the clocks. Then we'll go to Sun City and pack up the rest of them."

"See if Arthur got a good night's sleep." Bratton laughed, but I had a feeling he wouldn't have said it if he didn't have at least a suspicion about the antique dealer.

"I'll do that." I got Michael's attention, indicating he should do so, too.

***

James found his hunting knife. It was in the brush near

the fence covered with dead leaves and still in its sheath. He hid it under his arm and made his way to the men's restroom in the activities center. Once in a stall, he strapped the sheathed knife to his right calf, which made him feel more secure than he had in the last two days.

As he left the building, a sudden headache hit him. Something was wrong. He had taken the pills he'd gotten from the doctor. The headaches were worse and the anxiety hadn't improved.

In addition to his aches and pains and constant alertness, he lost large periods of time. He was fairly certain he'd taken a shower the other night and found some new clothes. The next thing he remembered was waking up and hearing voices below his attic hideout.

Had something happened during that lapse? Was he responsible for the injured person the people were talking about? Why couldn't he recall?

There was also the carbon monoxide incident. He remembered some of the details, but not enough to determine his involvement. He knew he'd gotten Ruby and her husband out of the house, but he had no memory of why he was there in the middle of the night.

He recalled how Princess had found him at Sharon's house. That was scary. But, he would love to know what happened before he fell asleep in the closet. Also, he wasn't sure what had happened to Sharon.

A crowd of people gathered near the front door of the activities center building he had exited. His curiosity got the best of him and he made his way to the front of the group to see why they were congregating. A white bus was parked in the circular drive near the curb with its door open. The bus driver collected tickets as people got on the bus.

James watched for a few minutes then moved toward the bus to get a better look at what was going on.

"Excuse me," a red-faced man said. "There's a line here."

James stopped. "Sorry. I'm not trying to cut in. I don't have a ticket. I was curious about where you're going."

The irritated man grunted. The woman with him offered a smile that looked as if she wanted to apologize for the man she was with, but had second thoughts.

"Where does this bus go?" James asked the woman.

"It's a tour bus. Today we're going to Austin for dinner and a play. There are a lot of bus trips planned for the year."

"Interesting." James gave the lady a smile. "Is there a schedule of tours posted somewhere?"

"Sure. It's all online," she said. "You can make reservations and buy tickets on the Internet."

"Online?"

She looked at him a few moments. "Or, you can buy tickets at the office. The bus schedule is posted on the bulletin board outside the office." She pointed. "Right in there."

"Thank you." James entered the building and walked in the direction she'd pointed. He found the bulletin board and looked over the schedule. He memorized the events and times for the rest of the month, but his hope deflated when he saw it was for residents only.

At first, he'd hoped a bus tour might be an easy way

to leave Sun City. Now he wasn't sure if he could do it. Still, he needed to get out of this town. With all the close calls he'd had and his memory lapses, it was only a matter of time before he would be found out and arrested. There was no telling what all he was guilty of. For now, he'd better stay at the campsite. No one had found it yet.

***

On our way to Salado, I called Dennis to give him an update and to ask if Kim had been to see him.

Dennis answered on the first ring. "Hello."

"Good morning. Hope I didn't wake you. I forget retired people don't get up as early as working people."

"No problem. I'm an early bird. I'm usually in the dining room by six every morning for breakfast. What's up?"

"Just wanted to give you a status report. I've sold the ten grandfather clocks to Arthur for two thousand dollars each. He's picking them up today."

"That's good to hear. They're probably the most valuable items Sharon had. The rest is probably junk."

"We'll see." I still had this funny feeling Dennis knew more than he let on. Could he have been involved in the attempted raid at the barn last night? I knew he wouldn't have been there himself, not at his age, although he may have sent someone. But why? If he wanted what we found in the house, he could have taken it and not hired me.

I wanted to ask him what he knew about the artifacts,

but I didn't. Instead, I began with the question about his daughter. "Have you seen Kim recently?"

"Kim? Is she in town? You didn't tell her where I live, did you?"

"No. I haven't talked to her. We're not positive she's here. Someone shot at Arthur as he approached the Salado house yesterday and he thought it could be her."

"Kim? Shooting at Arthur?" He sounded surprised.

"Like I said, we don't know for sure. Just going by what Arthur said. You sound like you don't think she'd do such a thing."

"I don't. It seems unlikely she'd shoot at anyone."

I remembered something Dennis said that bothered me. "Why don't you want me to tell her where you live?"

"Ah, ah..." He stammered but soon regained his speech. "She'll blame me for her mother's death."

"Why?"

"For not being there to protect her."

"From what I've heard, Kim and her mother weren't close." Every time I talked to Dennis, what I knew about the family got fuzzier instead of clearer.

"They weren't. But, with Kim being a nun and all, most of their conflicts had to do with Kim's concern about her mother's soul."

I wondered if I should tell Dennis Kim wasn't really a nun. I decided not to. I'd save that for a later discussion. It confused me he didn't know more about his daughter. Someone had lied and I wanted to find out who before I let him know what I knew.

"You're going to need to talk to her at some point," I said. "I would think you'd want to work with her about what happens to her mother's property." Especially since she wasn't a nun.

"There's no need to worry yourself about all that. Legally, it all belongs to me and I want you to dispose of it. If Kim should challenge that, tell her to see me."

"So it is okay to give her your address?"

"Uh…no. Just my phone number."

"Okay. I don't know if I'll see her anytime soon, but if I do, and if she asks, I'll give her your phone number."

"Yes. That's fine."

"We're at the house now, so I'll say goodbye."

"Thanks for the update. Have a good day."

***

Michael and I got to the Salado house before Arthur arrived. We went in and had sifted through a couple of the boxes before a rental truck parked in front of the house. We didn't find anything of value, just used clothes, books, and family photo albums.

I opened the front door before Arthur knocked and I was surprised to see a woman with him. "So, you brought some help after all," I said.

The woman was dressed in a cowboy style shirt with tails tucked into white jeans. She was slender and the silver buckle on her belt lay flat. She brushed back her brownish blond hair and moved toward me, not stopping until our faces were mere inches away. I didn't back down.

I could have heard her whisper, but she chose to shout. "I don't know who you are, lady, but this is my house and I want you to leave. Now!"

She put hands on hips and waited. Michael moved up behind me and Arthur took a step backward, moving away from us all.

CHAPTER TWENTY-THREE

"You must be Kim," I said, forcing a smile without giving an inch of territory. I could be stubborn when I felt like it.

"I am. And you must leave."

I held my ground. Michael was at my side. "I don't intend to leave. I have a power of attorney from your father, who owns this house. All you have is..." I didn't want to be rude.

Michael didn't mind. "A loud mouth."

"Be nice, Michael."

Kim's eyes glared and her nostrils flared even as she moved back, but only slightly. "I don't care what Dad told you or what he gave you. Mother said I could have the houses and everything in them. When he abandoned her he lost his interest in it all. If he told you anything different than that, he's lying. I'll take you both to court to prove it."

"You need to talk to him, not me. I am authorized to sell everything, houses and contents. Talk to him and have him tell me. Right now the clocks are for sale and Arthur offered to buy them." I looked at Arthur. "I assume that's why you're here. Do you have the twenty thousand dollars we agreed on for the ten grandfather clocks?"

"Yes." He took a tentative step into the house.

"No you don't," Kim said loudly.

She turned to me. "We're not going to pay Daddy for what is rightfully mine."

Arthur didn't agree or disagree. Instead, he walked into the house and went into the living room.

I crossed my arms. It occurred to me that I usually gave a hug to people I met for the first time, or just happened to meet. But even I had limits. "Then you don't get the clocks. I'll offer them to the next higher bidder."

Michael turned toward me with eyebrows arched. If I could have answered his silent query in front of our visitors, I would have said, "I know, Michael, there are no bidders."

Arthur seemed nervous. Probably because of the bluster in Kim's voice. "What happened to the floor?" he asked.

Kim all but ran over to where he was and they locked eyes.

"We're remodeling," I said. "Getting the place ready to sell."

Michael came to my aid. "Yes. Turns out there was once a sunken family room and we're converting it back to the way it was. The house should sell easier that way."

Arthur looked toward Michael. "Did you find anything under the floor?"

Michael didn't look at me or waver in his lie. "Under the floor? No. Why do you ask?"

Arthur turned his palms up. "Because it's strange to have a fake floor that large without someone using it for storage."

"That's right," Kim said. "What'd you do with what you found?"

She talked to Michael, ignoring me. But I jumped into the conversation anyway. "What do you think was there?"

"How should I know?" she said, hands back on her hips. "Now I want you two out of here. If you don't leave at this moment, I will call the police."

I moved up to her and matched her stance by placing my hands on my hips. "Really? You're going to call the police? That will be interesting. Arthur has already told them you were the most likely one to be shooting at us yesterday."

She glared at him. "You what?"

He shrugged, but moved toward the door.

"You idiot," she said, following him.

Kim yawned about that time, reminding me of our early morning visitors. Arthur yawned, too. Did he do it because he saw her yawn? Or had they both been up all night?

I wanted to fuel the anger Kim exhibited toward

Arthur, and perhaps entice one or both of them to say something they otherwise wouldn't. "Yes. He even said how good you were at deer hunting and how you would have shot him if you'd really wanted to."

"Is that what he said?" She spoke louder and her face turned crimson.

I pushed on. "Yes. So you go ahead and call the police. They're looking for you and I'm sure they'd love to talk to you." I pulled out my phone. "Why don't I call them for you?"

She grabbed Arthur's arm and walked briskly toward the door. "You haven't heard the end of this. I know what you're doing and you won't get away with it."

She was outside walking toward the truck and I was on the front porch. "And neither will you," I said.

Michael snapped a photo of the truck's license plate while I called the police.

***

It was warm enough for James to lay on top of the sleeping bag he'd stolen from someone's garage when he first moved out of Sharon's house. Even though trees surrounded his campsite and helped hide him, he'd selected a sleeping spot with a clear view of the sky. He loved to look at the stars and often marveled at the vastness of the universe.

Truth be told, James preferred to sleep outdoors. He'd moved to the inside places during the colder weather, but now the temperature was such that he could stay overnight at his campsite. When he was in Vietnam and Cambodia he'd spent many nights alone camping out while forced to find food or water to survive.

His spot on Mills Creek was lonely as well, but he liked it. When necessary, he could hunker down at the campsite for weeks. He could bathe in the creek when he had to. He didn't want to take a chance on getting spotted at the fitness center.

The main problem he had at the campsite was having water to drink and food to eat. Sharon had supplied both, but now she was gone. He could kill animals and cook them, but that increased the risk of discovery. Plus, he didn't have a way to store leftovers. He'd still have to leave the campsite from time to time to replenish his supplies. But, he vowed to only go out when most people were asleep. Doing otherwise was too dangerous.

After dark, all he'd have to watch for were the COPS, Citizens on Patrol Service. The Sun City volunteers who drove around all day and all night, watching for anything out of the ordinary. He'd managed to escape their notice for months, so he knew he could keep doing it. Especially if he spent most of his time at the campsite.

As he lay on his sleeping bag, observing the stars, a plane flew by. Red and green lights glowed like tiny multicolored stars as the aircraft crossed overhead. It reminded him of the times in Cambodia when he'd waited to be rescued by air and taken home. He half wished someone might find him now and help him out of this jungle.

He heard another engine in the air, this time much lower. He couldn't see it, but it sounded like a helicopter. He remembered all the times he'd been onboard military helicopters. His heartbeat accelerated at the memories. They were both good and bad.

***

Michael and I went to Sharon's Sun City house even though we didn't expect Arthur to show up as scheduled. It was apparent that Kim would tell him what to do and he would do it.

Lieutenant Bratton's car was parked out front so I'm glad we didn't give up for the day and go home.

We found him in the backyard staring over the fence.

"What brings you here?" I asked.

"I'm not sure. We had another incident. And I keep thinking about this James character and how he's been on the periphery of several strange occurrences. I was hoping he might stop by today so I could talk to him."

"What happened this time?"

"Someone died or was killed outside the fitness center the other night. I'm surprised you haven't heard about it. Gossip seems to travel fast around here."

"Seems that way," I said. "But we haven't opened for service in days. We've been going between here and Salado, and moving our findings to the farm. There hasn't been time to be librarians. You don't know if foul play was involved?"

"Not yet. The morning cleaning crew found the body outside the fitness center. He was naked, with a bath towel nearby. We checked the men's dressing room and found a shower running. However, we didn't find any unclaimed clothes."

"What was the cause of death?" Michael asked.

"The coroner is still examining the body, but his first impression is that the victim was struck or fell on something that broke his nose in a way that drove the bones into his brain."

I shook my head and said a silent prayer for the man's family. "Terrible way to go. Did you find anything that points to James?"

He pondered my question for almost longer than I could stand, but I waited.

"Maybe. This is a long shot, but James was in the Navy and possibly in Special Ops. And, as I told you, some of his military records are sealed."

"So?"

"Sealed records could mean he worked as a special agent and was most likely skilled in hand to hand combat."

"I see. But what motive would he have?"

"That I don't know." He laughed. "This isn't funny, but when I first looked for a possible motive, I thought perhaps he stole the poor man's clothes."

"Interesting. Did you check with the victim's family to see if anyone remembered what he wore when he left home?"

"Yes. He left home in a beige track suit."

"So you're looking for James to see what he's wearing?" Michael asked.

"I guess I am."

"We'll watch for him, too." I didn't feel hopeful about it though. We'd only seen him a couple of times plus that incident when I saw someone from Sharon's backyard.

"If I could pull it off, I'd like to get a search team and sweep the area between here and the next bunch of houses." Bratton took another look toward the tree line behind Sharon's house before we all turned and walked around to the street.

"We haven't talked to Samuel yet. How did things go at the barn?"

Bratton smiled. "Great. That FBI Art Crime Team I mentioned flew in overnight on a federal plane and were at the barn when I got there. They were impressed."

Michael gave me his "I told you" look. "So, the stuff we found was stolen."

Bratton nodded. "Yes. The FBI identified all of the items as being stolen from churches in South America. They want to talk to you about exactly where you found each item and what you know about who might be responsible."

Michael and I looked at each other and nodded at the same time.

"We can't prove it," I said, "but I bet Sharon and Dennis' daughter Kim obtained the items while she worked as a computer tech for some convents there. Arthur Duncan, who calls himself an old boyfriend, probably received and hid the treasures. I'm not sure how she got them to him, but they both act guilty."

"No proof yet?"

Michael shrugged. "They're dirty. Arthur is the one

who's buying the clocks. I wonder if he thinks the artifacts are still hidden inside. Also, I bet they're the ones who tried to break into the barn last night. They were both yawning while we talked to them this morning."

"You saw Kim?" Bratton asked.

I smiled, remembering how she'd so brazenly forced her way into the house and then slipped out quietly. "Yes, she came with Arthur to pick up the clocks. But she thought she'd just take them without paying."

"Gigi didn't let her get away with it," Michael said.

"All I did was tell her the Salado Police were looking for her and she got out of there in a hurry. Actually, I think Kim lost interest in the clocks after seeing that the artifacts had been removed."

Michael pulled out his phone. "Before I forget, here is a photo of the license plate of the rental truck they came in."

Bratton copied the numbers into his notepad.

"One thing I think is important," Michael said, "is the way they looked at each other when they saw the fake floor we'd pulled up where we'd uncovered some of the religious artifacts. It made me think they were the ones searching the place and hadn't thought to look under the floor."

Bratton nodded. "Which means someone else hid the artifacts."

Michael smiled. "Exactly."

I added my two cents. "That means someone else is involved with the theft. We need to link them all to the thefts."

"I agree," Bratton said. "Now that we have specialists connecting some dots, maybe they'll find something that will let us charge Arthur and Kim. What we need to know is how they smuggled the artifacts to Texas and who did it. I'll give the FBI all the information we have on those two."

"We'll help any way we can," Michael added.

I remembered Bratton's plan to look for tracks at the farm. "Did you find any sign of who may have visited the barn this morning?"

"Yes. Nothing that will help us make an arrest, though. Samuel went with me and we found footsteps in places where they shouldn't be. We tracked them to the road and saw where a car had recently parked. I turned the information over to the investigators. Maybe we'll get lucky and identify who was there."

"Thanks," I said. "Let me know if there's anything we can do."

Bratton stared at me as if debating with himself. "Have you had a chance to talk to Ruby about James?"

"No. Sorry." With all this other going on I'd forgotten about that. "I'll call her right now and set up a meeting as soon as possible."

"Thanks," he said. "I keep thinking she'll tell you something she won't tell me."

As soon as Bratton left I called Ruby. She said she'd meet me at the bookmobile tomorrow. She sounded different somehow. Cautious, perhaps.

CHAPTER TWENTY-FOUR

James woke with a bright orange light flooding his space. He was usually up before the sun reached this position, but then he remembered how his quandary had kept him awake late into the night. He'd read somewhere once that the brain continued to work on problems after a person fell asleep. He smiled. Perhaps it was true. For he now understood why he was there and why he couldn't leave. At least not before getting paid for risking his life carrying out the mission. After he got the money he could go anywhere he wanted. Maybe back to South America. No one would look for him down there. He'd have enough money to live on for the rest of his life. She'd done the dirty work. He was the shipper. That's all.

Something was wrong. She should have been there

by now. They were to meet at Sharon's house. All he could do was wait for her to show up.

He walked to the creek and cleaned up. Even shaved. He'd gotten used to not having a beard, but sometimes it was difficult to take off the stubble. Today he did it with cold water, a bar of soap and a rusting razor.

He searched his backpack for food. There wasn't much left. He'd make another raid tonight after the locals were asleep. He found a package of peanut butter crackers and washed them down with a lukewarm cola. Not bad, but he could have eaten two or three more packages. He headed up the hill to see if she was there yet.

***

It took a while, but I talked Ruby into sitting. She'd been pacing around since she'd gotten there. From my last meetings with her, Ruby didn't seem to be the type to worry about what she wore or whether she had her face made up. Today she looked even worse. She hadn't combed her hair and it looked as if she'd slept in her clothes.

Michael stepped out at my suggestion, hoping Ruby might talk more freely with only me listening. It wasn't yet clear if she would talk at all.

"Ruby, we're trying to find James. Do you know where he is?"

"Is that why you wanted to talk to me? I've been trying to avoid him. Ever since he tried to kill us I've gone out of my way to stay away from places I've seen him."

"Lieutenant Bratton said according to your husband, James pulled you out of the house and saved your life. Both your lives. Seems you'd want to thank him."

Ruby squinted. "James is a sneaky one. I think he tried to kill us. Left us for dead and then changed his mind."

"Why would he do that?"

She paused for too long, but I waited. I looked out the window and saw Michael walking back and forth in front of the house with his phone to his ear.

Ruby finally spoke. "I think I can tell you this, but only if you don't tell the police. I'm afraid to tell law enforcement everything I know about James because they could arrest me."

"I can't promise to keep quiet if I learn a crime was committed." She'd probably shut up now, but I had to be honest with her.

She kept talking. "That's just it. I didn't commit a crime. James seems to think I did. He must have imagined it all. He's crazy. The problem is the police may catch him and he'll blame me and it'll be his word against mine."

"Seems your word would override his."

"You'd think so, but he's going to say I asked him to kill my husband."

"Did you?"

"No!" She paused. "Well, jokingly, maybe."

"Tell me what you said."

Ruby stared at the ceiling as if trying to remember. "We were flirting. I'd described myself as a widow so he wouldn't get hung up about my being married. Being a widow made me seem available. I guess that's why I did it. It was a mistake, but it happened. Then, later at my house, when he wanted to come in, I had to retract what I'd said and the only way I could think of was to say I *wanted* to be a widow."

"I can see how that could be taken the wrong way. Especially when you're talking to someone like James. Did he tell you about his military background?"

"Yes, but he didn't say anything to make me think he was a hired killer."

"We're not sure he is."

"I am."

I remembered Ruby's car being seen in Dallas. "When did you decide he could be a killer? You told me you'd loaned him your car. Were you two that close?"

"No." She scowled. "I felt bad about lying to him and leading him on, so when he asked to borrow the car to go to the VA, I let him. He's a convincing liar, that's for sure." She paused. "The seriousness of loaning him my car didn't hit me until the next day when he didn't bring it back."

"What do you mean?"

"Didn't the lieutenant tell you? My car was spotted in Dallas near the scene of a possible murder."

Bratton had told me, but he hadn't mentioned Ruby knew. "James said he was going to the VA in Temple. He didn't mention going to Dallas, too?"

"No. Now the police have my car impounded and my husband is trying to find out why. He's notified the insurance company. Everything is such a mess."

"I'm sorry. I'm sure you'll get it all ironed out soon."

"I hope so. To make things worse, I can't talk to my husband about what happened."

"I'm so sorry. I'll pray for you. Is there anything else you can tell me about James that might help the police find him?"

She looked up and stared out the window before she turned her gaze back to me. "He said he'd been in the Navy, but he looked more like a combat veteran. Tough, tanned, good condition, always alert, watching his surroundings."

She paused and I waited, not wanting to break her train of thought.

"You know, there are a lot of men and women around here who have been in combat. James seemed to still be at war."

"I can see that, based on the way you described him, but he's our age, right? He couldn't be in the service now."

"No, he's too old. Still…"

"Where did you meet him?"

"At the pub. I was there alone having a drink when he came in for dinner. I ended up helping with his bill. I should have known then he'd be trouble."

"When did you see him next?"

"When he didn't return my car, I went looking for him. I started at the pub and finally found him sitting on a bench at the Veteran's Memorial behind the activities center."

It sounded like James stayed in the same general area. Always between Mills Creek and the fitness center, except for his excursions to the VA in Temple and his wife's place in Dallas. "Have you thought of anything else about James since you talked to the lieutenant?"

"I forgot to tell him that James said he lived in the Mills Creek Estates and that I would find him in the directory. That part turned out to be a lie. I found two full columns of Johnsons in the Sun City Directory, fifty or so, and not one *James* Johnson. None of the Johnsons lived in Mills Creek."

I gestured toward the outside. "This is Mills Creek Estates, isn't it?"

"Yes. That's why I came over here that day looking for James, remember?"

"I do." I could tell she had run out of information for me and starting to repeat herself so I brought the meeting to an end. "Thank you for talking to me, Ruby. I didn't hear anything that will make you look guilty. I hope you don't mind if I talk to Bratton and tell him everything you've told me. I think it will help."

"Okay." She seemed less tense now. "Thank you. It's helped to talk. I just hope the police don't have to tell my husband everything that happened."

"I'm sure they'll only tell him what's necessary." Of course that could mean anything, but she smiled.

As she moved toward the door, she turned to me. "I hope they catch that man soon. He scares me."

Bratton was right, Ruby did open up to me, probably more than she had to him. Still, she didn't say much that might help locate James.

After Ruby left there was little time left to open the library for readers. I hadn't fulfilled my obligation to my patrons lately and felt terrible about it. I decided right then we'd make sure to open for service first thing tomorrow. The carpet people would be working, but that was okay. All I had to do was get them started and then Michael and I could check out books.

***

The next day we parked in front of Sharon's house and opened for business. I hadn't told anyone, but I questioned how much time I spent on the work for Dennis. I didn't trust him or Kim. Why on earth would I want to help them? It didn't make sense. Then, during my morning prayers I got a strong nudge to continue with the investigation. Naturally, that meant to continue helping Dennis since doing so aided in the investigation. Doing the right thing wasn't always easy.

Once we had the library open, I turned it over to Michael. "I won't be long. The carpet people are here and I want to make sure everything is on schedule."

"No problem. I don't see a rush of patrons heading our way."

I looked out the window and didn't see any sign of life. Besides us, the carpet company truck parked in Sharon's driveway was the only vehicle on the block.

"I see what you mean. The neighbors may have given up on us since we've been here so sporadically lately."

"You go on, I can manage the rush." Michael laughed. "Actually, if no one shows, I'll have more time to test the security on that defense department system for Chris."

"Okay, dear, but don't get into trouble."

"I won't. And you remember I can't tell you anything I learn about James."

"I understand."

I found the carpet layers in the master bedroom finishing up in the large walk-in closet. I complimented them on their work then walked through the house and garage. There was still some clutter. Boxes and grandfather clocks were stacked in the garage, but the rest of the house was pristine. I was glad Princess had stayed home with Samuel again today. She'd only get confused by the new carpets since she'd had free range of the house for so long.

In the family room, I couldn't resist looking out the windows over the back fence and wondering if James was looking back at me. I stared toward the trees for several minutes when I heard the front door open. Must be Michael coming to ask me a question about a book.

"There you are!"

It was a familiar voice, but one I didn't expect to hear. I turned to see Kim.

"Where's my father?"

CHAPTER TWENTY-FIVE

James leaned against a large tree in the wooded area behind Sharon's house and looked through a pair of binoculars. All he'd seen so far was three men moving around in the house. Probably the carpet layers again.

When was she going to get there? He chided himself for getting involved with someone so unbalanced. If she didn't show soon, he would have to leave. With or without the money. It would be a shame to not get paid, but staying was dangerous. Besides, he'd set aside some of the booty for insurance. It wasn't enough, but it might at least cover his cost.

As much as he loved the outdoors, the campsite was uncomfortable and boring. Was he getting too old to sleep on the ground? Pebbles felt like boulders under his sleeping bag and he missed fresh cooked meals. He wanted to get back to Galveston and the relative luxury of his boat. He could do without close relationships, but he missed the occasional human contact.

How much longer could he wait for her and not get caught? To be honest, he'd always felt a thrill when he was involved in a dangerous task. The joy was gone for this endeavor. It was time to take his losses and move on.

Tomorrow.

If she wasn't there by then, he'd take off for the coast.

He knew exactly how he would do it. All he had left to do now was work out a few details. With the plan formulated, he relaxed, staring once again through the binoculars. In a matter of minutes his wish was granted. There she was, talking to the nosy librarian.

***

"I thought I'd find you here," Kim said. "First Salado, now here. Would you please keep your nose out of my business?"

"I beg your pardon. This is my business. I've been hired by your father to sell this house and everything in it."

"But, the house is mine."

Her voice had an ugly edge to it. I wanted to tell her to quit whining, but I knew it would only make her madder than she already was. I kept quiet.

She didn't. "He has no right to sell the house."

"That's between you and Dennis," I said.

"What about Dennis?" Margie had sneaked in again.

Kim turned to her. "Who are you?"

"Who are *you*?" Margie asked.

"Margie, this is Kim, Sharon's daughter. Kim, this is Margie, your mother's next door neighbor. I'm surprised you two haven't met."

Margie looked Kim up and down. "You don't look like a nun."

Kim swirled, tightened her lips and pierced her eyes like a child about to throw a fit. "I'm not a nun. I never was a nun. I worked in convents as a computer specialist." She ignored Margie and turned to me. "Where can I find my father?"

I didn't understand why Dennis didn't want to see his daughter, but I had to abide by his desire. "I'm sorry, but he was emphatic about me not telling you. I don't understand it, but I must bow to his wishes."

Kim turned to Margie. "Do you know where he is?"

"I do," Margie said, "but I can't tell you. I've been sworn to secrecy also." Margie added a grin that said she enjoyed telling Kim that.

"Ridiculous," Kim said as she walked out the back door toward the fence.

Margie moved close to me. "Thanks for not telling her where Dennis is."

"To tell the truth, I think we should. Why wouldn't he want to see her and get everything worked out?"

I pulled out my phone and called Michael. "Is there a car out front?"

"Yes. I couldn't see who got out of it. Any problems?"

"It's Kim. Get a photo of the license plate."

"Okay."

"Quickly. Then come in here."

"Will do."

As soon as I finished the call, Margie started talking. "I can tell you why Dennis doesn't want to see her." Even though Kim was outside and wouldn't be able to hear her, Margie spoke softly. "You've seen how volatile Kim can be. Last time she was here, Sharon told me Kim attacked her father with a butcher knife. He's afraid of her."

"That's terrible." But then I remembered Margie had said she didn't know Sharon well and didn't know she was married. Which Margie could I trust?

Kim returned before I could quiz Margie. She walked past us, toward the front door. "Don't think you two have won. There's no way you can keep me from my inheritance. You'd better not be here when I return or you'll both be sorry."

She kept going until she was out the front door. It slammed so loudly, one of the carpet layers came running to see what had happened. It wasn't until then that I remembered Dennis said it was okay to give Kim his phone number.

***

James climbed into the front seat passenger side of Kim's car and waited.

She paused ever so slightly before she opened the door and climbed in. "How'd you know it was my car?"

No greeting. That was just like her. "Glad to see you, too. Easy. It's the only rental on the block. Are you sure it's safe to drive around in a rented car?"

"Don't worry. I have mother's credit card and driver's license."

She started the engine, backed up and did a U-turn.

Kim motioned toward the bookmobile. "You know there was a guy sitting in that vehicle, don't you? I hope he didn't see you get in my car."

"He went into the house just before you came out. You didn't see him?"

"No. Maybe he went to the bathroom. Doesn't matter. Long as he didn't see you."

James sat up straighter when they got to the City Market. "We need to talk. Turn in here."

Kim stared at him. "Don't tell me what to do."

"Look," he said, "I know this place better than you do. I'm the one who has been stuck here waiting for you. Then, when your mother died, I had no place to stay. What took you so long anyway?"

"I would have been here sooner if you hadn't killed my mother. Was that necessary?"

"I didn't kill her. That ditzy next-door neighbor did it."

Kim looked at him in disbelief. "All I know is her death caused me to lose my treasures. Everything I've worked for is gone."

"You can't blame me. I delivered it to your mother just the way you told me to. Then, when she died and everyone started poking around, I moved the boxes to Salado. Again, your idea. Not mine."

"You still lost it all."

"I did everything I could to hide the stuff."

She shook her head. "Yeah, sure. Like that pathetic fake floor in Salado. Anyone could tell it was a cheap addition. The librarians emptied it before we got there."

James stared at Kim, feeling the throb in his chest that often occurred when he was losing control. If he didn't need this woman, he knew what he would do with her. There was a dam nearby and a lake deep enough to keep her body hidden for months.

He shook it off. "Why'd you want to put the stolen treasures in your mother's house in the first place? We should've rented a storage room somewhere. Any place would have been better than the house."

Kim pulled into the Legacy Gardens near the dam and parked.

James nodded. "This is a good place to stop."

"I know. Last time I was home, Dad said Mother was losing her memory. That, plus the fact that no one in the neighborhood ever visited her, made storing the crates in the house perfect."

James loosened his seatbelt. "Why didn't your dad take her with him when he moved out?"

"He tried. She wouldn't go."

"If he thought she was getting that forgetful, why'd he leave her alone?"

"He couldn't force her to go with him. She was intelligent enough to fool most people. You lived with her for a while. What's your opinion? Did she need help taking care of herself?"

"She took care of basic needs, I guess. She had food delivered, so she didn't cook or get out of the house much. Meals on Wheels, I think. She got excited when the home library service started. I don't think she read many books, but she seemed to enjoy talking to the librarian."

"Did the librarian come into the house?" Kim squinted at him.

"Only once before Sharon died."

"The library service." Kim hissed the words. "That's when our troubles began."

"Maybe." James paused. "Perhaps Sharon was more alert than any of you thought."

"Why do you say that?"

James locked on to Kim's eyes before answering. "The day the librarian found your mom dead, she had a stack of books with her. Books that Sharon had requested."

"So?"

"The books were all on South American art and antiques."

Kim gasped. "Really? You think Mom found the stolen objects and used the library to learn more about them?"

"Based on the books she requested, I think so."

Kim paused. "Still, she was a collector. She may have had an interest in the artifacts you stored in her house without knowing they were taken illegally."

"True. I'm pretty sure she didn't know they were stolen because she gave some to Margie."

"What? She gave my artifacts to her next door neighbor?"

"Not much. That's when I started hiding them and moving them to Salado."

"If she hadn't died, she may have eventually figured out the artifacts were stolen and we would have been found out." Kim beat her head on the steering wheel softly a few times.

After a brief silence, Kim continued. "How did you get along with Mom?"

"What do you mean?" James became defensive before he realized she didn't mean the time Sharon tried to kiss him.

"Did she buy the idea you were a friend I met in Buenos Aires?"

"Sometimes. Other times she thought I was Dennis." He didn't want to explain the details.

"Dad? And to think, Dad thought she was well enough to live alone?" Kim shook her head slowly, but James knew Kim wasn't too upset over her mother's health.

"I guess. Like I said, her memory would come and go. No one ever visited or stopped by to check on her other than Margie."

"Did Margie know you were living there?"

"No. I hid while she was there. I built a comfortable spot in the attic above the master bedroom."

"You probably took better care of Mom than Dad did when he was here."

"And I took better care of her than you did."

Her eyes pierced, but she quickly turned away.

James enjoyed making her flinch first. "About my payment...."

"We're not discussing that. I already paid you all you're going to get."

"That advance barely covered my expenses. I expect the hundred thousand we agreed on plus an additional twenty thousand to cover the extra time I had to sit around waiting for you to get here."

"You're kidding. You should have to refund the advance. You didn't do your job. None of the objects are here, are they?"

"It was *your* plan. It's not my fault it didn't work. I did the risky part, getting the stolen goods out of the country and into the United States. I delivered everything according to the agreement. Since your mother's death, I've had to live in the woods waiting for you. I intend to get paid." He stared her down again, but then he cringed inside as he remembered Kim's ire from the first time they met. She'd responded to an ad he'd placed in a *Soldier of Fortune* magazine. He'd been living in Buenos Aires and she lived in a convent nearby. Her anger was directed toward the Catholic Church at the time, but he could see she had a temper.

Her response was brash and she sounded like a child out of control. "The only thing you're going to get is a place to live for the rest of your life in a Texas prison. And don't think you can take me with you." Kim's voice rose. "Some soldier of fortune you turned out to be. You let that old librarian con you out of everything. Now the FBI is involved. They have many of the artifacts and they'll eventually return them to the original owners. All my work wasted."

"That's not my fault," James said, beginning to get angry himself. He grabbed her arm and squeezed her left biceps to convey his strength and the importance of what he had to say. "I want my money. I don't care where you get it. You can sell those two houses and pay me."

"I can't sell the houses. I don't know where Dad is and that librarian has his power of attorney."

"I know where Dennis lives. Go talk to him and get him to switch that power of attorney to you. If that doesn't work, let me know and I'll make sure the librarian is out of the picture."

Kim's eyes narrowed. "Where is he?"

"He's living in Royal Gardens in Temple."

"How do you know?"

"I hear things. Living in the attic has some advantages. When nobody knows you're there, they might say anything."

"Okay," Kim started the engine. "I'll go talk to him. But, I need the money for myself. I'll give you enough to relocate. The FBI is going to zero in on you soon."

"I'm not leaving until I get paid. And I mean all of it. Not some relocation fee."

"Take it or leave it. I'm not going to pay you anything else. You didn't deliver as promised. You're crazy."

He hated that word. He wasn't crazy. He had PTSD. There was a big difference. He pulled the knife from the sheath on his calf and held it against her neck. He wanted to slice into that slender neck and watch her bleed, but he also wanted the money she could get for him. The money she owed him. "Listen, lady. I've wasted enough time on this job. I want to get back to my boat. I'm not leaving until I get what you owe me. My memory is a little fuzzy, but I may have killed some people around here. One more won't make much difference."

Kim had pulled away from the knife until her head was crammed against the door window. Her eyes showed fear he'd seen before. He may have enjoyed it more than he thought he should.

"I'll get the money. Then you'll leave?" Her voice was a mere whisper.

He grinned as he pulled the knife away from her neck. "Gladly. In the meantime I'll be at the campsite on Lake Georgetown. Do you know where it is?"

"Yes."

"Good. I need to hide out for a while. As soon as you get the money, come find me." James got out of the car and walked toward the lake.

CHAPTER TWENTY-SIX

Michael e-mailed a photo of the car Kim drove to Bratton along with a brief message of her actions while she was at Sharon's house. With that done, we concentrated on library business.

We checked out a few books before the day was over, but mainly we visited with friends. Several said how they'd missed us and asked if I'd been ill. We must be doing some good. Still, I had a feeling we wouldn't be back tomorrow. I needed to go to Temple and talk to Dennis. I wanted to get him and Kim together. Now I knew why he was hesitant about seeing her, but it still had to be done. She could be explosive, but I thought it was all talk. I couldn't imagine her actually harming him even though she had threatened him with a butcher knife. According to Margie anyway.

"Michael, it's time to go."

He jumped up and started his routine to prepare for departure.

"I want to stop at the pub," I said as he drove away from Sharon's house.

"You want to *what*?"

"It was something Ruby said. I told Lieutenant Bratton about it, but we can do it more easily than he can."

"Do what?"

"Look for James."

"James?"

"Yes. Remember how Ruby said he was always somewhere between this neighborhood and the community center. We're going to make a quick check of all the places where he's been spotted."

"Okay." Michael's stomach growled. "Should I get a sandwich while we're at the pub?"

"Not enough time. Besides we're having beef stew and cornbread tonight. The stew's in the slow cooker so it'll be ready when we get there."

"Okay. I'll wait." He rubbed his stomach.

I went in to see if James was there. What I saw was six TVs, each showing a different sporting event and four people at the bar. James wasn't one of them.

Next we stopped at the City Market where I made a walkthrough while Michael double parked. Unless James was in the men's room, he wasn't there, either.

Same for the fitness center and the library. When we got to the Veteran's Memorial, I asked Michael to walk with me because I didn't want to go there alone. There were too many places where someone could be hiding. Still, no sight of James.

***

The next morning, we went to Royal Gardens in Temple instead of our regular library stop in Sun City.

Michael waited while I went in to see Dennis about his daughter. I wanted to get the two of them together to talk about the estate. Even though I didn't like Kim and felt she might be behind the thefts of the religious artifacts, she still deserved to have some say in the distribution of the family assets. I was prepared to end my business arrangement with Dennis.

I found him in the dining room sipping a cup of coffee. Empty breakfast plates were on the table.

His face registered surprise when he saw me but he quickly recovered. "Ms. Helmsley, I didn't expect you today."

"I know. I need to talk to you, face to face. Mind if I sit?"

He gestured toward the empty chair next to his. "Please. Would you like some coffee?"

"No, thanks."

"What can I do for you, dear lady?"

"It's Kim."

Fear washed over his face as he looked toward the door.

"Don't be alarmed. Margie told me about Kim threatening you. I don't think she would hurt you, but we could set up a meeting someplace public where she wouldn't cause a scene. It's important that you two talk and work out what to do with Sharon's estate. Kim feels it should all go to her."

Dennis leaned back, fingers entwined, "Perhaps if she'd been a proper daughter and helped care for her mother, I'd agree."

"Care for her mother?" I wasn't sure what he meant by that.

Dennis ignored the question. "I really thought the convent would be the answer. I guess she washed out there, too."

"About that." I was hesitant to be the one to tell him, but this conversation depended on him knowing why she was in South America. "She was never a nun. Your daughter worked on computers for several convents."

Dennis laughed. "I know. She worked in a convent. It was easier to say she was a nun."

"That means she didn't take a vow of poverty as you implied. Therefore, I can no longer help you sell the houses and their contents. I suggest you talk to Kim."

A coarse feminine voice broke into our conversation, and got louder as its owner drew closer to the table. "Talk to me about what?"

Dennis stood and glared at me. "I asked you not to tell her where I was."

"I didn't." I got to my feet also.

Kim smirked as if she were enjoying the disruption she'd caused. "That's right. A friend of mine gave me the location. When I went to the front desk they sent me here. Where's Dad?"

I turned and didn't see Dennis anywhere. He sure

could move fast for his age. "He was standing right there."

"Not him. My dad."

For a second I thought I'd misunderstood what Kim said. But then I knew. And what I realized shocked me and caused temporary speechlessness.

A door slammed nearby. I heard what sounded like dishes hitting the floor.

Kim laughed so hard she had to wipe away some tears. "Look at you. It's all over your face. You got conned by that old man, didn't you? He's the one who gave you power of attorney, right? Well, guess what? That's not Dad. That's Mom's neighbor, Jack Cummings."

I didn't think it would do much good to chase after him, whoever he was. Even at his age, he could outrun me. I wondered why he'd pretended to be Dennis. Maybe he was also pretending to be Dennis' age and was actually a little younger.

I hadn't responded to Kim, but she wasn't finished. "I guess everything you did with that fake POA is illegal. You may even go to jail, lady." She laughed again as if she was enjoying my misery.

I didn't believe that, but I hated what had happened. I should have checked him out. I mentally went through everything that had occurred when I first met the man who said he was Dennis.

Margie had told me about him living at Royal Gardens. Annette, the woman at the front desk told me he was in the dining room, like she told Kim today. Margie may have lied, but the woman working here was either lying or she'd been conned. An idea hit. She could tell me his room number.

I left Kim cackling in the dining room and went to the check-in desk. Annette was typing on a computer keyboard.

"May I help you?" she asked without looking up.

Can you give me Dennis Coleman's room number, please?"

"You didn't find him in the dining room?"

"Yes, but he left in a hurry. I thought I should go check on him."

The woman looked at me with eyebrows raised. "Really? He didn't come through here."

"He went out the back way."

"I see. We don't give out suite numbers, but I can call him and ask him if I can send you up to his room."

"That'd be fine."

Annette called, but no one answered. "I'm sorry. I guess he didn't go back to his room."

Or, he's there and doesn't want to talk to me. "Thank you anyway."

I told Michael about my adventure with the man we thought was Dennis. He was as astounded as I had been.

"Should we call the police?" he asked.

"We should. Not sure what to tell them. But, if they can figure out what's going on, maybe they can get the staff to let us in Mr. Coleman's suite."

"What are we looking for?"

"Clues. Anything that will tell us what's going on." I wished I knew someone in the Temple Police Department.

CHAPTER TWENTY-SEVEN

Michael and I sat in the bookmobile in the Royal Gardens parking lot rehashing what had happened and planning what to do next while keeping an eye out for Jack.

Jack Cummings, who had been impersonating Dennis, had made a run for it. Kim was gone, too. We could only assume Cummings was Margie's husband and that meant they'd both been lying to me. My mind thought of several ways to sneak into his suite and have a look-see, but, when I told Michael, he advised against it. Breaking and entering or some such. Strange how these things happen. You teach your children right from wrong only to have them throw it back at you at the worst possible times.

He was right, of course, so I knew I had to meet some

lovely Temple PD officers. My experience has been that police officers are so suspicious at first, little communication takes place. Perhaps Bratton could break the ice with them.

While Michael walked across the street to the coffee shop to get two to go, I called Bratton and gave him a brief summary of what had happened.

"You know the guy I've been working with, the one I thought was Dennis Coleman..."

"Hold it right there." He sounded ticked off. Perhaps I got him at a bad time.

"Yes?"

"When you say 'who you thought was Dennis Coleman' gives me the idea he isn't. So skip over to the good part. How do you know it's not him? Who is he really? Why did he pretend to be Coleman?"

"Well, if I knew all that I wouldn't have called you." I didn't care if I made him mad or not. He was the investigator, not me.

I tried to soften my response because of my respect for him, and partly because I needed his help. "I'm sorry. It's just so frustrating going for weeks trusting someone and then finding out everything I've done is a lie. I don't know how I'm going to pay for that new carpet in Sun City he conned me into buying."

"I'm sorry too, ma'am. I didn't mean to sound so gruff, but nothing has gone right today. Tell me about this guy?"

"I met him in the dining room in the Royal Gardens in Temple. Same place we'd met before. This time Kim came in unexpectedly."

"His daughter?"

"Well, that was my understanding. But then she proceeded to inform me the man I talked to wasn't her father."

"Was she telling the truth?"

"I think so, because the man I'd thought was Dennis took off running. And, he was fast for an octogenarian. By the way, I think he lied about his age."

"Probably not her father, then."

"Margie had warned me he was afraid of his daughter because she attacked him before. So maybe that's why he ran. Either Margie lied or Kim lied."

"Who do we believe?"

"I haven't told you everything yet, but I've got reservations about Margie which makes me believe Kim. In this situation, at least."

"Ms. Helmsley, I don't know how you do it, but you manage to get yourself into some messy situations."

"I know." I'd heard that before.

"Okay." Bratton had a little laugh in his voice now. He continued. "Please tell me why you trust Kim, a person who has evaded the police and who just might be an art thief instead of Margie Cummings, the retired school teacher who lives next door to the late Sharon Coleman?"

"Because Kim said the man I thought was Dennis is her mother's next-door neighbor, 'Mr. Cummings.'"

Bratton didn't respond right away and I knew he must be consulting that little notebook he always had with him. "So, you're saying the man you thought was Dennis is really Margie's husband."

"Right."

"That's odd. When I talked to her, she said her husband Jack was a petroleum engineer who worked abroad. Some neighbors verified her story. At least they'd seen him come and go."

There was a long pause, then he continued. "So who do we believe, Margie or Kim?"

"I think Kim is telling the truth about Jack. She seemed to enjoy the fact that Jack had conned me into working on the houses for him."

"I see. And Margie wouldn't want us to know that the man you knew as Dennis is really her husband, Jack."

I wondered what else Margie had said to misdirect us. "I think you should go pick up Margie before she has a chance to run?"

"I can't do that. Not yet. I'll talk to her, though, and try to find her husband if he's around."

"She's been lying about everything. Her husband is involved and he's run away."

Michael came in quietly and handed me a cup of coffee, steam oozing out of the sipping hole. "Remind him about the artifact thefts," he said.

I nodded and I set my coffee down to cool. "I wouldn't be surprised if these two are involved in the theft of all those religious objects we've found."

"We haven't connected them to any of that. We don't have enough evidence to arrest either one."

I understood what he was saying, but I was afraid they would disappear before we came up with the evidence. "Can't you bring them in to explain what's going on? If they don't give you the right answers, then arrest them for obstruction."

He laughed. "Ma'am, you've been watching too many police procedurals on TV."

I didn't care what he thought. I continued. "Also, I think we need to look around in Dennis' suite before Jack has a chance to clean it out. That might take some local PD officers. Do you know anyone in Temple PD?"

"Yes. I've worked with a detective there before. Let's see, what was his name?"

Silence fell for a few moments before he spoke again. "Never mind. I'll look him up and give him a call. Since Cummings and Coleman both have property in Georgetown, I won't have any trouble getting the PD there to fill me in on what they discover."

"That's a good idea. Be sure and tell them who I am and ask if I can look in the room."

"Hmm. That won't be as easy. I better come up there."

That made me smile. "That'd be nice, but grab Margie first. I don't trust her to stay in town."

We said goodbye.

I took a sip of coffee while my mind kept working at full speed. How could I convince the local PD to let me into Cummings' room? No matter how sure I was that Margie and her husband were guilty of something, what we knew wasn't enough to arrest them or look through their belongings. If I was a police officer, what could I charge Cummings with? There was one obvious violation of law. The Power of Attorney he signed and had notarized. But that wasn't so serious that the police could get a search warrant for his suite. I wondered if he'd used a real notary. I remember the papers had the notary seal on it, but he could have stolen it or faked it.

Michael broke my reverie. "You know the police are not going to allow you into Dennis' suite. There's no probable cause."

My grandson sounded more like a lawyer than a computer geek. "You're right. I was just thinking the same thing. We might as well go back to Sun City and open the mobile library."

"Not so fast. Didn't Bratton say he was coming up here?"

"Yes."

"Shouldn't we wait and see what he can do? I'm just saying, it doesn't look like we'll get to look into Dennis' suite. In fact, while you were talking to Bratton, I did some research and learned the police need a search warrant for a retirement home like this. Even hotel rooms."

"Maybe Bratton knows a way."

"I wish there was something I could do," Michael said, sitting his coffee cup down on the checkout desk.

I thought. "While we're waiting for Bratton to get here, there is one thing I'd like you to do for me."

Michael stood. "You want me to break into Dennis' suite? Tell me what to look for."

"No. That's not what I was going to ask. I'd like you to look around the place and see if you spot the baby blue Cadillac. I bet that's what Jack would use to make his getaway."

"Good idea. If it's still here, we can keep an eye on it in case he comes for it. We could block it with the bookmobile until the police get there." Michael went out the door.

"Where are you going?"

"To look for Dennis' car."

"You can drive around and look."

"I'd rather walk. The exercise will do me good. Will you be okay alone?'

"Sure."

Michael's mention of exercise reminded me how Samuel had taught me to love walking. What a wonderful man. I pulled out my phone and pressed his speed dial number to thank him for all he'd done for me and tell him I loved him. Before he answered, I heard the door opening. "Michael, are you back already?"

"It's not Michael."

I placed my phone gently on the dashboard and stood. "What are you doing here, Jack?"

"So, you already know who I am. I should have known you wouldn't waste any time IDing me."

"Luv? Is that you?"

Cummings looked around. "What was that?"

"The radio." I reached over and pretended to turn it off. "But you better get out of here now. The police are on the way." I hoped Samuel would get the message and call the police.

Cummings laughed. "I'm getting out of here all right. You're going to drive this contraption and take me where I want to go. Now sit down in the driver's seat and start the engine."

I was glad Cummings had raised his voice. It would make it easier for Samuel to hear him.

I didn't move. "Michael does all the driving. We

better wait for him to get back."

Jack laughed again, louder this time. "No. You're going to drive."

I stayed in the passenger's seat. "I can't drive this thing."

He pulled out a pistol and pointed it at me. "I know you're lying. Get in that seat and get this box of books on the road. Now!"

"Okay, okay. Just don't point that gun at me. It scares me so I'll never be able to drive." I moved into the driver's seat slowly and kept my eye on the gun the whole time.

"Now you're talking. Get that motor started. We need to get out of here."

"Just wait. I told you Michael is the driver. I've got to adjust the seat first. The way it is now, I can't reach the pedals. I hope I remember how to shift. That's the hardest part, you know. Shifting and clutching at the same time."

I moved the seat up, tried to press the clutch pedal, pretended I couldn't and moved the seat up more. "Now I'm too close." I moved the seat again.

"Lady, you're stalling. Get going or else."

I adjusted the rearview mirror. "I'm curious. Why didn't you take Dennis' Cadillac if you're in such a hurry to get away?"

"Isn't that obvious? It'd be too easy to spot."

Even with a gun pointed at me, I had to laugh. "A red double-decker bus isn't?"

"The difference is, here I've got you as a hostage."

I could see Michael out the window behind

Cummings. Either I'd stalled long enough for Michael to finish his search or Samuel had called him and informed him of the situation. Michael had probably called the police. All I had to do was continue to stall and hope Cummings didn't get fed up and start shooting.

"I'd rather be a hostage in the Cadillac if you don't mind. This vehicle is too hard to maneuver."

"Start the engine now." He poked me in the back with the gun.

I turned the key and the motor started. "Uh-oh. Do you hear that?" The motor sounded fine, but he didn't know what it was supposed to sound like.

He leaned in toward the dashboard. "Hear what?"

"That ping, the knocking. You don't hear that?"

"It sounds fine to me. Let's go."

To be honest, I could drive a vehicle with a manual transmission. That's all we had growing up. I just wasn't good at it any more. Still, I pretended to be worse than I was. I let the clutch out too quickly and didn't press the accelerator. This caused the mobile library to lurch forward before the motor died. Cummings almost fell. "Sorry. I warned you."

"You idiot. You're not trying. Let the clutch out gradually and give it more gas as you do."

I started the engine once more, let the clutch out slowly and gave it plenty of gas–while pumping the brake pedal with my left foot.

Cummings fell this time just as the gun went off. I don't know if he pulled the trigger on purpose or his tipping over caused it to go off. It didn't matter.

When I looked back to see where he was, I saw he

was flat on his back with Michael hovering over him.

I got up to help and saw the gun was near the hand Michael was standing on. I reached down and grabbed the pistol.

Bratton climbed aboard with gun drawn. "Except for that bullet hole in your windshield it looks like you've got everything under control."

I gave Bratton the gun we'd taken from Cummings and picked up the phone I'd left on the dashboard. "Samuel? You there?"

"Yes, luv. I prayed for you. Everything is okay, I presume?"

Tears filled my eyes and I thanked God for guidance, protection and…for Samuel.

"It is now."

CHAPTER TWENTY-EIGHT

I ended my call to Samuel and turned my attention to Lieutenant Bratton. "Wait until I tell you what happened."

"No need. Michael kept us appraised throughout the ordeal. We heard most of it live."

Michael beamed. I hugged him and Bratton. Cummings was on his feet with his hands cuffed behind him.

Bratton still had a huge smile on his face and clearly wasn't through talking about what Michael had done. That was okay with me. I was glad it was over and no one got hurt.

"Ms. Helmsley, that was pure genius the way you called your husband and then proceeded to broadcast everything that went on."

Cummings glared at me as the policeman escorted him out.

"Well, genius is a bit strong. How about lucky?" Then I remembered how it had happened. "Most likely, Divine intervention. I had been thinking how wonderful my life had been since I married Samuel and decided to call him and thank him for all he did for me. Cummings entered the bookmobile about the time Samuel answered. So, instead of hanging up, I placed the phone on the dashboard hoping Samuel would hear what was happening and call the police. I guess he did."

Michael took my hand. "He didn't. What he did was better. He called me and I called the police."

"Michael also called me," Bratton said. "Samuel told Michael what was going on and he relayed the information to me and the Temple police. Michael was ready to pounce when the time was right."

I hugged Michael again. "And he did. How did you stay up with us? I drove around the parking lot some. Just enough to make Cummings think I was doing what he said."

Bratton turned to Michael. "Why weren't you on board when Cummings got here?"

I answered for Michael. "I'd sent him to look for Dennis' car."

"Did you find it?" Bratton asked.

Michael pointed. "Yes. It's just around the corner there."

"Good," Bratton said. "I'll tell the Temple police about it. When I got here, Michael, you were standing over Cummings. How did you follow them, son?"

"There is a ladder connected out back. We use it occasionally to wash the top or to get to the air conditioner when it needs service. I climb up there sometimes to adjust the satellite dish we use for Internet access. I jumped on the ladder and hung on. From there I could see Cummings." Michael looked at me. "You almost knocked me off with all that stopping and starting, but that's also what knocked Cummings to the ground and let me get the gun from him."

Bratton patted him on the back. "Good job, son. And, you too, ma'am. I'm supposed to give you the warning. You know, the one about letting law enforcement do its job, but I know you've heard it many times. But, really, you both must be more careful." He winked.

Something about all that police mumbo jumbo gave me a solution for searching Cumming's suite. "That's it. The real Dennis is missing and the impersonator may have information about him in his suite. That should give you probable cause to search his room."

Michael nodded. "Sounds right to me."

Bratton smiled. "Me too. I'll give the local police the background and I'm sure they will have the search warrant within the hour. Who knows, there could be some imminent danger for the missing man if we don't move fast."

***

James rode a "borrowed" bicycle to Lake Georgetown, but ditched it behind a row of trees before he got to the ranger station. It wouldn't matter that he'd entered on a bicycle, and he would have if the bike had been his. With his pack and sleeping bag, he looked like any other camper. When he got further in he saw that most of the others had cars or trucks. Some pulled boats and all had fishing gear.

He picked a campsite in the developed area as far away from the other vacationers as possible. It was close enough to walk to the restroom where he found flush toilets and hot showers. This place was much better than his Mills Creek campsite.

He'd stopped at a convenience store on the way over and loaded his backpack with beef jerky and other food that didn't require refrigeration. He had enough to last for several days, maybe a week. If Kim didn't come up with the money soon, he'd go after her and Arthur and take what they had. He was ready to get back to his boat in the Gulf.

After setting up his campsite, he walked to the lake and watched as a young couple worked together to position their Bayliner 160 onto a boat trailer that had been backed into the water on a concrete ramp. The woman had the wheel, but she had trouble centering the boat on the trailer because of the wind. She reversed the motor and moved away to try again. The man remained calm and waited. Then, when she had the boat aligned perfectly, he gave her a thumbs up and a sincere smile. She revved the engine and slid the boat onto the trailer, and turned off the motor. He hooked the safety line and cranked it until the boat was properly in place on the trailer.

Watching them work together reminded him of what

he never had. He'd married, even had a couple of kids somewhere, but the only reason he remained married for so long was because he was never home. He was a career warrior with no time for a family.

The activity on the water also made him think of his boat sitting in dry dock in Galveston. After unloading the crates he'd brought into the country for Kim, and knowing how far inland he had to go, he'd decided to have his boat checked before he returned to sea. That was another reason he needed the money from Kim. He'd called the boat maintenance company a week ago and they said he needed to pick it up soon or they'd start charging him rent.

The young man James had been watching on the ramp climbed into the pickup truck and pulled the boat out of the water. Water dripped off onto the ramp. He stopped when the stern was out of the water. The wife, or girlfriend, climbed out and they worked together getting the boat ready for the road. She attached the straps that connected the boat to the stern of the boat while he removed the bilge drain plug and waited while water dripped out. Then he replaced the plug. When they were done, they climbed into the pickup and drove away.

The couple got their boat out of the lake just as the sun started to set. With the hills to the west, the sun would not be visible soon. The clouds reflected the deep orange and gold and the sunset was unbelievably beautiful. James couldn't remember when he'd last stopped to enjoy a sunset.

He felt safe at the park. No one would think to look

for him there. Still, it wasn't the time to let his guard down. Staying alert kept him alive in Vietnam and Cambodia. He didn't trust anyone. Even in this lovely Corps of Engineers park site, he prepared for the worst. He stuffed his sleeping bag with leaves and placed it near the fire pit. Before going to sleep, he put his backpack at one end of the sleeping bag to look like his head. He found a protective place a safe distance away to sleep. It wasn't easy. As soon as he got comfortable, he saw movement in the shadows, perhaps an animal. Skunks, armadillos, and other creatures searched for food in the dark in this part of Texas. But this intruder was larger than an animal and headed directly to his sleeping bag.

"James? Wake up!" It was a stage whisper, loud enough to be heard in the next campsite.

He quietly made his way around the campsite until he was behind the prowler he assumed was Kim.

"James? Is that you?" She poked the bag of leaves.

The rustling sound of the leaves muted the sound he made as he moved up behind her. When he was close enough, he grabbed her from the back.

"What? James? Wait. It's Kim." She twisted to get free. He held on, covering her mouth with one hand while holding her tight with the other.

"I know it's you, Kim, but I don't want you to wake the neighboring campsites. Just relax. Talk softly." He released his hold on her mouth.

"You scared me," she whispered.

He let go of her arms. "I wasn't expecting you so soon. Do you have my money?"

She reached over and punched his sleeping bag. "You filled this bag with leaves, didn't you?"

"Yes."

"Why?"

"It keeps people like you from getting too close."

He moved to the picnic table and sat on the bench. "Why are you here?"

"To give you an update. That guy at the Royal Gardens isn't my dad."

"What? Who is he?"

James couldn't see her face in the dark, but he could tell by her voice, she found it amusing for some reason.

She continued. "It was Jack Cummings. Mom's next door neighbor."

"Are you sure?"

"It was definitely him."

"Strange. Why would he impersonate your dad? Did you ask him where Dennis is? We need him to sell the houses."

"There wasn't time to ask Jack anything. That librarian was there. As soon as I said he wasn't my father, he hightailed it out of there and the librarian said she was going to call the police. That's when I left."

"What a mess. Did anyone ever tell you your family is dysfunctional?"

"Did anyone ever tell you *you're* dysfunctional?"

James felt his anger rise, but he decided to ignore her. He'd do whatever he had to...until she had his money. "How are you going to find your dad?"

"I'm not. I'm going to let that librarian find him for me."

"How do you know she will?"

"Because she's meddlesome."

"Yeah. That's why she has the treasures."

Kim sat next to James causing him to move away. "We'll use her to find Dad and then we'll get him to give us the money we need."

"Now you're talking." Whatever it takes…

Kim sat silently for minutes and James suspected she was processing everything that had happened and working on a plan. He didn't trust her, but he respected her logical mind. Other than that, she was a self-centered, uncaring person.

When she finally talked, she had questions. "You said Margie killed Mother and now we know Jack impersonated Dad. Why?"

James shrugged. "I don't know."

"Didn't you say you hid in the attic when Margie visited?"

"Yes, but they didn't say much. Neighborhood gossip mostly."

"How can you be sure Margie was the killer?"

"That day was different. They argued. Something about Jack. It sounded as if Margie accused Sharon of flirting with him or something like that. Kissing or attempted kissing."

"Had Jack been in the house, too?"

"A couple of times. But only when Sharon was asleep. Thinking back on that time, I suspect Margie may have seen Sharon trying to kiss me."

"You?"

"Yes. It was a time when she wasn't thinking clearly.

She thought I was Dennis."

"Oh, good grief. What did you do?"

He didn't want to tell Kim he wasn't thinking clearly either and had thought Sharon was his sister, Wanda Jean. "Nothing. I pushed her away and tried to explain who I was. But, if Margie was looking through the window, she may have mistaken me for Jack."

"So, Margie was angry and accusing Mom of flirting with Jack. What happened next?"

"There was this thump and then it got real quiet for a minute. Afterwards I heard Margie ask Sharon if she was okay…there was no response. Next thing I heard was Margie calling Jack on the phone."

"Did he come over?"

"No. He only came over late at night. The neighbors thought he was out of the country working as a petroleum engineer. I don't know why they lied about him being gone."

"So you heard Margie's side of the conversation. What'd she say happened to Mom?"

"She told Jack she'd barely pushed Sharon and she'd fallen and hit her head on the fireplace. She tried to wake her and couldn't."

"Did they discuss calling 9-1-1?"

"Margie suggested it, but it was clear Jack didn't want her to."

"You didn't call 9-1-1 either, did you?"

"No. I couldn't without being found out. We would've lost everything."

Kim glared at him. "I wonder why Jack was against calling for help."

"At first Margie was concerned about getting arrested for murder. Later in the conversation, though, it seemed Jack was more concerned about getting the stuff out of the house before EMS got there."

"What stuff?"

"Now that I think back on it, I suspect they were talking about the artifacts. Since all this happened, my access to the house has been limited. I haven't done an inventory. I'm not sure if they stole some items before the librarian took it or not."

"Maybe we should go visit Margie and see if she has anything that belongs to me."

"Don't you think the police have come up with the same conclusion now that they know Jack is on the run?"

"Probably. That means we better hurry. Come on, my car is just down the road."

"Wait. Let me grab my gear." James dumped the leaves out of his sleeping bag.

"Don't take time for that. I'll bring you back here when we're done."

"I'm afraid we're about done, one way or another. I'm not coming back here."

***

The local police looked in Dennis' suite first and declared it "uneventful and boring."

That's when they let us in, Michael, Bratton, and me. We had to stand in the middle of the living room and search with our eyes. No touching allowed.

It didn't take long.

When I saw it, I looked at Michael and he nodded.

Bratton saw our silent communication. "What?"

I stared at the slender wooden table behind the sofa. "There. That cross. Wouldn't you say it matches one of the crosses we found in Sun City?"

Michael smiled. "It sure does."

The local detective turned to Bratton. "So, you think that cross was stolen? Why?"

Bratton reached into his pocket and came out with a business card. "We're not experts, but that cross looks like one we found in Georgetown and learned it had been stolen from a church in South America. The FBI Art Crime Team has taken custody of ours and I'm sure they would like to hear from you." He handed over the card. "Here is the phone number. I bet they'll want to come here immediately to see the cross and to see if there are any other missing artifacts in this suite. You may also want to alert the FBI team about the Cadillac in the parking lot I told you about. After all, it's been known to contain stolen articles."

I would have loved to dig around more and maybe find some clues that would lead us to the real Dennis. But I could tell Bratton was willing to leave the search to the local police.

Bratton walked us to the bookmobile. Before I climbed in, I turned to him with the question that had been in my head all morning. "What's going to happen to Jack Cummings now?"

"I'm not sure what charge they'll come up with, but if it was me I'd charge him with abduction and then pump up the bond until the FBI gets here to see what all is in his rooms."

Michael cleared his throat. "Is it possible his wife could get him out on bond?"

"Wife!" I'd forgotten about Margie. I turned to Bratton. "Did you arrest her yet?"

"No. I was on my way to talk to her when I got that call from Michael about you."

"We better go talk to her. Fast. No telling what she'll do when she learns Jack is in jail."

Michael nodded. "Since we found that cross in Temple, I wonder if there are more artifacts in the Cummings' Sun City home."

"Okay," Bratton said. "Two reasons to go check on her now. I'll see if I can get a search warrant by phone and meet you two at the house. Do not, repeat *do not* approach her until I get there. Do you understand?"

"Yes, sir."

CHAPTER TWENTY-NINE

Kim and James found Margie's garage door open and her standing near the car's closed trunk. Two suitcases were on the concrete floor, one on each side of her.

They parked in the driveway and ran toward Margie. James grabbed her arm and held tight. Kim pressed the button that lowered the garage door so the neighbors couldn't see what was happening.

Kim flashed the evil grin James had come to love. "Going on a trip?" she asked.

Margie shook her head.

"What happened? Did your husband call and tell you to pick him up somewhere?"

Margie's eyes grew, but she again shook her head. This time more emphatically.

Kim peered through the car windows. "Give me your

car keys." It was a command not to be ignored. James felt the fear of his captive oozing out onto his hand.

Margie pointed to the purse on the garage floor. "Th…th…there…"

Kim grabbed the purse, searched the contents until she came up with a car key. She looked it over and punched a button. The trunk lid popped up partway. She put the purse in the front seat of Margie's car.

Kim tossed the keys to James and lifted the trunk lid. "Nothing here. Where are my artifacts, you thief?"

Margie shrugged.

Kim walked rapidly toward Margie while holding up an arm as if preparing to hit the scared woman in the face.

"Wait…" Margie pointed to the suitcases. "In there."

Kim smiled. James wasn't sure if she would have hit the older woman or not, but he wouldn't put it past her.

Kim opened both pieces of luggage and dumped everything onto the floor.

James saw two silver communion sets among the clothing.

Kim wrapped the treasures in some of Margie's clothes and placed them in the trunk of the car. "Very good. All you have to do now is tell us where the rest of my property is and we'll let you go."

Margie looked frightened. More than before. "The rest? Liz took everything else. I don't have more."

"Why can't I believe you? Come on, we'll search the house." Kim walked toward the door to the house.

James twisted Margie's arm toward the door to follow Kim. "Kim, let's make this fast. Since we thought to come here, the police will too. They may have nabbed Jack by now and are on the way."

"I thought of that. We'll just check the obvious spots and get out." She gestured toward Margie. "But if she doesn't find me a few more treasures, I'm taking her with us."

Margie stopped. "There's nothing in the house. I'd already packed everything in the suitcases...and a few in the spare tire storage area."

"Spare tire." Kim drew her arm back again, ready to slap Margie. "And...?"

"And the rest are in Jack's suite in Temple."

James snorted. "I bet the police have everything from there by now."

"Don't be too sure." Kim turned to leave. "But I bet there's more in Temple than here. And, like you said, the police should be here soon."

"Let's go." James pulled Margie by the arm toward the garage. "What should we do with her?"

"Take her with us."

Margie protested. "You said you'd let me go if I told you were everything was."

Kim laughed. "Isn't she cute? She kills my mother and then believes me when I say we'll let her go."

Margie's face turned white. James couldn't resist a snicker for Kim's sake, but he didn't like the way Kim treated Margie. She wasn't the enemy. He'd have to keep an eye on Kim. She was a powder box about to explode.

In the garage, Kim explained the plan. "The trunk has the artifacts in it so let's take her car and leave my rental here. The cops are looking for it by now, I'm sure. After they come here, they'll know to look for Margie's car, but it'll be at the lake where no one will notice it for days, perhaps weeks."

James asked Kim. "How are we getting out of here without a car?"

"Arthur will pick us up."

"Oh, great." James wasn't impressed. "Don't you think the police are looking for him also? Maybe you think he's a good fence, but he's not the brightest young man I've met."

"Don't worry about Arthur. He'll take care of us."

James watched Margie in the back seat. "What are we going to do with our guest here now that she's heard Arthur's name?"

Margie made a soft crying sound. "I didn't hear anything."

Kim backed the car out of the garage and drove toward the exit on the lake side. "See, no need to worry. She said she didn't hear anything. Besides, she has to go with us to Temple and get us into Jack's room." Then she laughed. Long and hard.

***

When Michael and I got to Margie's house, Lieutenant Bratton's car was parked in front and he was at the front door.

He walked toward us shaking his head. We climbed out of the bookmobile. "No one home?" I asked.

"No one responded." Bratton walked around the side of the garage then looked at us. "Wait here while I check the side door."

Michael and I waited in the driveway. In seconds, the garage door lifted and Bratton stood inside the garage. Around the space where a car would normally park was a messy pile of clothes. Two opened, upended suitcases stood empty nearby.

Bratton dug through the clothing as if searching for clues to what had happened. He paused, walked toward the interior door to the house. "Due to what I see here, I feel obligated to check on the safety of Mrs. Cummings. You two wait here."

The mess in the garage didn't make sense, but I suspected Jack called Margie after he ran out of the dining room and before the cops nabbed him in the bookmobile. He probably told her to make a run for it. But, why would she dump her suitcases in the garage?

"What do you think happened, Michael?"

"It's weird, and you may think I'm seeing more in this than there is, but I'd say Margie was getting ready to leave when Kim showed up. Kim searched the suitcases, looking for artifacts. Since she knew the police would be here soon, she dumped everything out to speed up the process. Kim then drove off in Margie's car."

"Then where's Margie? And where's Kim's car?"

Michael considered that briefly. "Kim kidnapped her for some reason. And her car is probably parked nearby."

I looked at Michael with new eyes.

He stared back, waiting for my response. "Well? Have I seen too many crime shows on TV, or could that have happened?"

"It's entirely possible. Good job."

Bratton came through the interior door with his phone to his ear. "Okay, let me know when you find the car."

He gave Michael and me his attention. "No one in the house. I called in Margie's missing car. All we can do now is wait. Maybe we'll hear something soon."

"Michael has an idea. He thinks Kim might have been here looking for something valuable and dumped the suitcases. Afterward, she abducted Margie."

"Hmm. That would explain a lot. I better call back and let them know we may have a hostage situation. Good catch, Michael." Bratton gave us one of his rare smiles.

***

When they turned onto the lake road, James stopped before the approach to the ranger's station. "So where's Arthur?"

"Don't worry. He's never let me down. Unlike you, I might add."

A pickup truck approached slowly, stopped when it was close enough to see the driver's face.

Kim climbed out. "That's him. Right on time. Get Margie and let's get out of here. You may want to drive her car into the woods a short distance. Make it harder to spot."

James looked in the back seat. "Where is Margie?"

Kim turned around. "What?"

Arthur pointed. "Is that who you're talking about?"

Margie ran toward the woods.

Kim started after her but quickly stopped. "Somebody shoot her."

"With what?" James asked.

"Then catch her." Kim had both hands on her hips.

"Go after her yourself." James laughed as he said it. "I'm not running into those woods in the dark. We don't need her that bad."

"But she'll talk." Kim sounded frantic.

"About what? We'll be gone before she can do any damage. Besides, she's wanted by the police. She'll keep her mouth shut."

James parked Margie's car and got the artifacts out of the trunk. Arthur had his truck door open to receive the treasures. James then moved Margie's car into the trees and took the keys with him. Kim grabbed Margie's purse.

When they were all in Arthur's pickup, he turned it around and headed out. "When you called you said you were going to use Margie to get into the room in Temple. Now what?"

James shook his head. "We'll get in." He couldn't believe the idiots he was forced to work with.

Kim held up Margie's purse. "I bet she has a key to his suite in here."

***

As we were leaving Margie's house, we saw a car behind the gazebo at the end of Mills Creek Drive. Bratton called in the plates. When he got off the phone, he told us what he'd learned.

"The records show the vehicle was rented by Sharon Coleman. However, the rental occurred after Sharon's death. Odds are, Kim used her mother's ID and credit card to lease the vehicle. This verifies Michael's suspicion that Kim took Margie and her car."

My phone rang. The caller ID said Margie Cummings. I showed Michael and Bratton the screen. "Maybe. Maybe not."

Michael punched the speakerphone button.

"Hello."

"Liz?" It was a whisper.

"Margie?"

"Yes."

"Are you okay?"

"I think so."

"Is Kim with you?" I thought I'd check.

"No. But how did you know…?"

"We're at your house now, and Kim's car is here. Are you safe?"

"Yes. James and Kim took me to the lake and Arthur met us there. While we were switching cars, I ran for it. Had to. They were going to kill me because I know too much."

"Slow down, Margie. Did you say James?"

"Yes. James and Kim are working together."

I checked Michael and Bratton's reactions and could see they were as surprised as I was.

"I never would have guessed that. But, the important thing now is that you got away. That's good. Where did you get a phone?"

"It was in my pocket. They took my purse, but no one checked my pockets."

"Good. Now tell us exactly where you are and we'll come get you."

Bratton made a signal for me to wait. "Ask her if she knows where Kim was going."

"Did you hear that, Margie? That was Lieutenant Bratton."

"Yes. They said they were going to look for stolen artifacts in Dennis' suite in Temple. They were taking me to help get into his room, but they can still get in. My key to the suite is in the purse they took."

"Okay. We'll notify the police to watch for them."

I decided to see what else we could learn. "Margie, I noticed your suitcases had been dumped out in the garage. Did they take your artifacts?"

She was silent for so long I thought we'd lost the connection. Finally. "Yes. But I only had a few."

"Thanks. I know that was hard to say. But, it'll help us recover everything and get it back to the churches."

Margie continued talking as if wanting to confess everything. "Jack had a few items in Temple."

"Yes. We found those."

"Is he okay?" Margie's voice shook.

"He's in custody. I'm not sure of his status. We'll talk more about it when we are sure you're safe. Now, tell me how to find you."

"I'm on the lake road about a mile off Highway 2338. I'll walk toward the highway now and wait if I get there first. Are you coming now?"

"I'm on my way. Look for the bookmobile."

After I ended the call, Bratton walked toward his car. "You pick up Margie and I'll go to Temple for the three there."

"Okay. What do you want us to do with her?"

"I'll meet you at her house, but give me a little time."

"No hurry. I want to ask her about Dennis."

"Good idea." Bratton drove off.

***

Arthur drove around the Royal Gardens parking lot looking for police cars. When he didn't see any, he stopped near the back door. Kim wanted James to stay with the pickup while she and Arthur went to search Dennis' room.

They had been gone for about ten minutes when James spotted an unmarked police car. It was made more noticeable by the way it sped in, stopped quickly, and the way the occupant exited and ran into the building.

The guy running in was in plainclothes, but he was a cop. No doubt about it. Kim and Arthur were in trouble and it wouldn't do much good to wait around. Still, he couldn't move. They may be dumb, but they were the closest thing to comrades he had. He couldn't abandon them. What if they came running out and needed him to help them get away?

He waited. It wasn't long before another police car arrived, this one marked, and two uniformed officers went in. Still, James waited.

Then he saw police leaving the building with Kim

and Arthur in handcuffs. Now it was time to leave. He headed south in minutes, staying away from I-35.

His mind worked as fast as his vehicle. It was all over now. End of the line for Kim and Arthur. James had a chance to get away, but where? There were a few artifacts in the backseat of the pickup, but everyone would be looking for Arthur's pickup soon. The artifacts wouldn't be a quick fix, though. Without Arthur and his connections, it would take James months to turn the stolen goods into cash. James couldn't pawn them or sell them to legitimate silver and gold dealers because they looked like historical artifacts. He gritted his teeth in frustration.

***

We picked up Margie on Highway 2338 near the entrance to the lake and took her home to wait for the police. She invited us in. As soon as we were seated she said she wanted to use the bathroom. I guess it was possible she'd sneak out a window, or overdose on pills, but I didn't think so. I had the feeling she was glad it was over.

She returned shortly, with her hair combed. "Do you and Michael want anything to drink? I'm having some iced tea before I go to jail."

"Do you have a cola?" Michael asked seemingly unfazed by her comment.

"Now, dear. I don't think you'll be in jail long."

We followed her to the kitchen.

"There are some cold drinks in the refrigerator. Help

yourselves."

Michael found two root beers and handed one to me.

Margie fixed her tea and sat at the kitchen table.

We joined her.

I wanted to hold her hand and pray with her, but I was also worried about Dennis. "Margie, do you know where Dennis is?"

"He went fishing."

"Fishing? When was that?"

"About the first of December, I think."

"He's been gone a long time. Did he say why he left?"

"Said he was fed up and couldn't take it anymore. Sharon drove him crazy. He'd leased a place at the Royal Gardens in Temple, but hadn't moved in yet. She refused to go with him. She was losing her mind and he wanted to enjoy what few years he had left."

I couldn't believe a man would leave his wife knowing she was having memory problems. "He said that?"

"Yes. He wanted to pay us to care for her. He asked me to check on Sharon every day and call him if there was an emergency."

"Did you contact him when Sharon died?"

"No." Margie suddenly found something interesting on the floor.

That shocked me and I guess I voiced my anger. "Didn't you think the death of his wife was an emergency?"

"Yes, but I couldn't call and tell him I killed his wife now, could I? Besides, Jack wouldn't let me."

CHAPTER THIRTY

"You what?" I never would have picked Margie for a murderer.

"One day I saw Sharon with her arms around Jack, trying to kiss him. He rejected her, of course. Still, I asked her about it later. She denied it, but I gave her a good shove to let her know I was upset with her actions."

"Don't tell me. She fell and bumped her head?"

"Yes. I murdered her."

I gave her a hug. "Sounds like you didn't mean to hurt her."

She whimpered. "I didn't. I'm so sorry. Do you think I'll have to spend the rest of my life in prison?"

Michael shook his head.

I patted her back. "No, dear. You should have called

for help, but I'm pretty certain you won't be charged with murder."

"Really?"

"Yes. Now I want you to tell me why you and Jack had the artifacts. But first, give me the emergency number you have for Dennis."

Margie went into the bedroom and came back with a notebook. She read off the number. "Dennis is in a place where there's no phone or Internet service. He said to call this number and ask the person who answers to go get him."

I called Bratton and gave him the phone number and the instructions on how to contact Dennis. Bratton told me they'd caught Kim and Arthur, but James got away. I relayed the information to Michael and Margie.

I patted Margie on the arm. "Now, tell me about the artifacts."

Michael took a drink of his root beer and leaned forward.

"It's all so terrible I hate to talk about it. I'm ashamed of what we did. You may not believe it, but we used to be decent people." Margie shook her head slowly and didn't make eye contact with me.

"I know this is not an excuse for what we did, but it explains why. In 2008, we got hit hard by the financial downfall. Before we could move our funds, the value hit rock bottom. We've been struggling ever since. We eventually withdrew everything we had to live on. We have social security, but it's not enough to pay the bills. Jack tried to go back to work, but he'd been retired too long and no one would hire him."

"Didn't you tell everyone he'd gone abroad to work?" I asked.

"Yes, but that was because we didn't want anyone to know he had taken Dennis' place at the retirement home in Temple."

"Why did he do that, ma'am?" Michael asked.

"Because we'd found a way to solve our money problems. Sharon had all those old gold and silver items and she didn't know where they came from. She gave me a few pieces one day and told me she'd found more. She said a guy named James brought them to the house."

"Did she say who James was?" I asked.

"Only that he was a friend of her daughter Kim. She told me Kim was in a convent in South America so Jack and I assumed she was a nun. We could see the objects Sharon gave me were valuable, but I never dreamed they were stolen. Sharon told me to take more if I wanted. She didn't want them in her house. So we started moving other pieces out of her house and into our house and Jack took some to the suite in Temple."

"Did you get many pieces?"

"No. We planned to, but before long, everything disappeared. We think James caught on that we took them and started moving them out of the house. Sharon said one day that James borrowed the car to drive to Salado where Sharon and Dennis had another house. We decided James hid the articles there. I learned later, from you, that he'd hidden some in the base of those clocks Sharon had here. So we went to Salado and got all the ones in the clocks there."

I thought about everything that had happened and

some of it began to make sense. But there were still many unanswered questions. "I don't understand why Jack pretended to be Dennis and hired me to clean out the houses."

"There were still a lot of artifacts missing. When I learned of your reputation as a detective, Jack suggested we should get you to find the artifacts for us. We didn't count on you moving them out to your barn. We went out there to retrieve the items, but Sharon's dog ran us off."

Michael laughed and I pictured tiny Princess protecting the farm. "So that was you?"

"Afraid so. Sorry."

"With most of the artifacts in the hands of the Feds, why did Jack continue to pretend he was Dennis? By that time you knew the artifacts were stolen. It led to his eventual arrest."

"Stubbornness, greed, I don't know. He was always that way. Once he set out to do something, he kept at it. Even if what he did made things worse. I tried to get him to leave Dennis' suite while he could, but we didn't know how much of the treasure was still out there possibly available to take. He kept thinking he could get more. We even talked about blackmailing Kim, but she scared us both. And James was worse."

There was a knock on the door. I gave a start. Could it be James? I looked at Michael.

"It's Bratton," he said.

"How do you know?"

He held up his phone. "He texted me to say it's safe to open the door."

I opened it and, sure enough, it was Lieutenant Bratton along with a female officer.

I gave Margie another hug. "Is there anyone you want me to call?"

Margie shook her head and let a few tears fall. "No. It's just us. No children and we outlived our close relatives."

I gave her another squeeze. "I'll come see you as soon as I can. And I'll continue to pray for you every day."

The female officer took her away and I gave Bratton a summary of everything we'd learned from Margie. He shook his head several times during the telling, even though I was sure he'd heard worse.

As we prepared to leave, Bratton looked directly into my eyes as if to get my attention. "Watch out for James. He's dangerous."

***

Along the way to Sun City, James kept a constant lookout for the police. He knew it wouldn't be long before Arthur's truck would be on the list of wanted vehicles. He stayed off the interstate and took the back roads.

He got to Sun City at dusk. After checking to see that there was no one nearby, he drove the pickup into the woods near his campsite behind Sharon's house. He laughed as he crushed one of the signs describing the area as environmentally sensitive.

He removed the artifacts from the vehicle and drove it into the creek. He'd hoped it would go under, but it didn't. Too shallow. The roof poked above the surface, reminding him of a giant turtle shell.

If the artifacts they'd gotten from Margie were the only pieces left, he'd have ditched the car somewhere far away and simply disappeared. But he had a few of the better-looking items hidden in his campsite. With Kim and Arthur in custody, he could take it all. All that was left, that is. It would take time to dispose of the collectibles, but he could eventually convert his stash to cash.

All he had to do now was hide out until the next bus tour. One was scheduled to leave from the social center in a few days and he'd be there with all his treasures. He would hijack the bus and disappear before anyone knew what had happened. No one would look where he planned to go. With a large bus, he wouldn't have a problem going through barbed-wire fences and he could take as many shortcuts as he wanted. The law would check the roads, but he'd be in the cattle fields. The cops would bring in the helicopters to help in the search, but by then he would be in a different vehicle and on his way to the Gulf.

***

Michael and I got home so late it wasn't until the next day that we caught Samuel up on all that had happened. He closed his eyes and shook his head slowly as I told him about Margie's confession. It was as if he hurt for her. When my tale ended, he reached out one hand toward me and his other toward Michael. At first I was confused, but then I took his hand in mine, feeling him tremble ever so slightly, and bowed my head.

Samuel cleared his throat. "Dear God, we don't understand why some folk do what they do. Still, You care for all, no matter their choices. We pray now for Your loving arms to be around Margie and her husband Jack. We also ask for guidance so that we may minister to them. We are mere humans and don't know what to do or what to say, but we will put ourselves close to where we feel we are needed and trust You will direct us. In Jesus' name, we pray."

My eyes flooded. "Thank you, dear." I looked at Michael and noticed tears in his eyes also. I think we had been so close to the action yesterday, we hadn't seen what Samuel did. Margie and Jack, no matter what they did, still needed our help.

Michael dabbed his eyes with his napkin and stood. "May I be excused?" He turned to walk out of the room.

"Yes, of course." I was glad to see his reaction to Samuel's words. I'd seen Michael grow into a man, but this was the first time I'd seen that his emotional side had matured as well.

Michael hesitated. "I haven't forgotten it's my night to clean up after dinner. Before I do, I want to test an idea for getting past that defense department security." He looked at the clock on the wall. "Now's the best time of day."

"It's okay, son," Samuel said, "we'll save the dirty dishes for you." He gave me a wink. I suspected he'd seen what I had and was making it easier for Michael to leave the room.

***

"I did it!"

It was about an hour later. Samuel still hadn't gotten the hang of automatic dishwashers, so he had washed the dishes by hand, while I put away the leftovers. We were reading, me the *Austin-American Statesman,* and Samuel an old *National Geographic* magazine.

"Did you hear what I said? I did it."

I hadn't seen Michael so excited since he he'd made the varsity football team in high school. Of course that was just before he got kicked off the team for smoking marijuana. "You did what?"

"I broke into the defense department's computer. I got past Chris' security blocks. I've read James Johnson's military records."

"Congratulations," Samuel said.

"I knew you could do it," I said. "So, what did you find out?"

"I can't tell you."

"What?"

"You remember. I gave my word. Chris is paying me to test his security software, and anything I accidently learn while logged in cannot be shared with anyone."

"Anyone?" I dropped the newspaper and stood. "But, dear, what you learned may help the police find James."

"I'm sorry. You know I can't tell you. I'd never get another white hacker job if I did."

"Can you tell me if what you saw would be useful to the police? Is it timely? Is it something we urgently need to know?"

"No, ma'am."

"Not useful or you can't tell me?"

He looked as if I'd beaten him in a game of checkers. "Don't do that!"

"I've got an idea." I was proud of my grandson for standing up for himself, but I knew the information he had might be critical to finding James. If I was right, the information Michael had might help us catch a killer before he struck again.

"What's that?" He looked at me with narrowed eyes.

"Contact Chris and give him your report on how you broke into the computer stuff. Then, ask him to get permission to report what you found to Lieutenant Bratton. And only to Bratton."

Michael nodded.

Samuel's eyes brightened. "That's it. Let the government people decide who knows what. If the Feds learn what is happening here, they may jump at the chance to communicate with the police department."

"Right," I added. "Be sure to tell Chris the FBI is involved in the stolen artifacts."

Samuel showed his agreement. "Excellent plan, luv."

"I can do that." Michael walked slowly across the room and picked up Princess. "Yes. I'll keep my word, live up to the terms of the contract, and the proper information will get to the people who need to know. Yes." He put the dog down and headed for the door.

CHAPTER THIRTY-ONE

The next day we checked out books in Sun City. Chris had promised to contact the Defense Department and apprise them of the situation in Georgetown. If they felt there was a need, they'd contact Lieutenant Bratton directly. We'd done all we could.

I sat at the front checkout desk, watching Princess nap next to the heater, even though it wasn't on. That's when it hit me. We'd been looking for James for days, but hadn't once thought to get Princess to help. She knew James and could probably lead me to him.

I jumped out of my chair and headed to the door. "Come on, Princess. We're going for a walk."

Michael was outside positioning the cart where we kept the most recent books along with ones people had requested. "Where are you going?"

"Princess is going to help me find James."

"What? Wait. I'll go with you."

"No need. One of us should be here for the patrons. Besides, I'm just going to see if Princess picks up a scent. If so, we'll call Bratton and let him know."

"Don't go far."

"I won't. Don't worry."

"Remember, I know things about James I can't tell you. Don't approach him. Promise?"

"Yes, of course." That made me even more curious, but I'd told Michael I wouldn't pressure him about what he'd learned about James.

I walked behind the Cummings' house where there was no fence blocking access to the woods like there was behind Sharon's. I hadn't put the leash on Princess, and decided not to. I would let her lead the way. The grass was taller out there and the little poodle disappeared from sight in places. She seemed to know when to stop and let me catch up. Then, on she would go as if following an invisible trail. My dress got caught on a wild prickly vine. I pulled it loose, but I wouldn't be wearing this outfit again.

The tree limbs were so low in places they blocked my vision and hit me in the face as I walked. Princess continued to stop occasionally and lock eyes with me before she moved on into the wooded area.

I wondered if my phone was in my purse where I usually kept it. Then I remembered I hadn't brought my purse. I felt goose bumps on my arms for no apparent reason and decided to turn around and go back.

Princess growled from the left at the same time I felt

something cold on the right side of my neck.

"What are you doing here?" It was James. Even though he whispered, he sounded more assured of himself than he had when I'd seen him before.

I hadn't seen or heard him, but he'd somehow gotten behind me without alerting Princess. "It's me, Liz."

"I know who you are and I know why you're here. I just didn't think you were dumb enough to come out here in the woods alone. Who's with you?" He continued to whisper, but I could hear every word clearly.

"It's only me. And Princess." Just as I said her name, I saw her hightailing it back toward Sharon's house. "I brought her out for a walk, that's all. What're you doing here?"

"Never mind. Where's that dog?"

"She was here a minute ago. I guess you spooked her. Let go of me. We need to talk."

"I'll let go when I'm ready."

Still standing behind me, he took the object away from my neck and I could see it was a knife. He grabbed my left arm and held it tightly behind my back. The arthritic pain in my wrist was enough to cause anyone to scream, but I didn't. Mainly to keep from giving him the satisfaction of knowing he hurt me.

He pushed me further into the woods and talked louder. "You think you're pretty smart, don't you? No one has found my camp and you were about to walk into it."

We entered an opening surrounded by dense trees with leaves covering the clearing from above as well as all sides. There was a gutted deer hanging from a tree. Blood pooled on the ground below. We walked close enough for me to smell it. Not so much the scent of death as the odor one gets on a farm.

"What am I going to do with you?" He looked at the deer and laughed, holding the knife in the air. "We'll see." He laughed again, louder this time.

I saw him in a different way than I had before. He seemed more like a maniac than a war-damaged veteran.

He directed me toward what appeared to be the center of the camp where a fire surrounded by rocks smoldered. A stick with partially eaten browned dough rested against one of the rocks. Another stick was covered with cooked meat, grease dripping to the ground.

James picked up a short rope and reached for my arm. He turned me around and tied my hands behind me.

"Why this? I came to talk to you. I won't run away."

"Yeah, sure."

I was never one to give up on anything or anybody, but as I assessed the situation I wondered what the Lord had in mind. Surely it wasn't my time to die. There was so much left to do. Michael was growing up, a man now, actually, and I'd hoped he'd give me a great-grandchild one day. And then there was Samuel, the man God had sent to show me what true marital happiness was all about. I wanted many more years with Samuel. *Please, Lord.*

These things passed through my mind so quickly I

marveled at the wonders of the brain. My attention returned to the present and I wished Michael had told me the secrets he'd learned about James. All I knew was that he was a sad, tormented man who was dangerous. Was it all because of his military experience? Was he mentally ill? Suffering from PTSD? Would he really rip me open like he did that deer?

I also wished I'd listened to Michael and not gotten myself into this situation. In hindsight it was a mistake to go into the woods alone. All along the way I'd known I should stop and turn back. But, the further I went the more tempted I was to continue. I thought I would see something and then turn back before I was spotted.

At least Princess got away. She must have sensed danger and gone back for help. Michael would see the dog without me and he'd call for assistance. Someone would help her soon.

I turned my attention to James. "Listen, I know you're hurting. I want you to know everything is going to be okay."

"Oh, shut up. Next thing I know you'll be praying for me."

"I am praying for you."

He laughed. "A lotta good it's done. You don't have to pray for me. I take care of myself. In fact, you're the answer to *my* prayers."

"What do you mean?"

"I sat here working on my escape plan and wishing I had someone like you to make it easier."

"You mean like a hostage?"

"No. I prayed for a talker. You and your big mouth

can help me get out of this Godforsaken place. And you arrived just in time."

"How can I help?"

"Don't ask so many questions. You'll know when I tell you."

He reached into a duffle bag and pulled out two smaller canvas bags, the size used for grocery shopping.

James unzipped his sleeping bag to expose a number of the church artifacts like the ones we'd collected and given to the FBI.

He looked at me and smiled. "I bet you thought you had them all." He divided the treasures between the two smaller bags.

"Before I untie you so we can leave, I need to tell you how it is." He locked his eyes on mine. "I've done some pretty horrific things in my life—but only because I wanted to serve my country. I was good at what I did, and it was all I knew. When they kicked me out all I could do was find my own wars. What I've done since is no different than what I did for Uncle Sam. You understand?"

"Yes."

"No you don't. Nobody does. Just pay attention to what I say. A mistake can be deadly. There is a tour bus leaving the social center in thirty minutes. We're going to be on it. Your job is to con the driver into letting us on without tickets. If you do that, I will set you free when we get to Austin. If you can't, I may have to stick you and anyone who tries to stop me from hijacking the bus." He held out his hunting knife and jabbed it toward me to make sure I knew what he meant.

"Please don't hurt anyone."

"That's up to you. Where is that guy who's always with you on the library bus?"

"He stayed home sick today." Sorry, Lord. Under the circumstances, I figured it was okay to lie.

"You're lying. I just hope he doesn't see you and try to be a hero. He's too young to die."

"He won't see us. Do you have something I could wear as a scarf, so no one will recognize me?"

He dug into the large canvas bag again and came up with a red bandana. It didn't match my blue and green flowered dress, but it would have to do. I didn't want Michael to try anything foolish.

James untied the rope behind my back. I put the bandana on like a lady's scarf.

"Let's go," he said. "Take one of those bags."

It was easier getting out of the woods than it had been to get in. We walked only a short way until we reached a sidewalk. I recognized where we were, and was shocked at how close I'd come to James' camp so many times.

When we got to the line for the tour bus, James grabbed my arm, leaned over to me, and whispered. "Okay. It's show time. Get us on board without a bunch of questions. It's probably fairly full by now since it's almost departure time. Try anything funny and people will get hurt. Not just you, but everyone around you."

James was right, I was a talker. If anyone could get him on the bus, it was me. The bus driver stood at the door and I noticed the people who entered before us showed him a piece of paper. Having never been on a

Sun City tour, I had no idea what it was.

When it was our turn to climb aboard, I gave the driver a hug. Although James managed to deflect my attempts to hug him when we first met, I hoped he would remember I was a hugger and not be alarmed by my hugging the driver.

I moved back and read the driver's name tag and saw an American flag pin on it. An idea overtook me. "Fred. How are you today?"

He was still reeling from the unexpected hug. "Fine, uh..."

"Listen," I said, holding up the canvas bag with the stolen artifacts, "I thought my purse was in here, but it's not. That's where I have our tour tickets." I hoped that was what they called them.

The driver listened patiently, but didn't respond.

"I called my girlfriend and she's on her way with my purse." I motioned to James next to me. "The problem is, my husband here needs to sit. He had knee surgery not long ago and can't stand for long. Would it be okay if we go on in and get a seat? I'm sure my friend will show up in plenty of time."

The driver nodded. "Sure. Go ahead." He looked at James. "Could I help you with that bag, sir?"

James moved slowly onto the bus. "Nah. I got it. Thanks, though."

As James entered the bus, I placed my canvas bag on the ground and took the American flag lapel pin off the driver's name bar. "Your pin is crooked. Let me fix it."

By the time I had finished with the driver's lapel pin, James had found two seats in the last row. I talked to several ladies along the way and then sat next to him with the canvas bag in my lap. I could've gotten away while I was still outside the bus with the driver, but I knew if I ran, James would panic and start slashing around with the knife.

He moved his head close to mine. "I was right about you being a talker. You've done good so far. Keep it up and no one will have to die."

I could see he had his hand in the canvas bag he carried. I suspected his hand was wrapped around the handle of the knife for quick access.

We waited for what seemed like an eternity. It was so long I kind of wished I'd run when I had the chance. The other passengers were getting antsy as well, but for different reasons. One called out to the driver that it was time to go. The driver said they were waiting for one more person. I hope he hadn't believed me when I said someone was bringing my purse.

A couple near the front of the bus exited, but did so leisurely. I suspected the delay was responsible for a restroom stop. Then two more people got off.

James whispered in my ear. "Something's wrong. People are leaving. They must have been warned. If this keeps up, we'll be the only one left. And you know what that means, don't you."

"What?"

"You'll be the only one I can hurt."

"Relax. It has nothing to do with you. They probably had to go to the restroom. You know how that happens as we get older."

That shut him up for a while, but soon he looked out

the window as if searching for signs of anything out of the ordinary. "I don't know. I can't see where they went. This delay may be a setup to wait for the police. Did you say anything about me to the driver?"

Another couple exited the bus.

"No. Of course not."

Something was going on. Not that many people would leave to go to the restroom. I needed to do something to get his mind off of whatever might happen next. I leaned in to him and talked softly. "James, I can tell you this. I suspected you may have something to do with Sharon's death, so I've been looking into your background. What I found was that you served your country honorably. We should all give you a big thanks for your service in Vietnam."

He looked at me as if trying to decide how to respond. He opened his mouth, but nothing came out.

I continued. "We've since learned that Sharon's death was accidental. So we know you didn't have anything to do with her death. I would hate to see you do anything that might harm yourself or others."

James stared into my eyes as if trying to see if I was sincere. I couldn't tell if he believed me or not and I thought he might do something rash like try to commandeer the bus.

I tried to think of other words to calm him. "Listen, James…"

"Ah, here he is," the driver said. "The man we've been waiting on."

I didn't recognize him at first, but soon knew it was Lieutenant Bratton. He wore a Hawaiian shirt, the kind that didn't tuck into your pants. A straw hat sat on his head on an angle. He carried a cane in his left hand and he leaned on it as he waved his right hand in the air apologetically.

"Sorry for holding you up, folks. My car broke down a few blocks from here so I called and asked the driver to wait for me."

There were some friendly boos, but most people laughed and greeted him like an old friend.

I looked at James and he looked suspiciously at the late arrival, but I could see he was more relaxed than he had been when some of the passengers got off the bus.

CHAPTER THIRTY-TWO

There were two empty seats on the back row next to where James and I sat. Bratton motioned his head toward the seats. "Hey, buddy, mind if we sit there? My wife will be here in a minute." Bratton emphasized the use of his cane to the point of dragging his left foot. He came across as weak and friendly.

James gave a non-committal shrug and Bratton walked toward him.

I'm not sure what happened next, but something must have spooked James. He had the knife out and lunged toward Bratton with it. The woman in the seat to my right screamed and moved further toward the window.

When Bratton pulled back I could see blood saturating his shirt near his right shoulder and the cane fell to the floor. James was on his feet with the knife pulled back and ready to swing toward Bratton.

I stood also and poked my canvas bag between James and Bratton. The knife blade went through the canvas as if it was paper then made a clinking sound as it struck something metallic. While the knife was embedded in the canvas, I jerked hard, the knife remained stuck in the bag and I pulled the bag, along with James' hand, until he let go.

Without the knife jabbing at him, Bratton subdued James and held him on the bus floorboard. Two uniformed officers ran in and handcuffed him.

The nearby spectators let out a cheer. Before long, the entire bus responded with applause.

I took off the bandana James had loaned me and held it tightly against Bratton's bloody shoulder. An EMT showed up quickly, entered the bus, and cared for Bratton. The whole rescue and arrest appeared to have been well-coordinated along with backup and support personnel in place before the action began. It was over in a matter of minutes.

The driver asked everyone to disembark to let the officers do their job. Bratton and I, along with the EMT, exited also. I grabbed both the canvas bags before I got off.

The medic led us to her vehicle, where Bratton sat on the back floorboard next to the stretcher. She removed the gauze she'd had him hold over the cut to stop the bleeding. With a pair of scissors, she snipped open his shirt around the wound and then tore it off his arm.

"Hey!" Bratton said, "I borrowed that shirt." He took

it off and was left with a white T-shirt with blood on the shoulder.

"Borrowed?" I asked.

"Yeah. My regular shirt and coat made me look like a cop so, after I explained what I was doing, some guy waiting to get on the bus gave me his shirt."

"You can buy him another one."

"I guess. If I ever see him again. I kinda liked that shirt he got from me in trade."

"Forget the shirt. Tell me how you found us on the bus."

"I got your signal."

"Signal?" I thought I knew what he meant, but I wanted to hear him say it. I wanted to know my spur of the moment idea worked.

"The distress flag."

That made me smile. "Really?"

"Of course. First, Michael called…"

"Is he okay? We need to let him know I'm safe. He'll be worried sick."

"Already done. He's on the way here now."

I looked around, but didn't see him.

"Anyway, because of Michael's call, I was in Sun City looking for you, hoping James would be with you. We even had a helicopter searching the area. That's probably about the same time the bus driver called 9-1-1. He reported the possibility of a problem. He described you and James…pretty accurately for a civilian I might add…and then he told me how you'd turned his flag lapel pin upside down. He didn't know why you did it, but he didn't want to depart with a busload of tourists knowing something could be wrong. The 9-1-1 operator told him to stall until we got there. Since I wasn't far away, it didn't take long. I called in for backup and medical support with no sirens. We had all responders park around by the tennis courts. We didn't want to spook James. All I had to do after that was change shirts and borrow a hat and a cane."

"And do some acting to go along with your costume."

"Acting?"

"You know, the cheerful man role."

"I'm always cheerful."

I wanted to laugh, then realized he meant it. "Never mind.

"Gigi?"

I looked around and spotted him. "Over here, Michael." He joined us at the emergency vehicle and I gave him a long bear hug. What ran through my head was how I hug people I don't know more than I hug my own grandson. I intended to change that. "I'm sorry, son. You warned me not to go alone, but James sneaked up on us. Even Princess didn't know he was there. Oh, do you have Princess?"

"Yes. She's the reason I knew you were in trouble. She came back and whimpered loud and long. That's when I called Lieutenant Bratton."

The EMT washed off the wound and put three butterfly bandages on it. "You need to go to the ER and get that tended to. It's a deep cut and wide enough to need stitches. Want a ride?"

"Nah. My car's here."

"Sir, you lost a lot of blood. Just look at this shirt. I

don't recommend driving."

"He can ride with us," I said.

"Okay." She looked at Bratton. "But if you get faint, call and we'll be back for you."

"I will." He looked at her ID. "Thank you, Shelda. I appreciate your care and concern."

After she drove away, a man appeared wearing a plain white tee with leisure trousers. He held a dress shirt and tie toward Bratton.

"Here's your shirt, Detective."

"And here's yours." Bratton held out the ripped and bloody Hawaiian one. "I'm afraid I ruined it, though. Could I buy you a replacement?"

The man's eyes opened wider. "No. That's okay. I'm just glad to be of service to the police. I hope your wound isn't too serious."

"I'll have to get a few stitches, but I'll be okay. Thanks for asking. Oh, and here is your cane." He held it out toward the man.

The man took the cane then looked toward me before returning his gaze to Bratton. "I hope you don't mind, but could I have the hat back? It was a gift from my grandson."

Bratton must have forgotten he had it on. He reached up and pulled it off. "Sure." He handed it to the man. "Thank you for the loan. It was more important than you might imagine. With your help we made an arrest, and may have saved some lives today."

The man smiled and then turned a crimson color. "Just doing my duty," he said.

We all waved goodbye and the man disappeared in

the crowd.

"That was nice of you," I said.

Bratton looked at me as if he didn't know what I was talking about. And, perhaps he didn't.

"Okay, we better get you to ER. Michael, where's the bookmobile?"

"In the parking lot." He pointed.

"Wait," Bratton said. "I just told her you'd drive me to keep her from bugging me. I'm okay. I can drive."

"No, you can't. Look at this shirt. You lost too much blood. Get in that bookmobile or I'm going to call Shelda back to pick you up. She'll offer you a nice stretcher and a loud bumpy ride to the ER. Whereas, I have a nice comfortable chair for you in the bookmobile. Which is it, Buster?"

Michael smiled.

Bratton didn't. "I'll go with you. By the way, what's in those bags? I saw how you've protected them."

Before I had a chance to tell him, he turned to Michael. "Your grandmother saved my life today, son."

He stared at the young man with such intensity I wondered if Bratton had tears in his eyes.

"She did?"

Perhaps it was the loss of blood affecting him, but he seemed to recover quickly from displaying his emotions. "Yes, indeed. She used one of those bags to stop James from stabbing me in the chest. Then she twisted the bag to keep the knife blocked long enough for me to get a jump on him."

"The reason I'm protecting these bags is because they contain more artifacts. Seems James had a little stash for himself at his campsite. Plus he probably had the ones he and Kim took from Margie."

"Good," Bratton said as we got to the bookmobile. "We'll need to hand them over to the FBI. And, we probably should check that campsite, too."

Princess loved having company. She snuggled up with Bratton all the way to the hospital.

***

A week later, Bratton called and wanted to know if he could come to the farm and give us a report. He wanted to meet us there so Samuel could hear it all too, but I noticed the only time Bratton could come was when we usually had dinner. I invited him to eat with us.

We managed to find plenty to talk about during the meal without getting into anything about James and the stolen artifacts. After we cleared the table, we found more comfortable chairs in the family room.

I poured Bratton another cup of coffee. "Did you find Dennis?"

Bratton took a sip of his coffee. "Yes. I talked to him by phone and then in person. He's back, but he's having a rough time with his wife's death. Blames himself. He had rented a getaway in the mountains where he couldn't be reached because of the strain he'd been under for so long caring for Sharon. He'd tried to get a doctor to tell her she needed more help than Dennis could provide, but she apparently fooled the doctor into thinking she was okay by saying it was Dennis who was having problems. That place in Temple, the Royal

Gardens, was his attempt to get help, but she refused to move there with him. He never lived there, either. Dennis asked Jack to watch his suite until he got back, so Jack moved in. The staff assumed he was Dennis.

"Dennis asked Margie and Jack to check on Sharon and get her help as soon as she would allow it. He gave them access to his bank account to pay bills to care for her as needed. He also gave them Kim's contact info at the convent. That's why they assumed she was a nun. Dennis knew she worked in IT, he just never mentioned it to Jack and Margie."

"Where is Dennis living now?" I asked.

"He's at Royal Gardens, but he'll be visiting the homes in Sun City and Salado to empty them and put the houses on the market. He's helping Kim as much as she'll let him. Since she spent so much time in South America, she hasn't gotten bond yet. She may go to trial before she does. Dennis visits her often and has hired a top-notch defense lawyer to help her."

Samuel cleared his throat. "Luv, we need to pray for Dennis, too. Okay?"

I patted his arm. "We will, dear."

Michael nodded with a smile, but I wasn't sure how to take it. I sometimes worried he didn't have the faith I prayed for him to have.

"What about Margie and Jack Cummings?" Michael asked. "What will become of them?"

Bratton looked at the ceiling, then turned to Michael. "Margie and Jack did some dumb things and they'll probably punish themselves more than the state will. As I said from the get go, I believe Sharon's death was an accident. Still, Margie thinks she caused it and she wants to go to jail for it. I'm not sure that'll happen. Just guessing, I'd say they'll both end up with probation."

"And James?" I asked.

Bratton winked at my grandson. "That's a different story. Michael knows more about James than we do, but he's not talking. And I respect that. I know only the parts of James' background the Feds felt required to tell me, knowing James was here and knowing how dangerous he is. But, the bottom line is the military will charge him first and I doubt he'll live long enough to get into the Texas criminal justice system.

"I told you about how James assaulted a doctor at the VA in Temple. The feds have a charge on him for that."

"Is the doctor okay?" I asked.

"Yes. He lowered his own blood pressure and pretended to pass out, using techniques he'd learned in a bio-feedback class. He was convincing enough to fool James. I don't think I could have done that myself."

Bratton finished his coffee and placed his cup on the side table. "If the Feds ever let James out, I've got a manslaughter charge waiting for him, and Dallas has a murder charge with his name on it."

"You told us he was wanted in connection with his wife's death in Dallas. Who'd he kill in Georgetown?" Michael asked.

"Remember hearing about the man who was found dead outside the Sun City fitness center?"

"I do," I said.

"We knew at the time the man had been killed by a karate chop taught in the military. We had a video showing James nearby at the approximate time of death. It wasn't until I saw him on the tour bus that I knew he was the man in the video. Around the time of the death, a workman replacing air filters found the attic area of a nearby rest room had been lived in. At the time, I didn't make a connection, but now I bet the occupant was James."

"In addition to the campsite where he took me."

"Yes. And the attic in Sharon's house." Bratton said.

"How did Kim and James meet?" Michael asked.

"Kim hatched up a scheme to steal the church's treasures and needed help getting the loot out of the country and to Arthur who was to sell the artifacts. She found an ad in a *Soldier of Fortune* magazine that led her to James."

"What a pair they were." I said.

"Well, they may have gotten away with it if Margie hadn't gotten jealous and pushed Sharon and caused her to hit her head."

"If Gigi hadn't found the body so quickly, they may have had time to get the treasure out of the house before anyone knew it was there," Michael added.

"That's true," Samuel said. "Sometimes it's beneficial to be assertive." He looked at me with a smile. "I mean that in the kindest way possible, luv."

"I know, dear." I turned back to Bratton. "What's going to happen to Kim and Arthur?"

"She'll be charged by the FBI for stealing antiquities from churches in South America. Those charges should give her free room and board in a federal prison for a while. We may file a few charges against her as well, but

I doubt it. It'll depend on what the Feds do."

"And Arthur?"

"It's not clear how much he was involved in the theft. Turns out he's more of a fence than the antique dealer he claims to be, but he's small-time. He never would've been able to find buyers for the stolen goods Kim obtained. That takes someone several pay grades above him. Right now, about all we can get Arthur on is aiding and abetting for picking Kim up when she kidnapped Margie. Even so, there's not much of a case against him since Margie got away before he joined the others. I'm sure the Austin police will keep an eye on him for a while, maybe even look into previous jobs he's been involved in. The FBI will also want to know what else he has fenced or tried to fence."

It turned out to be an interesting evening, as well as a way of closing out the adventure we'd all been a part of. I still wanted to meet Dennis, though, and I wondered if he might be kind enough to reimburse me for the carpet I'd installed in his Sun City house. It wasn't his fault that I'd been conned by Jack, but Dennis was the benefactor.

CHAPTER THIRTY-THREE

James opened his eyes, but didn't move. He assessed the situation the best he could as he remained frozen, using only what he could see and feel. He was on his back. A beige concrete ceiling connected to walls of the same color and material. The softness supporting him suggested he was on a mattress. He heard metallic sounds from time to time, but they seemed far enough away not to be a concern. There was a faint aroma of food in the air.

He turned to the left, his gaze following the wall down from the ceiling until he came to a window. Not a usual window; not one that could be opened. This window consisted of two opaque panes, each only a few inches wide and two feet or so high. The area around the window was painted blue.

He rolled to the right and knew he was in jail, perhaps a holding cell. There was a stainless steel sink and toilet in his view now. He focused on the bars that made up the door and saw a tray of food sitting in an opening.

He stood and walked cautiously to examine the food. Not because he was hungry, but because he was curious about where he was. The last thing he remembered was being captured on the tour bus. He'd taken the last of his pills before they could stop him, so he must have slept through everything that happened after that. He just wished he'd had some cyanide. That's what they gave spies. Why couldn't he have some, too?

He examined the contents of the tray. Coffee, lukewarm. Eggs, cold. Oatmeal, lumpy and crusted.

He looked back at the bunk. Single, no place for roommates. Temporary, then. What would they do with him next? Where was he? County jail? Military?

He reached out and pushed the tray through the slot. It landed with a bang, contents splashing and mixing on the floor.

A guard appeared in seconds. "Didn't like the food?"

James analyzed the man's uniform. Blue trousers with a red stripe down the side, beige shirt. A Marine. "Why am I in a military brig? I'm a civilian."

The guard stood back from the food on the floor. "I don't know. My job is to keep you here. And to feed you. Next meal is in four hours." He turned to leave.

"Wait." James said. "There's been some mistake. I shouldn't be here. My parents are going to be worried that I didn't get home last night."

The guard stopped and looked back, stared at him. "You're kidding, right. Your parents are alive?"

"Of course. Will you call them and tell them where I am? Please."

"What's their number?"

"Glendale 2…uhh…5157."

"That's not a phone number."

"Yes, that's it."

"I never heard of a number like that." He turned and walked away.

***

The next day after we'd had Bratton over for dinner Michael parked in front of Sharon's house. Even though she was no longer there, this location had become known as the bookmobile stop for Mills Creek Estates and surrounding neighborhoods.

Accompanied by Princess, Michael set things up as usual when we got there. I should have helped, but instead I stared at the commendation on the bulletin board next to the photo of me and the president. The new commendation was in appreciation for my help in getting the stolen artifacts back where they should be. The colorful FBI Art Crime Team logo brightened the bookmobile wall as well as my day. Michael got one also. He hadn't decided where to hang his yet, mainly because he wasn't sure where he would live. I bought him a nice frame like mine for when he was ready to put it on a wall.

He got a nice letter from the Defense Department

thanking him for what he'd done and, more importantly, offering him a full-time job.

I couldn't concentrate on work. I sat in the front passenger seat staring at the house and thinking about Sharon and what all had happened since that cold day not so long ago. So much had happened since the day we found Sharon's body.

Margie was still in jail and even with all she'd done and the way she lied to me, I kinda missed her. I'd been to visit her several times since she'd been arrested, and it was time to go again. She seemed like a different person now.

Princess ran into view before she circled around to Michael I knew we should keep her on a leash, but she loved to be free. She had been a part of our life since Sharon died. Jack had given the dog to me, but that was when he was impersonating Dennis. The proper thing to do would be to give the dog to the real owner. Just thinking about losing Princess made me sad. How'd I let myself get so attached to that dog?

Michael hadn't been there the day I found Sharon's body. He'd still been in college. Then he had graduated and had several job offers for work he loved to do. I suspected he'd take the one from the Defense Department. They said he could work from home most of the time. He didn't have a place he could call home and Samuel and I agreed he should get out on his own. He'd have to go to D.C. for meetings from time to time. So he may want to get a place there. If he did, I'd sure miss him. He'd grown into a fine young man and it had been a blessing to watch him mature. He'd come a long way from the time he was in prison.

As I gazed at the driveway, reminiscing, a baby blue Cadillac pulled in. I knew at once it was Dennis. Princess verified it as soon as the man stepped out of the car. She yipped in a way she'd not done as long as she'd been living with us. It sounded like she was in pain, but it was the sound of joy.

He walked toward the bookmobile, but stopped long enough to scoop her up and give her a big hug. Princess licked his face as she shook all over.

"I missed you too, girl."

I stood and waited for him at the door. "Come in."

He did, still holding Princess even though she was calm now. He was older than the man who had impersonated him, but his face was softer and his smile more sincere than the fake Dennis.

"You must be Dennis," I said. "Or someone Princess loves."

He put Princess down and held out a hand. "Dennis Coleman. And you must be Liz. I've heard a lot about you and I want to thank you for all you've done."

Instead of shaking hands, I hugged him, perhaps a bit longer than usual.

Michael came aboard. "Everything okay here?"

"Yes, dear. This is Dennis. The *real* one."

Dennis shook Michael's hand.

"This is Michael, my grandson."

"Nice to meet you, son."

I pointed to the librarian's spot. "Have a seat. Let's talk."

Dennis and I took seats but Michael said he had some

phone calls to make. He went outside.

I wasn't sure where to begin. "I only saw Sharon twice, but we took an instant liking to each other. I wish I'd known her longer."

"She was a wonderful woman and wife. I should have been here taking care of her. She didn't deserve to die alone. I'll never forgive myself for what happened." The tears in his eyes showed his sincerity.

"You're grieving now, but there'll be a time when you'll know you are not to blame. Think more about all the happy times you had together. God has forgiven you."

"I don't know why God would ever care about me. I left my wife alone knowing she was getting more forgetful each day. I wasn't there when she got hurt. The police say she died quickly, but who knows? Perhaps she'd be alive if I'd been there."

"Probably not."

His eyes narrowed as he looked at me. "And I'm sad about Kim. I raised an evil daughter. Who steals from the church? I find it hard to believe what I'm hearing about her."

"You can't take the blame for what your grown child did."

"I know I shouldn't, but I feel responsible." He bowed his head and paused. "You don't want to hear my rantings. I'm glad to meet you. I was here the other day and saw the new carpeting. The neighbors said you were responsible for that."

"Yes. I don't know if you are aware of it, but Jack Cummings pretended to be you and he asked me to prepare the homes for sale."

"Yes, I heard what Jack did. He also wrote himself a few checks from my bank account. Good thing I didn't give him access to all my funds. Don't worry. I'll reimburse you for all the money you spent on my behalf, plus pay you for your time."

"Reimbursement is sufficient."

"Just let me know the amount and I'll give you a check."

"I've got the receipts right here." I grabbed an envelope from the dashboard that I'd carried around for some time now.

He put it in his pocket without checking the amount. "I'll mail you a check tomorrow."

"Thank you."

Dennis started toward the door.

"Don't forget your dog."

Princess didn't move.

"She seems more at home right here."

"We both saw how much she loves you," I said.

"Yes, but now she's choosing to stay with you."

A strong feeling of love passed through my body as I realized what he said was true. "Do you mean…?"

"Yes. I'm planning to live in Royal Gardens and I think Princess will be happier with you. Would you mind keeping her?"

"I'd love to."

"Then she's yours. Thank you, dear lady."

He exited to what I knew would be the beginning of a new phase of his life…and I looked forward to Princess being a part of my family.

EPILOGUE

Michael stepped into the bookmobile and handed his phone to me.

I must have looked surprised.

"It's Chris. He wants to talk to you."

I took the phone and put it to my ear. Michael probably told Chris about our little adventure here and he was going to congratulate me on solving another case, such as it was.

"Hello."

"Liz, I need you to come to England. Right away."

I was stunned. Not even a hello. That wasn't like Chris. "What's wrong?"

"I can't say anything on the phone except that I need you. Can you come?"

"I guess. Where?" There was so much to do. What

would happen to the library service? And Samuel? Michael? Princess?

"Meet me at Angela's place in Hemington. As soon as you can."

"I need to tell Samuel and Michael how long I'll be gone. Can you tell me that?"

"No." Chris paused. "Because I don't know. Michael can work your library route while you're gone. I've already talked to him about it. He'll also be a part of our support team. Bring Samuel with you. It'd be nice to have someone here at the house while we're not."

"Where are we going?"

"I'll tell you all I know when you get here."

I felt myself shaking. Was it excitement or fear? I was getting too old for this type of adventure. "What about Percy and Jane?"

"I've already talked to them and they're in. You may want to coordinate your travel plans with them."

I was surprised. Percy wouldn't be able to leave his clients long and both Percy and Jane had made their children a priority in their lives. Maybe they knew more about Chris' plan than he was telling me.

"I'll need to talk to Samuel first."

"I understand. Call me tomorrow. And, no matter what you decide, I will understand and always treasure your friendship."

The line went dead. No time for hellos or goodbyes. I wondered who would take care of Princess.

ACKNOWLEDGEMENTS

This book was my first to be written with the help of a critique team. I think it made it my best book yet.

A special thanks to Dorothy Featherling and Wayne Dawson, the other two members of the team. They helped me in many ways. A major reason to join a critique team is to write on a regular basis. Left on my own, I can go for days, even weeks, without writing a word and find ways to justify the lack of productivity. A critique team is hard to ignore. We began with a goal of two-thousand words a week and later upped it to three-thousand a week. Sometimes what I submitted was short and not my best work, but the word count grew.

We met weekly and critiqued each other's work in writing and verbally. We limited the verbal critique to fifteen minutes per person. The corrections and suggestions received were valuable to me and resulted in changes in story direction and character development. In addition, I learned to be a better editor by reading and commenting on their work.

I would also like to thank my editor, Lisa Lickel. She did an excellent job correcting my mistakes and pointing out where more (or less) was needed.

Thanks to Peg Case for talking to me early on about the concept. Thanks to Liz Franklin for helping with the opening based on an oral account of what I planned.

Beta readers for this book were Malia Barth, Nell Newton, and Vivian Davis. A special thanks to all of you. This book wouldn't be the same without your input.

ABOUT THE AUTHOR

Sidney W. Frost is a former Stephen Minister, and a member of his church choir at First Presbyterian Church in Georgetown, Texas.

While singing with the Austin Lyric Opera Chorus, he was in 42 productions. He and his wife, Celeste, sing with the San Gabriel Chorale and have been in several Berkshire Festivals. They have sung with choruses in Texas, Massachusetts, California, Austria, Ireland, and China.

Until May, 2010, he was an Adjunct Professor at Austin Community College where he taught computer courses. He received the adjunct teaching excellence award in 2005. He has taught writing classes at the Senior University in Georgetown.

After completing service in the U.S. Marines, he

attended the University of Texas. He worked part-time at the Austin Public Library driving a bookmobile where he got his first idea for a novel. That book was never completed, but he has included the librarian and the bookmobile in all his books.

He has a Master of Science degree from the University of Houston and a Bachelor of Arts from the University of California at Long Beach.

Awards for his first novel, *Where Love Once Lived,* include First Place in the 2007 SouthWest Writers Contest, First Place in the 2007 Writers' League of Texas Novel Manuscript Contest, Third Place in the Fourteenth Annual Lone Star Writing Competition, Northwest Houston Chapter of the Romance Writers of America, and Finalist in the 2006 Yosemite Writers Contest.

The Vengeance Squad (Kindle edition) has been a bestseller on Amazon.com in the Religious Mystery category.

Love Lives On, the sequel to *Where Love Once Lived,* was published in 2013 and is growing in popularity in the Christian Romantic Suspense category.

The Vengeance Squad Goes to England, published in 2014, continues to increase in popularity here and in the United Kingdom.

AFTERWORD

Thank you for reading Murder in Sun City. If you haven't already, I hope you will read *Where Love Once Lived, Love Lives On, The Vengeance Squad* and *The Vengeance Squad Goes to England*. See my website, http://sidneywfrost.com, for the latest information about all my books.

If you would like to see images for this book, go to: https://www.pinterest.com/sidneywfrost/images-for-bookmobile-book-5/.

You may also want to visit the Christian Bookmobile:

http://christianbookmobile.blogspot.com/

This is where I talk about writing, review books, interview other Christian authors and occasionally talk about growing up in Austin, Texas.

I also respond to e-mail queries and would love to

hear from you: sidfrost@suddenlink.net.

I am also available to speak to your church or other group. Here is a list of classes I've taught or can teach:

- Basic Creative Writing
- Christian Fiction
- Novel Writing
- Memoir Writing
- Converting Memoirs to Novels
- Self-Publishing vs. Traditional Publishing
- Creating E-Books
- Book Marketing
- Grieving
- Job Search

The length of each class can be adjusted to your schedule.

Made in the USA
Middletown, DE
14 January 2018